DANTE'S END
THE JAILOR
BOOK ONE

ARIANA NASH

Dante's End, The Jailor #1

Ariana Nash

Subscribe to Ariana's mailing list & get the exclusive story 'Sealed with a Kiss' free. Join the Ariana Nash Facebook group for all the news, as it happens.

Copyright © 2022 Ariana Nash.

Edited by No Stone Unturned Editing. Proofread by Marked and Read.

"Havok" cover design by MerryBookRound. Hardback covers by Saint Jupiter.

Warning: The unauthorized reproduction or distribution of this copyrighted work is illegal. Criminal copyright infringement, including infringement without monetary gain, is investigated by the FBI and is punishable by up to five years in federal prison and a fine of $250,000.

Please note: Crazy Ace Publishing monitors popular international pirate sites for infringing material. If infringement is found (illegal downloading or uploading of works) legal action will be taken.

US Edition. All rights reserved. No part of this book may be reproduced in any form or by any electronic or mechanical means, including information storage and retrieval systems, without written permission from the author, except for the use of brief quotations in a book review.

All characters and events in this publication, other than those clearly in the public domain, are fictions, and any resemblance to real persons, living or dead, is purely coincidental.

First Edition - October 2022
www.ariananashbooks.com

BLURB

Monsters are made, not born...

Most called him the Jailor. Some called him a monster. If he had a name, nobody had survived meeting him long enough to tell it. They said he sat atop a mound of skulls and marked each death on his throne, like notches on a bedpost. Some tales told of how he had wings as dark as night, and of how he wore a crown of razor wire woven around four horns.

Dante had heard all the stories before.

The only tale he cared for was the one that said the jailor could bleed. If the jailor could bleed, then he could die, and Dante was going to be the one to finally kill him.

This is the story of how all those tales were wrong. And so was Dante.

Content warning: self-mutilation, sexual threat.

CHAPTER 1

efore:

THE BUTTERFLY BOY

HAVOK FIRST SAW the boy by the emerald pool—as different to Havok as night was to day. He chased butterflies by the water's edge, catching them in soft, pale hands, only to laugh and set them free. He could not hear the butterflies curse, but Havok did. Sunlight glittered off the water like it did from the boy's green eyes. He had hair as red as the fiercest of rubies and he stole Havok's breath in those first few moments, and perhaps his heart too. Although, Havok realized that too late.

A call rang out and the boy darted away, summoned back to his own people. Havok waited until the stars shone and the heat left the world, but the boy did not return.

The next day, Havok climbed through the same gap in the gnarled thorn wall, keeping his wings tucked close to avoid snagging them on the vicious barbs. The butterfly boy did not come that day. Or the next. Havok returned to the pool time and time again, his heart soaring in hope. Dragonflies flitted, butterflies danced in sunbeams, but the boy did not return.

And then on a day like any other, the boy already sat beside the pond when Havok took his place behind the hawthorn bush. He tossed stones into the shimmering waters. His hair had grown long enough to tie back from his shoulders. Some locks fell in feathered bangs over his eyes. His eyes, though, they were the same emerald, the same color as the pool between them. As before, the sight of Butterfly Boy stole Havok's breath and hurt his heart.

Havok hunkered down behind the undergrowth, peeking through thick leaves, and watched as the boy examined the stones at the water's edge. He picked smooth, flat ones—those seemed to skip the best—and he launched each stone, and those brilliant green eyes watched each hop, skip, and jump until the stone vanished beneath the surface.

Butterfly Boy was of the Lenola people. Havok knew that much but little else.

Those people were as mysterious and untouchable to Havok as the stars in the sky. The boy did not have wings, claws, or horns. The Lenolians had steel and steam. They tended farms with big, lumbering animals.

But Havok sensed Butterfly Boy was different from most Lenolians. He did not crush the butterflies, like so many of his kind. He let them go.

The boy sighed, folded his arms over his drawn-up

knees, and peered into the water. The butterflies asked him to play. They danced about him, calling to him, but if he could hear them, he showed no sign of it. Perhaps he didn't know their language, perhaps that was why he was sad.

Butterfly Boy stood, brushed grass and pollen from his handsomely stitched waistcoat and matching leather-laced trousers, and turned to leave.

Havok leaned forward, trying to catch a final glimpse of him. A twig snapped under his boot.

The butterfly boy's gaze speared across the pond. Havok froze, willed himself begone. If he wished it hard enough, he'd turn invisible and nothing could hurt the vanished.

The boy made a calling sound in his language, eyes narrowing.

A small iron dagger hung in a sheath at the boy's hip. He would not use it. He was different, Havok was sure.

Finally, Butterfly Boy looked away, but he did not leave. Something held him back. Some instinct perhaps, a sense of knowing. The butterflies teased around him, telling him he was being observed. Perhaps he *could* hear them? But just as the thought crossed Havok's mind, the boy swiped the butterflies away and disappeared down the trampled-grass path, back to his life beyond the pond.

Havok waited a while, as he always did, but day and night soon passed, and his hunger won over his desire to see the boy again. When Havok next crouched behind the hawthorn bush and scanned the opposite bank, Butterfly Boy wasn't there.

Havok's heart sank like one of the boy's skipping stones. Havok had so little that was new in his life: a den among tree roots, Khandra—his butterfly, and a menagerie of animal carvings he'd whittled to pass the time. Some, he kept behind the hawthorn as company. There were many now, carved in all shapes and sizes—birds and frogs, badgers and mice. Sometimes, he pretended they talked, like the butterflies, and he'd talk back. But everything was silent now.

Silent like the pond.

He parted the spiky hawthorn branches, trying to see more of the poolside. Perhaps the boy had found another spot to sit? The butterflies danced, but there was no sign of the boy.

What if he never came again?

Perhaps that was for the best. Their worlds were too different to mix. Havok rested back on his feet. He'd once seen the Lenolian's great city when he'd ventured beyond the thorn wall, with its sprawling streets and homes, its vast central spire, reaching high into the sky. Most Lenolians lived there, or so the butterflies said. Smoke sometimes billowed from inside their homes, and from the spire. Bad smoke. Havok had only been there once, and it had been so full of noise and smell, he'd fled. He could not venture there to search for the butterfly boy, could he?

A blur sprang from the bush and slammed into Havok's side, sending him sprawling. He gasped, thrust out a hand, and raked claws across a soft cheek. His attacker let out a cry, and then warm fingers caught Havok's wrist and slammed it to the ground. Cold iron kissed Havok's throat.

Havok panted, sprawled on his back, pinned beneath the solid weight of Butterfly Boy.

Fierce green eyes narrowed.

Had Havok been so wrong? Was the boy just like the

others? Would he kill Havok and grind his bones to dust to make potions? Would he take his wings and strip them of feathers to stuff his bed?

Butterfly Boy panted too. He swallowed, and his eyes narrowed some more. Words fell from his lips, but they didn't sound as angry as before. The boy cocked his head, and his tone lifted. A question?

Havok blinked.

The boy removed his dagger from Havok's neck and rose onto his knees, still trapping Havok's legs and tail. Eyes that had been cruel moments before, softened. His lips found a small smile. More words came, gentler now, and his smile grew.

Havok propped himself onto his elbows. The boy's gaze roamed downward, over Havok's naked chest, then back up to Havok's face, his horns, the chain and the shimmering gem-like pendant hanging from it and slung between the horns, the golden ring around his right horn. He appeared curious, and Havok waited, wary but curious too.

The boy's gaze sailed over Havok's shoulders to his wings, pinned awkwardly against the bushes. More words —smooth. He liked his wings?

The boy wasn't afraid. Nor was he angry. He sheathed his blade and clambered backward, taking his weight off Havok's legs. But he stayed crouched and looked around them at the patch of trampled grass and the animal carvings Havok had brought with him to play with while waiting. His gaze settled for a long time on those small wooden animals.

A strange uncomfortable sensation squirmed in Havok's chest. The same feeling he experienced whenever

Butterfly Boy's pretty face turned sad. Slowly, Havok rolled onto his side and plucked a carving from the rest. A butterfly, which seemed apt. He held it out. The boy scrutinized it and when he next spoke, the words were short and clipped. Had Havok displeased him? Did he not like the gift?

The boy arched an eyebrow, smiled, then reached out and took the wooden butterfly and dropped it into his pocket. It was his now. And he was no longer sad. This pleased Havok.

When the boy extended his hand again, Havok closed his fingers around warm, soft fingers. Havok's black-tipped claws contrasted against pale skin. The boy pulled Havok onto his knees and crouched alongside him.

He said something and half smiled, still reading Havok with his eyes. Blood dribbled down his cheek from where Havok's claws had caught him. Havok hadn't meant to hurt him. He reached out. The boy flinched, his smile vanished, and he froze.

Havok stilled too.

Was touching forbidden? He began to pull his hand back, but the boy's soft hand caught it. He smiled and nodded, and so Havok swept his fingers across the boy's cheek, admiring how his pale skin blushed.

It was good then? The touching?

The boy pointed at himself. "Dan-tay," he said, tapping his chest. "Dan-tay. *Dante*." He pointed at Havok, his tone rising in question again.

A name then. The butterfly boy had a name: Dante.

Dante pointed at Havok, asking for *his* name.

Havok shook his head. If he'd had a name, it had been forgotten. Just like he'd been forgotten.

The boy laughed, but it wasn't a cruel sound. Havok's heart skipped a little faster.

"Havok?" the boy said, and pointed at Havok's chest. "You. Havok."

A name? A name for Havok? The boy said a string of things that didn't make any sense but sounded nice, all the same.

"Ha-vok," Havok growled in reply. It didn't sound the same when he said it. His voice was different to the boy's, deeper, rougher. They had many differences. But it seemed as though those differences were far away when crouched behind the hawthorn bush.

"Yes!" Dante laughed again and his green eyes glittered. He might have been the most beautiful creature Havok had ever seen.

"Dante!?" a Lenolian voice called.

Dante lifted his head. Sorrow shadowed his eyes. Havok's own heart fluttered again but for a different reason. Dante's firm fingers touched Havok's chin, tipping it up. He said three words, then bolted from behind the hawthorn bush.

Havok stayed a while, heart racing, head full of new and wonderful memories. He had a name now. Havok. What a gift it was, to have a name. He would cherish it like he hoped his butterfly boy would cherish the gifted wooden butterfly.

IN THE MONTHS and cycles that followed, during the many times they met by the pool, Dante taught Havok his words, and Havok came to love three the most.

"I'll come back," Dante would say when he left, and every time, he did.

The next day, and the next. He taught Havok how to pick the best stones, how to skip them across the pond. He showed Havok a book but seemed dismayed when he could not decipher its contents. So Dante read the story aloud, and sometimes, he taught Havok to read. Another day, Havok told him how the butterflies wanted to play. Dante laughed, the sound so like before, when he'd been younger, smaller, and he'd laughed at setting them free. Together, now older, but still boys, they chased the silly butterflies around the pool, catching and releasing them, until he and Havok flopped side by side on the pond's sun-warmed, grassy bank.

Dante's hand found Havok's, and their fingers entwined. Havok liked these moments the best. The quiet, gentle moments, the touching. They made him feel safe, made him feel... not forgotten.

"You cannot tell," Dante said.

"I won't."

Dante's green eyes shimmered. "You're my secret."

As the days passed, Dante revealed snippets of his life—he was alone, like Havok, his family gone. He never smiled as he spoke of them. He only smiled with Havok, by the emerald pond, chasing butterflies. Havok had little of a life to tell him, so he showed him his wings and tail, turning shy when Dante studied them closely. When he touched Havok's tail, Havok's mouth dried and a rattle of nerves shivered through him, strangely *pleasant*.

One night by the pool, under the moonlight, while pale moths fluttered, Dante pressed his lips to Havok's and that strange, shivering feeling grew. Havok's heart soared to a place his wings could never take him. Like his name, the kiss was a gift from his butterfly boy.

"I'll come back," he said afterward. Then he was gone, vanishing into the night, like he'd done all the nights before.

But after the kiss, Dante did not come back.

The next night, Havok waited, but Dante did not come. The butterflies lamented his absence, said he was gone forever, but Havok knew he would return. He'd said he would. He'd touched Havok's face, he'd kissed his lips, and he'd said, *I'll come back*. Dante always came back.

All the warmth began to fade from the world, or perhaps it faded from Havok. The seasons changed, and the air turned cold. The butterflies went away. Frost froze the emerald pond. Havok waited, shivering on the bank, turning over stones, searching for the right one to skip across the ice. But it wasn't the same without Dante.

A day, a week, a cycle, more, he waited.

And then finally, one cold, dark day, the air full of storm, Dante came back.

But not alone.

The young Lenolian with him carried a hunting bow over his shoulder. They laughed loudly together and walked down the trampled grass pathway, hand in hand. Dante had brought a friend, but this one was different. He had winter in his heart. He smiled and laughed, and ruffled butterfly boy's hair, then murmured something in his ear that brought color to Dante's face, just like Havok's touch had brought color to Dante's face all those months ago.

"Wait, watch," Dante told his companion. "You'll see. It's a secret." Dante turned toward the pond and cast his gaze across its frozen waters toward the hawthorn bush, to Havok. "You can come out. It's all right."

Havok trusted Dante. The butterflies trusted him. There was nothing to fear.

All would be well.

Havok stepped out from behind the hawthorn bush, and because Dante loved to see Havok's wings, he spread each black feather wide, hoping to impress Dante's friend, even if doing so made his skin crawl. But Dante's friend did not smile. He snarled and reached for his bow. "*Monster!*"

Dante said something, tried to stop him, but the stranger nocked an arrow and let it fly so fast there was no time to react. Fire and agony exploded in Havok's left eye. Havok reeled, wings flapping, tail lashing. The agony burned, but more than the physical wound, something fierce and bright burned inside his chest too.

"Kill it now. Before more come! Why is it here? Dante, get off me—kill it! Summon the guards! Guards! A monster! Here!"

Havok clawed the arrow from his eye, opened his wings, and launched into the sky.

He wept blood and tears. Pieces of his heart crumbled. *Monster*. Was that what they thought? Was that what *his butterfly boy* thought of him?

Was Havok his *monster*?

Havok flew hard, wings beating, muscles ablaze. His sight blurred, eyes streaming. Had it all been a trick?

A net flew from below, spiraled around his leg, and pulled, yanking him from the air. He reeled, wings fighting to keep him aloft. A second net landed, falling over his wings, buckling them around him. He tumbled and turned through the air, falling too fast to think, to fear. Tree branches shattered under him, then he slammed into the ground, shocking him almost into unconsciousness. He lay still, but the world still spun. His heart thumped. He reached for his mark—the gem slung on a thin chain between his horns—instinct telling him to pull it free. But a hand caught his and yellow eyes blazed.

A club came down, striking the remains of his consciousness away.

The pain should have ended there. But it had only just begun.

CHAPTER 2

fter:

DANTE

OFFERING DAY.

It appeared to be a day of celebration. Market stalls lined the plaza, with traders selling anything from a new oil lamp to a wicker basket. The faces in the crowd were full of smiles, the people content to scatter their coin and buy themselves trinkets they did not need, if only to take their mind off the real reason they'd gathered. None could hide the thin edge of fear behind their eyes. Dante saw it and touched the dagger at his back as he wandered among them. He had a second dagger in his boot, more a paring knife, really, but a killing weapon in talented hands. Not his. He'd never had to kill anything larger than the wolf that had tormented local farmers, but he'd been preparing for this day for a long time. He was ready.

Behind the plaza, looming large, stood the jagged, gleaming black spire. Its shimmering edges jutted above the highest rooftop and weather vane, higher than the clouds, so high he wasn't sure it ever ended. As a boy, he'd wondered whether climbing it would take him to faraway lands. He'd even heard some had tried, but they'd fallen to their deaths or vanished.

The spire was where the jailor would come from, the monster. The spire was *its* domain, where legends told it sat atop a throne of bone and wore a crown of razor wire.

Dante didn't care for legends or rumor.

His gaze fell to a council chamber's rooftop, one of the highest around the plaza, and he spotted Ricard's crouched form tucked under the eaves. He caught Dante's gaze and nodded. He'd wanted to come, promised Dante he was ready. The others had argued Ricard was too young, but the boy was good with a bow, and they needed every arrow and keen eye they could muster. They wouldn't get a second chance.

Dante continued his final walk around the plaza, occasionally lifting his gaze to check the others were in their places, high on rooftops and balconies. They each gave him a nod. Good men and women, all of them. All wanting to end the terror.

With the circuit complete, he came to a stop near the front of the stage. Much of the crowd had moved forward, gathering together to watch the annual spectacle play out, grateful it wasn't them, relieved they each had another cycle of freedom.

Perhaps for them, this *was* a celebration.

The band members picked up their instruments and

began to play. The music was no different in tone to that they'd play at the fayre, or a joining ceremony, or any other special event. And everyone smiled as though this was the best day of their lives.

The crowd parted for a line of mismatched guards. Farmers, mostly, taking up the role of security for a single day each cycle. They escorted a man, dressed in an all-white gown. Dante didn't know his name—he probably should. If he succeeded today, this unfortunate man would be the last offering. The man in white wasn't shackled. They never were. He tried to smile, to put on a brave face. During the last few weeks, he'd had his every wish granted. He'd wanted for nothing, ate any dish he'd craved, fucked any man or woman he'd desired. Everyone in Lenola was so very *grateful* for his sacrifice.

"You're scowling," Calen purred in Dante's ear, then looped an arm around his waist and kissed him on the neck. "Look happy, won't you? Before you draw too much attention." He forced the words through his own pretend smile—just as dazzling as a real one—and tucked a lock of his floppy dark hair behind his ear. Dante clutched the back of Calen's head and swooped in for a more savage kiss than Calen's chaste one. Calen moaned and plastered himself close. His hand sank down Dante's back and clutched his ass. But the spark of lust soon fizzled to nothing under the threat of what was to come. With a chuckle, Dante pulled back. "Tonight," he promised, stroking Calen's cheek.

Calen smirked and pried himself from Dante's arms. "I'll hold you to that." He adjusted the bow and quiver on his back. The same age, almost thirty seasonal cycles, Dante had known Calen for most of his life. And in that time, they'd grown from friends to lovers to... something more, he supposed.

It was him Dante was doing this for. And so many like him. So Calen didn't have to hear his name being called and have his life reduced to a few weeks. So he could grow old, have the family life he wished for, and not live in fear of being offered up like meat on a platter to satisfy a monster's whims.

Calen tilted his head, shielded his eyes, and looked up. "You ready?"

"As I'm ever going to be." The knives at his back and ankle didn't seem like enough, the archers too few, and the nets not strong enough. It was too late now. They had to proceed.

The man being offered up had made his way to the center of the podium where the guards looped both his wrists to timber uprights. Before Dante's time, one of the offerings, struck by fear at the sight of the monster, had tried to run. The creature had torn down everyone in its way to get to its prize. Now they dressed the offerings in white, to make them stand out among the crowd, and fixed their arms with rope, making sure they couldn't flee so easily. Being offered was an honor. No man or woman could die more nobly than for the people of Lenola. But even the bravest of souls could crumble when staring death in the eyes.

The band had reached their musical crescendo and cut off, leaving a heavy, foreboding silence behind.

"It's going to be all right," the offering said, his gaze fixed on a woman standing alone among the crowd, her pale face streaked with dried tears. She didn't cry now, but she wasn't smiling either. She clenched her hands at her sides while rage and desperation locked her face in a fierce mask.

By the powers, Dante's heart ached. If he had to watch Calen stand there, watch that monster take him... This had to end. And it was going to end today.

"Here it comes," Calen whispered.

High above Lenola, where the clouds skimmed the spire, a pair of black wings corkscrewed downward. Every cycle it came, and every cycle they stood back and let it take one of their own. Some screamed. Some went silently. All of them wept. This cycle's offering let out a sob. His legs gave out, and he hung limp from the uprights.

The woman he'd leave started forward. If she climbed that stage, she'd die alongside her loved one. Dante shoved through the throngs of people and thrust out an arm, blocking her path.

"Get out of my way," she snarled, and pushed his chest.

He stood firm. "Don't."

She raked her gaze over him. "You've never loved or you wouldn't stop me. That's my man up there. I will not let him die alone!"

Her words struck at some unknown crack inside. He loved. He'd been loved. Hadn't he? He shoved those thoughts aside. "He's not going to die."

She blinked, and a silent, furious tear fell. Her gaze swept over his shoulder, catching Calen's approach. "The day will come when your true love is taken, when you can do nothing to stop it, and then you will know my pain."

Dante caught her hands, held them tight and fixed her under his gaze. "He's not going to die. Not today." He nodded toward the nearby rooftop where Ricard knelt, bow in hand. The woman's gaze followed his gesture. Her lashes fluttered. She looked for more of the resistance, all positioned around the plaza. "By the powers," she whispered, then grabbed Dante's shirt. "You must kill it. Make it pay for all of us it has taken!"

Nearby people in the crowd around them began to take notice. They saw the heated discussions, saw Calen with his bow, the dagger at Dante's hip.

"Kill it," the woman snarled again, but with force enough to suggest if they didn't, she would. Others had tried over the cycles. All had failed. Dante would not fail—for her, for Calen, for Ricard and Jean, Jarl, Lucane, and the rest of the resistance daring to stand against a monster. For everyone here, their eyes wide in hope and fear.

Calen nocked an arrow and lifted his head. He wouldn't miss.

Unease shivered through the crowd. Whispers of dissent sailed in the breeze. Dante hadn't meant to give their plan away. They'd be exposed. But there was little he could do now. The monster still spiraled, its wingspan growing larger with every passing beat of Dante's heart.

Now was the moment they'd been waiting for, their one chance to take the monster down for good, to save Lenola and its people.

Dante freed his grip on the woman's hands, nodded for her to stand firm, and raised his arm. "Hold."

The crowd stirred. The resistance waited under eaves and overhangs, arches and on balconies. All they needed now was for the monster to descend within range. A handful of members of the crowd scattered at the edges. The offering sobbed, oblivious to the commotion. More people scurried, spooked by Dante's actions and the sense of foreboding.

If they fled, the monster would know something was amiss and they'd lose the advantage of surprise. "Stay, damn you!" But it was too late, the crowd had fractured, people fleeing. They'd heard the stories. They knew defiance would incite its wrath.

Above, the monster's silhouette widened. Its tail lashed. Two prominent horns protruded from its head, while two more curved backward, over its skull. The beast was a creature of fang and claw, vicious and rabid. And like the wolf that had terrorized the farms, it needed to be dealt with.

"Hold!"

Ricard and the others were poised, arrows aimed high.

Calen's bow creaked.

It was close now, just one more spiral. The creature lowered its gaze, the light shifted, and Dante saw its face. Blind in one eye—the socket struck through by a vivid white scar—but the other eye had a fierce wildness, glowing as red as the gem slung on a slim chain between its horns. It grinned, flashing sharp, curved teeth, and veered from its flightpath toward the council chambers, *toward Ricard*.

"Fire!" Dante brought his arm down, praying to the powers he wasn't too late.

The monster dove straight for Ricard. He stood, arrow nocked, and with the bravery of a man three times his age, Ricard loosed the arrow. The monster yanked its wings in and spun. The arrow sailed past it in a blur and the monster slammed into Ricard, knocking him from the roof.

"No!" Dante rushed forward. He wouldn't make it.

Ricard flailed from the building's edge, reaching for the edge too late. He screamed as he fell, until the scream cut off. The crowd erupted, boiling into motion.

"Calen!" Dante barked. "Now!"

Calen freed his arrow; it went wide as the jailor shot vertically into the air. He nocked a second.

More arrows flew from around the plaza. The monster thrust its wings down, as agile in the air as water running between pebbles. One of Calen's arrows slammed into its leg, ripping a howl from it. Another arrow slammed into its side. Its back arched midair, and its flapping wings faltered. Yes! All it had to do was drop, and they'd smother it in nets. More arrows slammed into it. It bucked and twitched.

"Again!" It was working! "Fire the ropes!"

The monster flapped erratically, struggling to keep itself aloft. More arrows rained, some of these with ropes tied to weights. Another arrow sank into its wing, and the monster fell, landing hard on the stage. It tore the arrows from its side and leg. It bled, and if it bled, then it could die. And Dante was going to be the one to kill it. Bolting from among the screams and chaos, he raced up the steps.

"Dante, wait!" Calen cried. "Not yet!"

He couldn't wait. It had to be now. If it took to the air again, it would escape, and they'd never get a second chance like this one.

He freed his dagger and lunged toward the monster. More arrows sailed in, slamming into its shoulder, its back, stabbing at it like pins in a butterfly. *Yes, now! Strike its heart!* It had to have one.

Dante launched himself at the creature, dagger poised high over his shoulder.

The monster's hand shot out and locked around Dante's throat, jarring him to an abrupt stop. It cocked its head and its clear red eye narrowed.

Dante's boots dangled inches above the stage. He tried

to bring the dagger down, but the monster's fingers closed, choking off his air, blurring the world in black at the edges.

How?

Of all the thoughts, that was the clearest. How had this gone so wrong?

The dagger slipped from his fingers.

He tried to cling to consciousness, to fight the pounding darkness, but the battle was already lost.

The monster's smile grew, revealing sharp teeth. Arrows punched into its flesh and stuck fast, but it didn't seem to notice or care. As Dante struggled, the monster yanked him close. The red gem slung between its horns glinted and winked. A smirk played on the jailor's lips. A smirk Dante had seen before, so long ago. The creature by the pond from his dreams... The boy with horns and wings... It couldn't be the same creature terrorizing Lenola?

The wings. The tail. His careful, nervous touch, the way he'd tasted under Dante's kiss...

No, by the powers, no!

Its wings burst open, raining black feathers over the panicked crowd, and the monster shot into the air, taking Dante.

Dante's lungs burned. He kicked out, but his will had drained, choked by the monster's cold, iron grip.

It couldn't be Havok. Havok was a fantasy, a fever dream.

The monster pulled him close. Recognition sparked in his one red eye. And he laughed. That deep, rumbling laughter was the last thing Dante heard before darkness stole him away.

CHAPTER 3

*D*reams of blood and laughter plagued Dante. He groaned awake on a prickly bed, scanned his unfamiliar surroundings, and wished he'd stayed in those nightmares because he'd woken in a new one.

An open fire crackled and spat in a central pit, its flames making shadows dance over black stone walls. There were no windows here at all, just an opening into darkness above, where a roof should be. The bed he slept on was nothing more than straw stuffed into a roughly stitched mattress.

What and where was this place?

The failed attempt to kill the monster at the plaza came back to him in a rush. The beast had pushed Ricard from the roof, likely killing him. It hurt to think about, to know Dante had been the one to persuade Ricard to fight. After he'd watched the young man fall, the rest was a blur, with only the jailor's viselike grip around his throat remaining vivid. He rubbed his neck, then spotted the monster across the chamber, halting his spiraling thoughts. It stood with its back to the room, illuminated by the firepit's shifting light. It appeared to be shuffling items around a workbench. Black-feathered wings were tucked against its bare back, the arches adding several feet to its height. When opened, those wings would stretch across the width of the chamber, but folded closed, they were compact. Glossy feathers sparkled, as though wet.

Beneath the wings, at hip level, where its lower back met its ass, a thick red appendage arched from its body and twitched downward, tapering to a triangular point that tapped on the floor. A tail.

It wore slim, stitched-leather trousers tucked into knee-high boots. No armor. Only seeing the thing once every cycle, and then in brief snatches when it took the offering, meant Dante's knowledge of it was scant. Until now, he hadn't been sure if it wore clothes at all.

There was something familiar in the way it stood, one hip cocked, and how the tip of its tail flip-flopped...

But this creature could not be Havok, Dante's *secret* from so long ago. A secret none but Calen knew. There were other monsters, other jailors. This one was just the latest. Besides, Havok had been skinnier, all limbs and horns and—Dante's memory was foggy—but he remembered Havok's claws weren't as long or sharp. Not monstrous at all. Whereas this beast was ferocious, wild and bloodthirsty. And it was a threat to all of Lenola.

Dante eased his hand down inside his boot. His fingers skimmed the small knife's handle. *Still there.* He'd lost the larger blade during the fight, but it wasn't over yet.

All he had to do was creep over there and plunge the blade between the creature's wings, deep into its back. It had to have a heart, didn't it? It resembled a man, underneath the claws and tail and wings. So, then if it had a heart, it could bleed.

But the chamber was large, the distance between him and the jailor several strides. It would be better to wait for it to come to him.

He laid himself back down on the prickly, straw-stuffed bed and watched from half-closed eyes as the beast busied itself at the workbench.

Firelight shifted shadows around the chamber. Dante's eyes closed, for only a moment. Between one blink and the next, the monster *vanished*.

Dante jolted upright. A growl sounded, like something born in the depths of the earth, and the monster stepped in front of him, peering down. From Dante's sitting angle, the beast seemed taller still. Its black horns gleamed, and sharp teeth shone behind rippling lips. So close, it didn't seem real.

Angry welts marked where the arrows had punctured its chest. If it was wounded, then it was weakened.

Slipping his hand into his boot, Dante slowly, carefully withdrew the knife, making it appear as though he rested his arm over his knee—no threat. The monster's one-eyed glare remained fixed on Dante's face. He wasn't watching his hands. Dante's heart pounded. If he could punch the knife through the beast's chest, it would be over. *For Calen, for Ricard, you curse on all that is good!*

He lunged.

The monster's backhanded slap threw Dante to the floor so fast, he only realized he'd been struck when his head stopped ringing and he blinked at the woodgrain of old, filthy floorboards. He spluttered, swallowed the taste of blood, then felt the monster's presence loom over him too late to stop its grip from plunging onto his neck.

Dante slashed the blade, seeking any vulnerable part to cut. The beast shoved. His back slammed into hard stone, cracking his skull, and the monster held him pinned, wings spread, teeth bared, his eye a fierce red, like the fire of a furnace.

Dante impossibly, still held the knife. He twisted to swing again, but the monster caught his wrist and slammed that to the wall too. Pinned with his head ringing, heart racing, fear threatened to loosen his guts. But he'd be damned if he was going to die a sniveling offering. "We will never let you win." He spat into the beast's face.

The beast reeled from shock but held on. Dante slashed his knife, catching the beast's thigh, slicing open its leather trousers leg and parting the skin beneath. A roar tore from the monster, and then Dante was skidding across the floor, tossed like a doll.

He came to rest on his side—the knife glinting, still gripped in his hand. He could do this. *Get up.* He coughed, and a fiery agony scorched his chest. Something broken, a rib or two, perhaps. It wouldn't stop him. If he could get to his feet—

The monster's boot came down, crushing his wrist.

"No— No, don't!"

The beast's wings lifted, its smile grew, turning cruel, and it leaned in, threatening to shatter bone.

"Wait!" Dante raised his free hand, palm out.

The knife slipped from the fingers of his trapped hand. The monster bent down, scooped up the blade, turned its back, and casually strolled across the chamber toward the firepit. Pain snapped through Dante's wrist. He cradled it against his chest but he could move his fingers. It wasn't broken, just bruised.

The monster paused by the fire and glanced over its shoulder—wing raised— ensuring Dante watched. Its smirk was a humorous tease on its lips, a promise of more wickedness to come, and it tossed the knife into the fire, sending embers rising into the air. It laughed rich, melodic laughter and returned to the workbench.

Damn the creature.

Dante panted through his gritted teeth. Its strength was twice Dante's. It could break his neck in a twitch. It was playing with him, keeping him alive for sport. Why else hadn't it killed him?

Dante scurried back against the bed. He breathed hard around the pain in his chest, his arm burned, his fingers tingled. The creature might kill him at any moment. He had to get away. There had to be a way out, didn't there? But there were no doors, no windows, just the stone wall arching up like a great clawed hand, with Dante in its palm.

Unarmed and outmuscled, there was only one way to survive. To make it need him, *want* something from him. And when it lowered its guard, when it turned its back for real, then Dante would kill it. He just had to discover what a creature like the jailor wanted, and to keep that one thing out of reach.

If it wanted to toy with him, he'd let it. And he'd learn its weakness. Everyone had one, even monsters.

HOURS PASSED, the fire burning low and the pain in his chest easing. When the monster took itself to the fireside and began to unlace its trousers, Dante watched, curious as well as wary.

It set its boots to one side, stepped from its clothes, and sat on a rickety wooden chair, picked up a needle and thread, and began to stitch the cut in its thigh. It didn't flinch or moan or hiss. Either it didn't feel pain or had a high threshold.

The missing eye might have taught it to withstand agony. But there were other cuts on its legs too, pale, slim scars, each one like tiny lash marks. Similar cuts scattered across its arms and back. Old scars, deep enough to remain forever.

Dante turned his head, but his gaze crept back. Strange, to see its bare legs. He'd known parts of it were man-like, and he'd obviously known it had legs, but to see them naked beside the fire toyed with his notion that the monster was *other*. Its thighs were firm, muscular but lean, in a way that men honed their bodies for wrestling matches or guard duty. He'd known it to be pale, but its skin was smooth, almost silk-like.

It poked the needle into its thigh with claw-tipped fingers, swept the needle through its flesh and tugged on the thread, as though it were stitching the trousers that lay beside its feet, not its own leg.

Dante's gaze skipped higher. He hadn't meant to look *there* and tore his gaze away. So it was *very* man-like, right down to the cock between its legs. But then, he'd known that too, because Havok... Well, he hadn't seen Havok's dick, but he'd known he'd had one. Back then, as a boy, Dante had been envious of his wings, his claws, even his horns. He'd watched Havok, when he'd chased the butterflies around the pond. And when they'd grown older, he'd watched him in different ways. Studied his body with a different kind of interest. Havok had been so... carefree, so bright, so full of fun. He'd been everything Dante wasn't. But this beast wasn't Havok, although it did appear to share a similar design.

This one wasn't the first jailor. There had been others.

Each of them had swooped from the skies and taken their prey. They were an inevitable curse, like the turn of the seasons. Winter came every cycle, and so did the jailor. In Dante's lifetime, he'd known one other. That one too had wings and horns, but it had been less man-like and more... monstrous.

He wasn't even sure why they had called them jailors, but Dante supposed it fit. The people of Lenola were in a prison of the monsters' making.

He looked up—straight into the monster's eye. It watched him, as he'd watched it. It assessed, studied. What did it think of him? It gave a huff, like a snarl, but more dismissive, and then stood, showing Dante *everything*. The sight yanked a gasp into his bruised chest and set him coughing. By the time he'd recovered, the monster had reapplied his trousers and boots and returned to his workbench.

Certainly, a man in some aspects, but nothing like one in others. If it was half man, could it reason, did it think like a man? What did it want? If Dante could discover that, he could use it.

With the monster at its bench again, Dante rested back on the mattress and winced around the ache in his chest. As long as he was alive, this could be an opportunity. Nobody had gotten so close to one of these creatures and survived. Those it took were never seen again, presumed dead. But Dante wasn't dying here. He'd learn everything he could, and he would escape. This place, this monster, it wasn't his end.

"Do you speak?" he croaked.

The monster didn't react, just continued to shift what appeared to be strips of fabric around the worktop.

"What do you want?" he added.

Nothing. Perhaps it didn't understand words or language. It probably communicated in growls, which was going to make finding out its desires all the more difficult.

"Why do you take us? Tell me that, at least?" Desperation slipped into his voice. The monster wasn't even listening anyway. "You must have a reason? Why every cycle? What do you do with us?"

Nothing.

"Hey!" Dante stared at its back, its wings, its resting tail. He was overthinking this. The monster was a creature, it didn't reason, it didn't think, it just acted, like a dog or some other wild animal. It had needs, and that was all. "You're just a beast, aren't you? You don't even know what you're doing, I don't know why I'm bothering talking to you. You don't understand a word... I should talk to the master, not the pet." He pushed to his feet, breathed around a new throb of heat in his chest, and wandered toward the fireplace. If the thing didn't think, then reasoning with it would be impossible, and getting out of here was going to be more difficult than he'd already feared.

The monster had stilled.

Was it something Dante had said? What *had* he said—something about a master? "Is that it? You have a master?"

Its wings ruffled. It grabbed another fragment of fabric and now that Dante had moved a little closer, he saw how the creature was making something, stitching it together like it had its wounded thigh. Would a thoughtless beast be capable of crafting?

If he moved closer still, would it lash out? It didn't seem interested in killing him, yet. But that could change at any moment. Better to hang back, watch and learn.

He settled beside the firepit and studied the chamber

from the new angle. Still no windows or doorways, just the opening above and the night sky, where a few stars peeked between shifting clouds.

Several patchwork rugs were strewn about the floor in an effort to make the space more comfortable. There appeared to be an area for preparing food, with a few stacked bowls and some fruit in a rack. This was a *home*. He hadn't expected this. A slaughter chamber, iron bars, implements of death like the legends said, yes, but not a comfortable den.

The pain in his chest throbbed. He tried to stretch it out, but moving made it worse. "I think you broke something."

The monster either didn't hear or didn't care to listen. It left its workbench and strode to the kitchen area. There, it rattled around the crudely made wooden cupboards, dunked something into a bucket of water, then threw the cloth at Dante. Dante swiped it out of the air in time to stop it from slapping him in the face. Water splashed him anyway. "What's this for?"

The monster ignored him and returned to its workbench, tail swishing.

He'd get more conversation from a brick wall.

He shifted on the chair, winced at the twinge around his ribs, and then eyed the cold, wet cloth. Was it for his chest? If it didn't want Dante hurt, what by the powers did it want with him? He unbuttoned his shirt, poked at the mottled bruising appearing on his skin, and applied the cloth. Cool relief quenched the heated pain.

"Did you leave this cycle's offering alone?" Dante asked after too long a silence. He didn't expect an answer and didn't get one. Was Dante the offering now? Calen would think him dead; he'd blame himself.

But if Dante was alive, did that mean the other offerings might still be alive too? No, they'd be here, and there was no sign of anyone else.

Dante had to get free, get back to the city. Nobody ever came back from the jailor, but he could be the first.

If he climbed the kitchen countertop, he might be able to get a foothold on the stone walls and climb up, but the walls curved inward, designed to keep non-flying people inside. "Just another prison," he muttered.

He couldn't try to escape with the monster watching. But it would leave eventually, and then Dante would get a good look around, maybe climb up the rock wall, although his broken ribs would slow him down, but he had to try. There was no knowing when the monster might tire of his company, might end him...

CHAPTER 4

When Dante next awoke, warm sunlight illuminated the den, diffused through a wispy layer of clouds. He glanced around, checking for the monster nearby, but found the chamber empty. This was his chance. He shoved to his feet too fast, sparking his broken ribs, swore, and stumbled across the floor. The fire had burned down to embers. The monster had been gone a while and could return at any moment. He needed to move *fast*.

A weapon.

Then escape.

He hurried to the kitchen area and searched for a knife or something sharp among the cups and bowls but found only a small mixing stick that wouldn't hurt a firefly, and certainly not a monster. The workbench, though, that was a wonder of needles of different sizes. Dante grabbed the largest he could find, slipped it up his sleeve, and dashing back to the kitchen area, he climbed onto the countertop and started to scale the wall. His ribs screamed. Gritting his teeth through the pain, he heaved himself up the rocky surface, one reaching hand and foothold at a time. Too fast, and he risked falling, too slow and the monster might swoop back down and catch him fleeing.

The top of the wall seemed to get farther away the more he climbed. Agony burned through battered muscles. He hadn't eaten, the wall was too smooth, too high, damn the powers—he wasn't going to make it. But he *must*. He couldn't give up. He'd never given up in his whole life, not when he'd been abandoned as a boy, not during the times he'd been haunted by nightmares full of ice and loneliness and found solace in the sweet but addictive ragvine; he'd always fought on, even when there had been so little worth fighting for.

For as long as his heart beat, he'd always fight.

His foot slipped. He clung on, nails hooked into jagged rock, hanging high over the floor below, saving himself for a few gut-wrenching seconds, then fell.

The drop was short. He struck the floor with a hard thump, slamming his head and jarring his teeth. But the impact shuddered through a timber floor, not rock. He'd landed on one of the many woven rugs, and beneath it, timbers had bounced. Was there a hollow, a way out?

Rolling over and back on his feet, he flung the rug aside, revealing the sweetest damn thing he'd seen. A trapdoor.

He grabbed its iron ring and heaved the heavy door open.

Steps spiraled down into the dark. *Yes!* It didn't matter where it went; anywhere was better than here. He hurried down narrow, dust-covered steps, into cold, dank air. With every step, the gloom thickened. Something pale loomed around him. Indecipherable shapes, mounds of... sheets? No... Whatever it was, it didn't matter. He froze. There, on the next step, lay a smooth, pale bone. Small, picked clean. A chicken bone...

The strange, hulking shapes around him came into focus as his eyes adjusted to the dark. Not mounds of blankets... His heart lurched. Mounds of *bones*. So many, all scattered, like heaps of trash. And among them, hundreds of skulls.

Dante stumbled and fell against the steps. The offerings. These bones... they'd been people. People the jailor had taken. Fathers, sisters, sons. Loved ones.

This wasn't a way out. It was a basement of the dead.

He raced up the steps, slammed the trapdoor closed, and threw the rug back in place, hiding the horrors beneath.

Breathe. By the powers, he had to breathe, to think, to escape!

He whirled, vision doubling, and fell against the kitchen countertop. So many dead... He'd known, of course. They all knew the people it took were dead, but... The jailor hoarded their remains.

Panic tore through him. He couldn't get out, there was no escape, and his bones would soon be lost among those beneath the trapdoor.

The swish of feathered wings sounded above. Dante froze.

The beast landed lightly, wings sweeping up dust, and when it pulled those wings in, it turned toward the workbench—the only thing it seemed to care about. Dante dashed for the bench ahead of it and grabbed the scraps of fabric it had been working on. But the supple, cool material draped over his fingers wasn't fabric. It was leather. Leather... made from the skin of his offerings. Lenolian skin.

The monster's growls bubbled behind him.

"You want this?" Dante raised the wretched leather garment. "Then take it."

It stalked forward.

Dante slipped the needle from his shirt sleeve, rested it against his palm, and as the monster reached for the garment, Dante stabbed the needle toward its one remaining eye.

The monster whipped its head to the side, and the needle plunged down, catching its cheek. The metal sunk in, ripping flesh. Dante withdrew it, to strike again, but the monster grabbed him by the shoulder, slammed him into the workbench, and reached under the bench, from where it retrieved a sword as tall as Dante. The blade kept on coming, its sharp edge gleaming.

This was it. This was his death. His end. He bucked and struggled, but the beast's heavy hand pinned him still, the blade poised over Dante's chest, over his heart. Madness blazed in its red eye. Blood dripped from the tear in its cheek.

Dante was about to die here, too soon, too late. He wished he'd done more, wished he'd told Calen he loved him, even if it hadn't been true.

The monster's top lip rippled and with a final snarl, he plunged the blade down, slamming it into Dante's side. Dante gasped. Pain and heat washed through him.

The monster leaned in, face-to-face. "You leave me no choice," it growled in a deep, smooth voice. A voice Dante knew, a voice from his past. A voice he'd heard laugh, tell him secrets while keeping Dante's. No, it couldn't be. He wouldn't do this. This wasn't him.

"Havok?" Dante rasped.

CHAPTER 5

*N*ightmares swirled with memories, old and new, weaving together, impossible to pick apart. A boy with wings and a tail, sitting by the emerald pond beside the hawthorn bush. A boy, a monster, a secret.

Something was *very* wrong.

Shivers wracked Dante; sickness rolled over him.

A needle pierced flesh, and pain sparked like a firework. He saw Havok and the monster, two sides of the same coin, saw him/it stitch Dante's sweat-glistening side. It smiled, it laughed, and it stabbed its needle into Dante's skin. He was dreaming, wasn't he? This had to be another nightmare. He'd always had them, been tormented by dreams of monsters and ice.

"You are feverish," the deep, growling voice said.

Kill it! A woman screamed. An arrow flew across the pond and slammed into Havok's eye. Calen's arrow. Dante had brought Calen to the pool and ended their fairy tale. *It's a monster, Dante!* He saw his hand in Havok's, saw Havok's smile, heard his laugh, he knew how his lips tasted, soft under Dante's. He hadn't wanted to believe.

But fate wasn't giving him an option. The truth was as clear as day. The boy by the pool was the jailor who hid bodies beneath his feet.

HE WASN'T sure how many days or nights had passed. He only knew he didn't want to move from the cot. Moving meant he'd have to face the truth. His side throbbed. When he lifted his shirt, the neat little stitches reminded him it hadn't been a dream, at least not all of it. The monster had stabbed him, and then stitched him back together as though Dante were some kind of living doll.

The monster.

Undeniably Havok.

It—*he* sat in his chair by the firepit, one leg bent, his demeanor relaxed, and from there, he watched Dante. He'd been there a while now. Days, perhaps. He caught Dante's gaze and his lips lifted in a one-sided smirk.

He'd heard every word Dante had said but chosen to remain silent. Why? A cruel game, another way to isolate Dante?

Havok wasn't an ignorant beast, but he'd let Dante believe it.

He took the offerings because he could and kept their bones under his floor because he wanted to. He might not have been a beast, but he *was* a monster.

"So, you do talk," Dante croaked. Dryness scratched his throat. He reached for the cup beside the bed, sniffed the water, then wet his lips, and Havok's gaze tracked every movement.

"Only when I have something to say. Unlike you," Havok said. His tone sparkled with wicked intelligence.

Dante should have seen it before now, should have recognized him earlier. Although, if he was honest, some part of him suspected all along. But he hadn't wanted to believe how he'd once befriended the jailor, how Havok— a figment of is past—was very real, and now warped and twisted.

"Your prattle is tiresome." Havok sighed. He leaned an arm on the chair's rest and propped his chin on his knuckles.

"You could have replied."

"And encouraged you?" His laugh coiled around Dante like his tail had used to. The thought made Dante shudder.

This creature disgusted him. Dante tried to rise, but his stitched wound protested. He got an arm under himself instead and levered himself upright. He still wore his shirt, but it was a bloody mess. His clothes were filthy, creased, frayed. He stank of stale sweat and old blood. He needed to relieve himself, but the walk to the area and the hole in the floor set aside for that seemed like an impossible distance. By the powers, had there ever been a worse hell than this?

"Why don't you just kill me?"

Havok flicked his black claws. "If—when I want you deceased, you will be."

That didn't answer Dante's question. "Then what *do* you want with me?"

Havok's glare thinned. He leaned forward, making the chair creak, and pinned Dante under his gaze. Some instinctual part of Dante tried to shrink under the weight of the jailor's gaze, but ignoring those urges, he glared back. What did Havok see? Just another Lenolian to add to his collection of bones, or a person with a life he'd been taken from?

After too long a silence, Havok straightened again and examined his claws. "Perhaps I am bored? Perhaps you are to be my personal plaything?"

Dante closed his eyes and sighed. "What happened to you?" he whispered. On opening his eyes, the monster's smirk had vanished, a single raised eyebrow in its place. "You were better than this," Dante said.

"Have we met?"

"You don't remember?"

"Tell me what I have apparently forgotten, and we'll see."

He didn't recognize Dante? "*Havok*? You don't recognize the name?"

"That's twice you've called me that. Three times, if we're to include your delusional ramblings." He rose from the chair, swept his wings behind him, and made his way across the chamber to the workbench. "I don't recall such a name."

"Then what *is* your name?"

"Well, I..." His tail knotted and lashed, writhing like a snake with its head severed. "My name is none of your concern."

He didn't remember? Or was this another game, like the one where he'd pretended to be mute? Dante didn't know what to believe around him. In truth, he knew for certain only two things: Havok was the jailor, and he killed people, tossing their bones into the basement. A fate awaiting Dante. "Never mind. I was wrong..."

"Know many *monsters*, do you?" Havok's tone crawled with irony.

"Then you admit it?"

"Admit what?"

"You're a monster."

"I am perceived to be many things. I admit to only being myself. I cannot control how others, like you, see me."

"You kidnap and murder my people. That clearly makes you a monster. That and your appearance."

"My appearance?" He gave a snort. "Well then, you have me all figured out."

Was he mocking Dante? "You deserve to be alone in this wretched place."

"Hush now. Your prattle is the buzz of a fly."

"Fuck you."

He chuckled, making his wings rustle. Was all of this amusing? He'd brought Dante here to play with him, then kill him, and he laughed?

Dante got to his feet. The wound in his side barked again. He clutched at it and started forward. "Take me back. You can do that. Just take me back and leave Lenola alone."

"Quiet, pet." The peaks of his wings lifted, like the shrug of a man's shoulders. "I'm concentrating."

Dante shuffled forward, gaining strength with every step. "I knew someone like you. It was a long time ago. We were just boys, but he was better than you are, braver, kinder. He was everything you're not. You don't have to be like this. You can be like he was. Take me back, make it right."

Havok's wings flexed, relaxing some, feathers spreading. He continued to focus on his work at the bench, keeping his back to Dante. "If I return you, I'll be forced to take another. Is that what you want, to condemn another to your fate?"

"What?" Dante's approach stalled. Unlike this beast,

Dante wasn't malicious. He'd never deliberately hurt another soul. "I... No. That's... No—"

Havok turned and between the fingers and thumb of his right hand, a needle gleamed. "Quiet," he growled. "Or we'll see how my little pet fares with his mouth sewn shut."

The threat wasn't idle. He meant it and had the strength to carry it through. Dante pinched his lips together and shuffled toward the corner and the hole in the floor to relieve himself.

He'd preferred the monster when he hadn't spoken, when he'd been a *thing*. Now he was a he, and an asshole. But he *was* Havok, even if he didn't remember those days and nights by the pond. The missing eye, the gem between the horns, one horn with a golden ring, the emotive tail, and his lopsided smile—now pulled into a thin smirk, but its origin was the same.

If Dante could make Havok remember who he was, then Havok might release him—or further condemn him, considering their last meeting. It had been Dante's actions that had taken Havok's eye, scarring his face, and chased him away for good. He still recalled, vividly, how Havok had fled, vanishing above the treetops.

Havok had never returned to the pool. Dante had waited.

Perhaps Havok didn't *want* to remember, the same way Dante hadn't wanted to see the jailor had once been his forbidden friend. But now, Dante's own survival depended on it.

HAVOK TOOK to the air the next morning, wordlessly leaving Dante alone in the den.

Perhaps wherever he went during the day was his real home? If he had a life outside this, it was probably filled with more murder and mayhem. With Havok gone, Dante rummaged through cupboards. Under a blanket, he found stacks of old, moth-eaten books. Their pages were dog-eared and their covers torn. Some had names scrawled inside. They'd once belonged to people. Why did the jailor have them? Had he stolen them from his victims as trophies?

Dante approached the workbench next, and the garment the jailor seemed so engrossed in stitching. He reached out to touch it, but held back, knowing its grisly origins. It appeared to be a full-length coat made of patchwork leather. He scowled at the thing. If it *was* skin, dwelling on it would change nothing.

He eyed the walls, but the wound in his side was a long way off healing, and if he chanced a second climb, he'd rip the stiches.

Resigned to staying confined, he fixed himself a drink from the fresh bucket of water, ate some fruit and bread, and whittled the hours away until the sky turned dull and the shadows swelled. He stoked the fire, keeping the cold night air at bay, and waited for Havok's return.

As time wore on, stars gleamed above. The quiet was broken only by the fire's crackling and the wind rattling through the chamber. He couldn't remember it ever being so quiet in Lenola, certainly not in the city. Perhaps, when he'd been a boy, and he'd spent long days and nights alone on the farm... But even then the crickets had chirped and distant dogs had barked. The den existed outside of those normal sounds, in a bubble all of its own. Had the jailor carried him far from Lenola? The stars looked the same, so Lenola was nearby. Strange, then, that all he heard outside was the occasional howl of the wind.

Dante dozed, woken by sunlight and his grumbling stomach. Still no jailor. He fixed himself some more water and a little food, studied the coat again, with its fine purple stitching. A hideous garment, even if the skill required was beyond anything Dante could make.

He found a pile of folded shirts and trousers, didn't think too hard about where they'd come from, and decided he needed them more than its previous owner. Stripping out of his bloodied clothes, he wiped himself down with cool water and threw on the fresh clothes, replacing his boots.

When the jailor still hadn't returned, he eyed the sloped wall, debating whether to make another escape attempt. No, he'd wait for his wound to heal.

The day surrendered to another cold night, and still the jailor did not return.

Dante paced. How long had it been? A whole day and night? Perhaps this wasn't a home at all. He couldn't escape, and he was trapped here, so then this was a prison? *His* prison. He chuckled, realizing the laugh sounded akin to madness and not caring. Of course Havok would leave him here. This was all his game to play, and Dante's to figure out.

As prisons went, he supposed there were worse than one with a warm fire and adequate food.

He dozed, waking every so often when the fire died down and the cold had crept into his bones.

Another day came and went, another day of watching the skies, another day of pacing back and forth, the den getting smaller with every lap, another day of reading the stolen books. As soon as Havok returned, Dante was going to tell him everything. Their past, how Dante had been the one to name him, to teach him to talk, to *read*. How they'd played together with the butterflies, catching and releasing them.

If he came back.

This was the second time Dante had driven himself crazy, waiting. After Calen had shot Havok, Dante had turned on Calen, ripped his bow from his hands, and tossed it into the pond. He'd raged, pushed him, almost punched him in his fury. Until Calen had looked at him as though he'd lost his mind for caring for a monster. *Was* he mad? He felt it sometimes.

Back then, he'd waited for Havok by the pond, waited for days and weeks, waited until he'd been sick with it. And that was where Calen had found him, weak and rambling, searching for an imagined friend who was never coming back.

He'd abandoned the farm after that, gone with Calen into the city, found work to tide him over. And they'd never spoken of the monster, or the farm.

Those memories haunted his dreams, memories of being abandoned again. He despised being alone. Hated it more than having the jailor here, because it made him remember darker days. Days like this, when he'd been so alone, he'd talked to the walls, so hungry he'd eaten the leather from his boots...

No, he wasn't going back there. The past was irrelevant, or so Calen would say, when he'd found Dante lost to the ravages of ragvine and nursed him back to sanity.

Was Havok doing this on purpose? Torturing him? Did he know, somehow, how the loneliness killed Dante with his every heartbeat.

On the third night alone, Dante stared into the fire and poked at its radiant base, sending embers dancing into the darkness. The almost silent swish of feathered wings sounded, and where the embers rose, a descending shadow made them swirl. Something above moved, spiraled, *fell*.

Havok landed hard in a crouch with one knee bent, one wing twitching, head bowed and chest heaving. He held his grand sword in his right hand and leaned on it as though it was the only thing holding him up. A rivulet of something dark slithered across the floor, soaking into his rugs. *Blood*. Dante shot to his feet. The rage and madness he'd been harboring during the past few days fled. Havok was hurt? He took a step closer.

Havok jerked the sword up, its tip trembling. His every breath sawed through clenched teeth. A smear of blood stained his pale cheek and a bloody handprint marked his pale neck, where he'd been *held*. Streaks dribbled from multiple cuts all over his chest. He clutched his middle, and blood oozed from between his fingers.

"By the powers—" Dante stepped closer, ignoring the sword's tip pointed in his direction.

"Back!" Havok slashed. "Stay"—he swayed—"back." His eyes rolled, the sword clattered to the floor beside him, and he collapsed onto his front, chin slamming into the boards and his eyes closing.

This was Dante's chance, his opportunity to kill the jailor. He just had to pick up that sword and bring it down through his neck. The jailor would be dead, and no more Lenolian people had to suffer.

He toed Havok's limp hand resting over the sword's handle, checking for any sign he was conscious. Nothing. Havok was out, but not dead; his shoulders and wings rose a little with his every haggard breath.

Dante knelt and pried the enormous weapon away from his claws, then wrapped both hands around the long handle and heaved the heavy blade over his shoulder. The neck. Right there, just bring it down where the locks of silver hair fell against the nape and cleave his head from his body. It would be over. It was the right thing to do. There wouldn't be another chance like this one. He had to take it. *Take his head...* See it done. *Kill it.* Save Lenola. That's what a good person would do.

His palms sweated. He tightened his hold, raised the sword. He had to do it, for all the bodies beneath his feet, for all the lives the jailor hadn't yet stolen.

The memory of holding Havok's hand charged into the forefront of his mind. The sweet smell of summer grass, the tinkle of water into the pond, how the butterflies danced in sunbeams, and the feel of... that kiss.

No, he had to kill the monster.

That was what he'd planned days ago in the plaza. For Calen. For Ricard.

Just let the blade fall... It was heavy enough that he didn't even have to swing it.

He swallowed around the knot in his throat and fought to keep his hands from shaking.

But if he killed Havok now, he'd be trapped in the den. Havok was his only way out. If Havok died here, so did Dante.

It didn't matter, killing him was right.

But he'd remembered the soft look in Havok's eyes when he'd said he'd been forgotten, when Dante had asked him about his family and he'd asked what a family was.

"You're my secret," Dante had told him.

By the powers, he couldn't do this.

He dropped the sword with a loud *clang* and fell to his

knees beside Havok's great wings. He was too weak, too soft, he couldn't do the one damned thing that needed to be done? A sob almost fell from his lips. Another failure, another weakness. He rubbed his face and when he focused again on Havok's limp form. Blood crept from under him. Deep, deliberate lacerations marked Havok's arms. Someone or something had sliced into him time and time again. "Who did this to you?"

Didn't matter. Nothing mattered. Just that Havok couldn't die if Dante was going to live. He hauled Havok's cumbersome weight into his arms. The wings flopped, limp and useless, and Dante fought to roll Havok onto his back. The gut wound was the worst of it and would have already killed a Lenolian man.

"I hate you, but you're not dying today."

He grabbed the water bucket, some clean cloths, and got to work.

CHAPTER 6

ost of Havok's wounds had clotted on their own, but a few were too deep for his body to fix. Those needed stitches.

Dante heated one of Havok's many needles over a candle and set about cleaning the wounds, then stitched the worst of the cuts. His mah had taught him how to sew before she'd been taken. The principle was the same, except the fabric was the blood-slick flesh of a mass murderer. As he stitched, he battled with the same argument over and over. He shouldn't be fixing him; he should let him bleed. A dead jailor was better for everyone. A few times, he even set the needle aside, only to curse and pick it up again.

As he worked, he snuck a few glances at Havok's face. The permanent snarl had vanished now he was unconscious, and its absence softened his sharp lines. The face from Dante's memory was in there, behind thinned cheekbones and a sharp jawline. He'd grown lean as he'd aged. Although some of that sharpness would probably vanish if he ever genuinely smiled. The golden ring around the more curved of his front horns was still there, lost in a splash of silver hair. He assumed someone had given him that ring, the same as someone had given him the gem that he wore slung between his horns. Unless he'd stolen the jewelry, like he'd stolen the books.

On Havok's lower back, hidden until now by his wings, was a small blue butterfly tattoo. A tiny thing, inked there like an afterthought. Dante never would have seen it had he not been so close.

He knew so little about him—didn't want to know. Just because he'd met Havok when they were younger didn't change the fact he was still a butcher, a monster. Their shared past changed nothing about today.

With the cuts cleaned and stitched, Dante tucked a folded blanket under his head, then remembered the bones beneath the trapdoor and yanked the damn thing back out again, letting Havok's head thump against the floor.

"I just need you to get me out of here," he told the sleeping jailor. He picked up a stick by the fire and stabbed the flames, stoking them higher.

The sword still lay on the floor, mocking him. It wasn't too late. He could still kill the jailor. All of Lenola wanted the monster dead. Dante was failing them, failing Calen... He snarled and tossed the stick into the fire. A part of him hoped—no, *wanted*—Havok to be the same as when Dante had first met him. He was waiting for a miracle, for Havok to realize he wasn't vicious. But the hope was useless. Havok couldn't be redeemed, the bones were evidence of that. The best outcome was that he learned of a way out, and after that there would be no excuses left. He'd have to kill Havok.

A BITTER CHILL plucked him from a dreamless sleep. The flames in the firepit spluttered. Dante checked the opening above, saw stars and no sign of clouds or rain, but the air was bitter, contracting over the skin of his face and chapping his lips. The cold's sudden onset didn't feel... *right*.

He glanced over at the sleeping jailor, still on his back on the floor, where Dante had left him. Nothing appeared amiss, until he spotted a thin jagged layer of ice sparking and cracking across the floor, spreading from the far wall toward Havok. The ice sheeted outward, leaping in jerky motions. Its leading edges touched Havok's wing, climbed over the glossy feathers, encasing each one in a crystal cocoon. More ice rushed in from around the room, gaining in fits and snaps. It poured in, jagged and sharp, a thousand frozen knives all destined for Havok.

Dante lunged from the chair. "No!"

He jolted awake, gasping. The fire blazed, wood spitting. There was no ice, and no Havok either. Only a few smears of blood remained on the floor where he'd lain.

"Nightmares?" Havok's smooth, always mocking tone jerked Dante's attention toward the kitchen area where the jailor leaned against the countertop, eating soup from a bowl, legs crossed at his ankles, tail twitching alongside him.

If it weren't for the few angry cuts on his chest and the stitches keeping them together, Dante might have assumed the entire event, from Havok falling from the sky to stitching him up, might have been a dream.

"No. It was nothing." He twitched in the chair, looking for any pools of water or sign that the ice had been real. It had *felt* real. He shivered, leaned closer to the firepit, and spread his hands to soak up the warmth. It had been many cycles since he'd dreamed of the ice, but this was the first time it had come for someone else, not Dante.

"You have my thanks for not killing me, and for your medical assistance. Although your needlework is deplorable."

The sword had gone. Havok had been quick to squirrel that away again. Dante blew into his cupped hands and eyed the jailor. "You owe me. So take me back, and we'll call it even."

"Soup?" he asked, ignoring the suggestion.

Dante's stomach growled, answering for him. Havok smirked, prepared a bowl of hot broth, and handed it over. Dante eyed its steaming contents without taking the bowl. It smelled wonderful, full of herbs with a meaty base. It was probably delicious.

"It's not poisoned," Havok insisted.

He eyed the meat floating in the golden liquid. "What's in it?"

"Why?"

Was the meat... Lenolian? Should he tell him he'd seen the bones? Would it wipe that smile off his face?

His mouth watered, but he couldn't stomach anything the jailor made. "I'll pass."

"You'll need your strength." He returned the bowl to the kitchen countertop.

"What for?"

Havok waved his spoon and finished off his own meal. "For when you inevitably try to kill me again."

"I could have taken your head when you were out cold," he grumbled.

Havok set his own bowl aside and faced Dante,

DANTE'S END

cocking his head. The gem on its chain slid across his forehead. "What is your name?"

He almost snapped that Havok already knew it and demanded he stop playing this ridiculous game, but if they were talking, then he might be able to get some answers out of him.

"Dante." He watched Havok's face, searching for any twitch of recognition, but the jailor just looked curious. Did he truly not remember him? All those days by the pool, the stories they'd told each other, how he'd learned to speak?

"You say we've met, but I'd remember you. Your scent, your irritating voice—"

"Clearly, you don't."

"Hm... Then explain, in this reality of yours, how do you propose you and I met?"

Dante leaned back in the chair. "There's a pond near my old farm, outside the city, near the foothills. I'd go there sometimes..." He wasn't going to explain why, or what had driven him there, not to this Havok. He hadn't told the old Havok much either. The pond had been his escape, his sanctuary. "You watched me from behind a hawthorn bush."

Havok screwed up his face. "Unlikely."

"It's true. I didn't know you were there at first, then you gave yourself away, so I set up an ambush."

He scoffed. "I don't believe you."

Dante snorted. "I don't care what you believe. It happened."

Havok narrowed his eyes and appeared to consider this new information before lifting his head again. "What purpose did watching you serve?"

Dante studied the beast now. Far stronger than he'd

been then, scarred by old wounds, missing an eye—Dante's fault—but he'd been through much. Perhaps he'd deliberately blocked out his past? "Honestly, I think you were alone."

Havok's mouth twitched at one corner. "Go on."

"You told me, when you'd learned to talk—which took some time, by the way—that you'd been forgotten. We were young back then, and neither of us cared to speak much of our lives. But you were sad, so I didn't ask any more."

"Forgotten?" His tail, now resting on the floor beside his boot, ticced gently, suggesting he was curious.

Dante shrugged. "When we'd first met, I'd never seen anything like you. I assumed you were... unique. Later, that changed."

"How so?"

"I don't want to talk about it."

"Why not?"

"Because... it doesn't matter. What we did, back then, I didn't know what you were, what you'd be. I shouldn't have..."

"Shouldn't have what?"

Liked you, kissed you, wanted more... Dante shook his head and rubbed his face. "It doesn't matter. None of that matters. You're different now, and so am I. Talking about it doesn't change how you're keeping me a prisoner here for some fucked-up reason and you need to be stopped."

"Do I?" His smirk was back. "How do you propose to do that, Dante?" When he said Dante's name, the sharp points of his teeth showed.

"I should have killed you already."

"Yet you had the opportunity and did not act."

A decision he was regretting more with every word

that left the monster's lips. "Who cut you up, huh? Who did that to you? Maybe I should thank them. Maybe next time they'll finish you—"

The bowl came out of nowhere. Dante ducked, and it sailed past and smashed against the far wall. When he faced the jailor, he'd spread his wings and blasted upward, through the opening, vanishing into the night.

Someone out there had hurt him. And Dante had just found his weakness.

CHAPTER 7

They fell into a reluctant routine. Havok left during daylight hours, returning at night to add another patch of leather to his coat and check on Dante. After the bowl incident, Dante attempted to have Havok explain how he'd been hurt, but the jailor shut down. If Dante pushed too hard, Havok tossed out a few threats, then spread his wings and flew away.

But as the days progressed, Havok's moods darkened. His sneers gained sharper edges, and his tone turned cruel. He threatened to stitch Dante's lips together to stop the questions and kept his sword close, always within his reach. But the sword wasn't for Dante. Havok was strong, like an ox. He could and had thrown Dante against the wall. He didn't fear Dante, but he feared *something*. And that thing had hurt him. Was it another monster? One of his own kind? It had to be; no Lenolian could gut him like his wounds had suggested.

Dante watched and listened and *learned*.

One evening, Havok removed the coat from the workbench with a flourish while Dante watched from the cot. He held up the garment and smiled, then flipped it over his head and thrust his arms through the sleeves. The long coat covered him from ankle to shoulders, with slits to allow it to fall around his wings. He'd spent weeks making the garment, and he appeared to be proud of it. But the real surprise came when he looked across the chamber to Dante, spread his arms, and turned on the spot, as though seeking his approval?

Dante arched an eyebrow. Did he expect to be told how fine he was?

"Come now, you must have an opinion," Havok urged. His wings fanned open, like they had at the pond whenever he'd wanted Dante to watch him.

Chuckling, Dante bowed his head, breaking their shared gaze. "I don't think you want to hear it."

"Admit it, you like the coat."

"No, I really don't," he said with a snort.

Havok huffed and strode to where a sheet covered a piece of old furniture. He whipped the sheet free, revealing an ornate full-length mirror. Dante almost laughed at the fool. A bloody murderer *and* vain?

Havok's smile died as he admired his reflection. His wings sagged and all the delight drained away, leaving him pale and withdrawn.

Dante's wretched heart did a strange little stutter, as though a part of him wanted to reassure Havok that whatever he was in that mirror, it couldn't be half as bad as it seemed. But before he could say something foolish, Havok tugged off the coat, balled it up, and threw it at the wall.

Did he hate the coat, or himself? Dante stayed silent, preferring to observe as the jailor began to pace. His boots clipped the wooden floorboards, his wings swept trails through the dust, and his tail writhed.

"Tell me about your Havok," Havok snapped.

Perhaps this was Dante's moment to get through to him, to make him see he didn't have to be a monster? "It was a long time ago... Fifteen cycles, roughly. I was around ten or twelve, I think. We were similar. You were taller than me, but back then I was the stronger one. We would er—" He cleared an ill-timed hitch in his throat. "You said the butterflies talked, and they wanted to play, so I'd chase them, trying to catch them. You'd try and stop me." He smiled, despite the circumstances, then frowned when he spotted Havok's glare. "We were young... You tripped me up once and I almost broke my nose on a rock," he said, with a chuckle. "Your face, when you realized what you'd almost done..." Havok's intense stare hadn't eased, and Dante swallowed. "You were kind then, unlike now."

Havok's snarl twitched. "You don't know me."

"No, I don't. And I don't want to. You're nothing like the Havok I knew."

"In that we agree. This Havok you speak of, he's someone else."

"I wish it were so, but no, you're him."

"How do you know?" He still paced, his strides choppy.

Dante sucked on his teeth and sighed. "The eye..." He gestured at his own and instantly regretted even mentioning it when Havok's eye widened. "I... Well, something happened, and you... There was an accident."

"An accident?" Havok snarled.

"I made a mistake," Dante hurried on. "I wanted to share you, to tell someone you were real, but that person didn't react well, and—"

"My eye?" Havok blinked. His frown cut deeper. Then

he stopped pacing and regarded his reflection in the mirror. The snarl faded, and he seemed to study himself, searching for something in his reflection.

"I didn't see you again after that," Dante continued. "I thought maybe you'd gone far away, or died. I wish you had, instead of becoming *this*."

Havok's wings spread a little. His tail wrapped around his left leg. "*This?*" He snorted. "And who are you to judge me so? I should kill you. This is—" He huffed through his nose, cutting himself off. "This is madness."

"We agree in that. Not the killing part, the madness." Dante got to his feet and marched across the floor to face the beast, tilting his head up to peer into his eye. They stood close, closer than he would have dared only days ago, but he sensed his time was running out. "Why do you do it? Why do you take one of us every cycle?"

"I wish I'd left you behind," he snapped. "I should have. Your being here solves nothing."

"Then take me back."

"No."

"Am I just to sit here and rot for the rest of my days? Why? What's the point? If you're going to kill me, then kill me, if not, let me go."

"Believe me—" Havok's hand shot out. He grabbed Dante's neck and lifted him off his feet. "—*I want to.*"

Dante grabbed at his arm, squeezing, trying to pull him off. His feet dangled, and just like before, at the plaza, darkness throbbed at the edges of his vision, threatening to spill in.

"I saw you in that crowd," Havok sneered. "Saw how hatred burned in your green eyes, Dante. Your people sought to trap me, to slay me with arrows. But none of them hate me as much as you. Why is that? Did you know me then? Was I your Havok, your secret, or am I something else to you?"

Dante spluttered, choking. He dug his nails in, trying to pry Havok off, knowing it would be in vain. Havok's thick tail spiraled up Dante's leg, squeezing hard, and the beast bared his teeth, so close Dante saw their gleam. "You are more trouble than you're worth, but if I return you, you and I will both suffer. Your people will suffer. It has to be this way." He flung Dante to the floor and reached for his sword, his tail still looped tight around Dante's leg.

Dante scrabbled backward. The tail yanked, sliding him across the floor, toward Havok, now armed, the sword shining in his hand. He couldn't take this; damn Havok, it needed to end! "Just do it then! Kill me!"

Havok raised the blade. All the fire and humor had snuffed out of his eye, leaving it dull and flat. But the gem, that glowed like living embers, fueled by rage perhaps, or some part of Havok that Dante had never understood.

The sword slammed down, missing Dante by a hair's breadth. Its tip slammed into the timber floor, and the sword thrummed, and Havok abandoned it there. He whirled and strode away, using his tail to yank Dante along behind him, and kicked the rug off the trapdoor.

"Wait—what are you doing?" Dante grabbed the thick tail and tried to unravel it from his ankle, but it pulsed, tightening, cutting off his blood, making his foot tingle.

Havok heaved open the trapdoor, snapped his tail tight, and flung Dante toward the dark hold in the floor.

"No, Havok, wait, don't." Too late. The edges of the floor dropped away and Dante tumbled down the steps. He caught the stone risers under him, stopping himself from falling into the chilling dark. Havok's tail unraveled from his leg and the trapdoor slammed shut. "Havok!"

Dante hammered on the door's underside. "Havok, please… Don't leave me down here."

Havok's boot slammed down, rattling the trapdoor. "Quiet! Be grateful you're alive. Most who find their way down there are not."

Dante perched on the edge of a step. He hugged his knees to his chest and closed his eyes. It was his own fault, for thinking Havok could be reasoned with. He'd forgotten what he was, what he was capable of.

He shivered in the cold and knew, just a few more steps down, around the curved stairs and out of sight, mounds of bones lay in silence. Bones of those he'd watched the jailor carry off, the bones of old and young, men and women, sons and daughters. The bones of both his parents, taken by a jailor, so long ago.

CHAPTER 8

He dreamed of chasing butterflies, of sunbaked grass and of Havok's tail snaking up his leg, climbing higher and higher. He laughed, batted it away, but the tail persisted.

A voice wrenched him awake... Not Havok's smooth timbre. A female. Her voice was brittle and sharp with a jagged accent. He lifted his head and peered at the thin strips of ochre light filtering through the trapdoor's timbers. Movement shuttered his view. Someone else was out there. He reached out to bang on the trapdoor, to call for help, but held back. Whoever it was, they weren't likely to be a friend.

"—will be ready soon," Havok said, in answer to a question Dante hadn't heard.

"And the skies?" the female enquired.

"Clear." Havok paused, then added, "For the most part."

"Visitors?"

"Nothing worthy of note."

"Good. You've done well, Beric. Come to my chamber,

when you can spare the time. I'll see you're rewarded accordingly."

"Very generous, Reina."

They were *familiar*. Havok sounded subordinate, so perhaps this female was his master, or whomever he reported to? Was she a monster, like him, with great wings and spiraling horns? Dante ached to see, and shifted on the step, face pressed to the wood. His boot brushed the small bone from the lower step, sending it clattering down into the dark.

"Vermin," Havok said, hastily. Then his boot came down and slammed on the trapdoor, jolting Dante back. "I'm working on eradicating them."

"Hm. See that you do."

A leathery blast of wings signaled her leaving, and in the quiet that followed, Dante considered all he'd learned. Another jailor, like Havok, or someone else?

The trapdoor rattled on its hinges but remained closed. "Fool," Havok growled from above it.

Dante thumped the door. "Next time I'll tell her I'm here and we'll see what your reward will be then, huh."

The trapdoor swung open. Light poured in, bleaching the details from his sight but Havok's distinctive silhouette was dark. "You'll do no such thing if you'd like to keep your male appendage between your legs."

Dante choked on any kind of retort—she was a monster then.

Havok crouched, arms resting over his knees. "She'll eat you, piece by piece, and make you watch every moment. Beginning with the fingers. Those are easily removed, and their absence won't kill you. Then the toes. Avoiding the main arteries, of course. The male appendage is entirely unnecessary for survival, so she'll eat that early on."

Sickness flopped Dante's stomach over. "Is that your reward? Or maybe you get to fuck her with *your* male appendage?"

Havok's laugh sounded bright and free, almost like his carefree laugh of old. It was so like the laugh he'd known as a boy that all he could do was stare, until Havok thrust out his hand, offering to help him out of the bone pit. Dante glared.

Havok shrugged and stood, turning away. "You'd do well to avoid her until the time is right."

"Who was she?" He climbed the steps and slammed the trapdoor on the bones.

"Your end, I suspect."

So smug, the prick.

Dante glanced around him, searching for anything that had changed, any sign of something he could use, but the den was the same. He spotted the coat, still crumpled on the floor, checked Havok wasn't watching, then rushed across the room and grabbed it. He flung it onto the worktop, grabbed a sleeve, and pulled, ripping the stitches apart.

Havok whirled at the sound. "What are you—no!" He lunged.

Dante brandished the torn sleeve. "Answer my damn questions or watch as I tear your precious coat to pieces."

Havok snapped his teeth together and flexed his wings. "You wretched worm of a man."

"Who is she to you?"

His nostrils flared. "None of your concern."

Dante yanked the coat's arm clean off and flung it at Havok. It didn't sail far and flopped to the floor between them. But the absolute fury on Havok's face made it worth it.

"I will kill you—" He started forward.

Dante grabbed a fistful of more coat, halting Havok once again. "Tell me!"

"Her name is Reina," he growled. "I answer to *her*."

Then it was as Dante had assumed. She was above him. His leader, if jailors had such a thing. "Is she like you? A monster?"

Havok bared his teeth. "For every stitch you unravel I will do the same to you."

He took a step, and Dante yanked a hole in the coat.

Havok froze. "Fiend!" he roared.

"You are going to tell me everything or this coat is rags."

Havok spread his hands, claws extended. "There is no creature, man or beast, I despise more than you."

"The feeling is mutual—Why do you take my people every cycle? What purpose does it serve?"

"This is as pointless as your existence..." When Dante bared his teeth and stood firm, he huffed. "You do not want to know. It's better for you if you live the rest of your days in your land of fantasy, believing I am all that is bad in your life. Die, blaming me, your monster, because there is nothing you can do to change your fate."

Dante frowned and shook his head. "What does that even mean?"

Havok held out his hand and said flatly, "Give me the coat."

"Answer my question," Dante countered.

"Are you deaf as well as terminally irritating? I already answered."

"No, you didn't. Why do you kill us? Why do you take one of us every cycle?"

"You don't want to know."

"Clearly, I do, or I would not ask!"

"Enough!" Havok's wings splayed, pushing down, and the jailor lunged. He slammed into Dante, driving him back against the workbench. Havok grabbed the coat, yanked, heaved, fought, but Dante clung on, sensing it was the only thing keeping him safe.

A great tearing sound froze Havok and from the horror on his face, Dante almost regretted his actions. What if Havok killed him now? Because of a coat?

"If you would just answer my question—" Dante said carefully, waiting for Havok to snap.

Havok tore the coat from Dante's hands with a roar, flung it down on the worktop, leaned over it, and shuddered with his every breath. "I curse the day we met."

Dante wet his lips and said quietly, "Then return me to Lenola and I'll gladly be gone from your life."

Havok's slow turn might have been one of the most menacing Dante had seen. The jailor hissed his every breath through sharp, clenched teeth. "If I take you back, they all die." Rage sizzled in his single red eye. "You will stay, you will be grateful, and by the powers, you will cease asking questions. It's that, or I kill you now and be done with you. Choose."

If he returned to Lenola, they all died? Why? What risk was there in returning Dante to his home? What did he know that made him dangerous? "All right," he answered, raising his hands. "I understand. No more questions."

He backed off while turning Havok's words over in his

head. He'd talked of fantasy, as though there was some other reality that Havok lived. Whatever it was had to be the reason he took people away, killed them, and collected their bones. It didn't make any sense, but nothing about Havok ever had.

Havok snatched up his needle and thread and muttered under his breath as he set about fixing the coat —a coat he'd hated on himself but treated as though it was the most precious thing he owned. Perhaps it was. Everything he did was a mystery. But if he believed returning Dante to Lenola endangered lives, then did he believe he was *protecting* the Lenolian people?

No, that was absurd. He killed people, he didn't protect them.

Dante returned to the cot and watched Havok stab his needle at his coat, his fine fingers working. The jailor's tail lashed against the floor, apparently without him noticing. He'd claimed, when they were young, that his tail had a will of its own. Dante had laughed that off, especially when the tail had been used to trip him, or grab his wrist, or slide up his trouser leg. The tail was probably the truest part of Havok, and it thrashed now. Furious. Conflicted.

If he believed he was protecting Lenola, who was he protecting it from? Was it whatever had attacked him? Was it Reina?

Havok worked for hours, until the day had shifted into night again. Dante fixed them both some bread and fruit, and left Havok's on the side of the workbench. Havok narrowed his eye at the gesture, then went back to stitching.

Dante settled in the chair by the fire. He'd assumed Havok was in control, was the master of all this, but with Reina's arrival, Dante realized he had been wrong. Havok answered to another. Which begged the question, was he trapped too?

He knew what he was doing, in his own mind... trying to rationalize Havok's behavior, trying to find the good in him. Even if it wasn't there.

The end of a small knife poked from the fire's ashes. His charred paring knife, thrown there right at the beginning of all this. He kicked it under the chair to cool, checked Havok hadn't seen, and after a few minutes, he picked it up and tucked it into his boot. It was blackened, a bit warped, but it held its edge.

"Do you have someone?" Havok asked without looking over. The growls had smoothed from his voice, leaving it softer.

"'Have someone'?"

"A companion?"

"You mean a lover?"

"Yes. That," he replied stiffly. "A lover, so you are not... forgotten."

"Yes. Although, not officially. To be partners in Lenola, you have to apply for a license. Families are restricted. Space is limited." And why was he telling the jailor any of this? "It's complicated." He didn't want to reveal too much about Calen, should the jailor get any ideas about plucking him out of the plaza too.

Havok fell silent, leaving Dante to wonder why he'd asked. "Do *you* have someone?"

"No."

Havok said no more, and Dante got the impression he wouldn't react well to those questions he despised so much.

"What do you do?" Havok asked, adjusting the coat on the worktop. He still hadn't turned around. "A skill? A trade or profession? Your purpose? Everyone in Lenola has a purpose."

"Oh, this and that."

Havok turned, peering around his raised wing. "This and that?"

Dante rolled his hands. "I do a lot of different things."

"Like what?"

Havok appeared curious. That was good. The more he talked, the more he'd reveal. "A little farm labor, some guard work, if required. Some of the families with more coin pay handsomely to keep it out of the hands of those who don't have as much. I try to keep my nose clean. It doesn't always work."

"All of that is menial. What is your *purpose*?"

Rubbing his hands together, Dante tried to think of a purpose, a meaning to it all, but there wasn't one. Lenolians farmed, it was what they were good at. Their goods were sold and shipped out of the city, he assumed to other cities. He'd never much thought about it. "What's *your* purpose?" The question came out harsher than he'd planned, and predictably, Havok ignored it.

Instead, he asked, "Are you good, Dante?"

The question was so unlike Havok, that he chuckled. "I don't know. I try to be."

"But you don't *know*?"

Where was this going? "I've made mistakes, like any man."

"Such as?"

Dante leaned back in the chair and shrugged. "I guess, I could have been better, done more to help others. I've never really had a direction, a goal, not since..." He trailed off, wary of venturing into his past, but Havok's curious gaze suggested he genuinely wanted to know, and maybe it was time someone heard his thoughts, even if it was the monster who would probably kill him. "I was going to be a farmer, like most Lenolians, like my father. But that changed, and..." Irritation and inadequacy made his insides simmer. All the nights he'd spent passed out, high on ragvine, all the coin he'd squandered. If it weren't for Calen trying to keep him focused, he'd have been a vagrant on the streets, with no life and no direction. "I have more regrets than I'd like."

"Such as rallying a resistance group against me?"

"No." Dante laughed. "*That* was one of the only things I've done that felt right."

"Even though you failed?" Havok's lips hadn't changed from the snarl all evening, but there was a hint of that hidden smirk in his tone.

"At least I tried?"

"Is trying enough?"

"Nothing happens without it."

Havok considered the words with a huff and returned to his stitching. "I tried..." he said after so long a pause it took Dante a moment to remember the conversation.

"To be good?" Dante asked, sensing he was getting close to something, but like walking on thin ice, one wrong step and he'd have a bowl thrown at his face. But Havok fell quiet again. The next question had to be asked carefully, without judgment, or he'd shut down. "Do you think what you're doing to Lenola is good?"

"I..." He jerked his head up and froze. Even his tail ceased twitching.

Dante glanced at the sky but saw only thick, grey clouds. "What is it?"

"*Hide.*" Havok whirled and grabbed his sword from beside the workbench. "Under the cot."

"What?"

"Go!"

A wave of hot, dry air blasted from above. Dante looked up. The clouds had descended, coming in so low he could almost lift his hand and rake his fingers through them.

Havok slammed into him, hauling him clean out of the chair. "Hey!" He barely caught his balance, staggered, twisted, and was about to demand Havok let go, when a pair of enormous leathery wings flew open behind Havok's, and a beast straight out of Dante's nightmares grabbed Havok by his left wing and yanked him off the floor. The creature threw Havok against the rock wall. He slammed into it and dropped, then lay spluttering face-down on the floor.

The beast folded its wings behind it and angled all of its enormous bulk toward Dante.

It was so unlike Havok, Dante's thoughts failed to wrap around what he saw. Talons for nails, a spiked, lashing tail, gnarled horns that spiraled. Where Havok was half man, this monster was all beast.

Havok was trying to rise, but the bigger monster stomped toward Dante. Havok was in no condition to stop it.

Dante snatched the knife from his boot—the tiny blade was woefully inadequate compared to this heaving mountain of muscle with wings. "Yeah? You want this?" He'd read once that the best thing to do when faced with an animal bigger than yourself was rage at it, make yourself loud and terrifying. Or was it to play dead? By the powers, both actions would likely get him killed.

What was he doing? With the beast distracting Havok, now was the perfect time to flee. Dante stumbled against

DANTE'S END

the cot. He had nowhere to go, but... *up*. He slipped the knife into his pocket and using the cot as a step, he leaped, grabbed the jutting segments of wall, and climbed. He couldn't slow, couldn't stop, couldn't look down. The wall began to lean inward, but Dante dug his fingers deeper into each nook. There would be no better time to escape.

Havok's roar sounded. The huge beast growled. All Dante could do was climb and hope he made it to the top, to freedom.

The brittle sound of bone snapping filled the den. The beast let out a roar like thunder, rattling the wall Dante clung to. He glanced down. Havok clung to the creature's back. He'd bent one of its leathery wings at an awkward angle under his arm. The beast circled, grabbing at Havok, trying to pry him off. Havok's own wings flapped manically. His tail had looped around the creature's neck, choking off its air. The pair danced, crashing into the chair The beast stumbled through the firepit, scattering burning logs across the floor. *Havok might actually kill the thing...*

But Dante was done with this nightmare. He grabbed the overhang from beneath, swung out, and used every last bit of strength in his trembling arms to heave himself over its edge.

Suddenly exposed, the wind howled around him. He searched for any sign of houses, for streets, for anything familiar, but the world was a swirl of grey cloud and the vastness of a hungry void. He wobbled to his feet. The wind whipped through his hair and tugged at his clothes.

The clouds; he knew, deep inside, that the ground was far, far below.

This was the spire.

He'd been imprisoned atop the central spire, high

above the city, for the entire time. Right in the center of Lenola, but too far away to reach it.

The wall shuddered, cracked, shifted sideways—toward the clouds, tilting Dante downward. He dropped to his knees, swallowed his heart in his throat, switched his grip to the rock near his feet, and scrabbled back the way he'd climbed. But a rush of heat and light shoved him back. Fire raged inside the chamber. Embers twisted in the air, driven by leaping flames, and among those flames, the beast slammed Havok—still riding its back—into the wall right below Dante, again and again. More rock shifted and split. Dante's insides lifted as the overhang crumbled, with him still atop it.

He slipped, the rock splintered, and he slid backward. *No, no!* He reached for the edge and missed.

Havok's hand shot out of the dark. His clawed fingers sank into Dante's arm, catching him as the rock fell away, leaving Dante scrabbling midair, suspended by Havok's grip.

"Don't—don't drop me!"

Havok smiled, and it was almost like his old smiles, when they'd been boys, wrestling in the grass, when Havok knew he'd won. He opened his mouth to say something—

The enormous beast swatted Havok aside, dragging Dante with him. Dante dropped, and landed in a roll among smoldering rugs, and the scattered flaming contents of Havok's chamber.

He had seconds to regain his balance, to fight.

The beast yanked on Havok's tail, lifted him, and slammed him down against the floor. Havok's growl rumbled. He turned on the beast, springing at its face. The beast's tooth-riddled jaw yawned wide, about to clamp down on Havok.

Dante bolted for the creature, slammed his paring knife into its tree-thick thigh, and yanked, tearing open its leathery flesh. Blood pumped, slickening Dante's arm. The monster roared, fixed its ice-white eyes on Dante, and released Havok's tail.

Dante backed up, his tiny knife suddenly small again and his victory short-lived. The beast was large enough to crush him in one of its huge hands and now it was coming for Dante.

Havok shot into the air, reeled, and swooped back down, wings tucked in, turning him into an arrow. He grabbed the monster's horns, jerking the beast's head back, briefly arching the creature's spine. "The throat!"

Dante let the knife fly from his fingers. The point slammed into the creature's neck, puncturing a main artery, gushing blood.

The beast reeled, clutched its neck, and gurgled dark blood from its lips. But it wasn't done. It tossed its head, flinging Havok toward Dante. Havok threw open his wings—and for a moment they were all Dante saw—until Havok barreled into Dante, knocking him against the crumbling rock walls. His teeth rattled, fireflies danced in front of his eyes, his ears rang, and then he was falling again—the ground having vanished. The wall had collapsed, falling away completely, and once more he tumbled through the air. In the spiraling chaos, he grabbed for Havok's reaching hand. They locked grips, and it might have been the first time Dante saw real fear in Havok's eye. "Hold on!" Havok yelled.

He beat his wings, lifting them away from the spire's collapsing walls, carrying them higher above the raging monster as it ripped the flaming chamber apart.

Dante clung to Havok, praying to the powers that

Havok didn't decide this moment would be his last and let him fall. Through the smoke and raining rocks, he caught a glimpse of sparking lights far, far below. To the city he'd called home, so small, its ant-like people oblivious to the pair of furious monsters raging above it.

What if the beast flew down there?

"We have to kill it," Dante shouted over the wind, but Havok's wings flapped unevenly, dozens of bleeding wounds painting his body,

Havok panted through gritted teeth, carrying them higher on battered wings. "Not today."

They hadn't won this fight, they'd survived.

The burning spire's top faded beneath wispy clouds. The clouds swarmed in, masking which way was up or down. Dante gripped Havok tighter. He breathed in wet air, bowed his head to the wind, and listened to the heavy beat of Havok's wings.

Wherever Havok was taking him, the horrible sinking sensation in his gut suggested it was going to be worse than the prison chamber they'd just abandoned. The creature had come from somewhere. Hideous and strong, it wouldn't be the only one of its kind.

Perhaps the spire hadn't been a prison at all, but a sanctuary. There were more terrible beasts outside of the chamber, worse things than Havok, and now the only thing protecting Dante from them was the one monster he'd tried to kill.

CHAPTER 9

Havok dropped Dante and he landed on wet soil with a grunt, grateful for the cushioning moss. Havok slammed into the ground nearby, wings still flapping. He tried to stand, staggered, and fell.

A horrible hollow snap sounded, and his right wing buckled. Havok yelped and dropped, this time on his hands and knees. He bowed his head, and his body heaved with every labored breath.

Dante's own body ached and protested, bruised and cut up, but not as bad as Havok.

"This... is... your... fault," Havok snarled.

"Me?"

"I told you to hide!" He rocked back into a crouch and clamped a hand over the cut in his shoulder. His wings shuddered, and his right flopped at an unnatural angle. Havok growled at it, seething from agony or anger, maybe both.

"I didn't know that *thing* was out there!"

Havok gave an exasperated cry. "Thought I was the worst of the monsters, did you?"

Dante was not going to waste time arguing. There could be more of those beasts close by. He eyed their strange jungle-like surroundings. Tree leaves shone damp, lit by a strange ambient light that appeared to be coming from bundles of blue-headed flowers. The air was thick and warm, and faintly sweet. A heavy fog prevented him from seeing any further than a few feet around them. Wherever they were, this place was nothing like Lenola.

"Run, if you want," Havok snarled, misreading Dante's glances. "You won't last the night."

"I *should*," he grumbled. Standing, he brushed leaf litter from his trousers and approached Havok's broken wing.

"Do it." The jailor's teeth snapped together. "See how far you make it without me."

"Maybe I will." Many of Havok's feathers jutted at odd angles. Some he'd lost altogether, leaving sparse patches behind. The right wing was kinked, its leading edge snapped. "It needs righting and splinting or it will never heal."

"No."

Dante huffed through his nose at the stubborn fool. Havok was as likely to lash out with his fists as he was his tongue. "You're just going to drag your wing along beside you like a wounded bird?"

Havok's only reply was to hiss between his teeth. "Come any closer and I'll finish what the gregog started."

"Is that what that thing was? A gregog? Are there more of them?" The sweating brush and drip-drip sounds took on an ominous feel.

Havok snorted and bent forward, leaning on an arm. Although in pain, he still had enough breath in him to laugh. "You have lived as a fool and will die as one."

"And you're a dick. How far are we from Lenola? Maybe, if this fog lifts, I can find help." He said the words, but no help was coming. Even if he could find someone, what would he say? Ask them to help fix the monster that had terrorized them their whole lives? And if he stumbled into the path of something like the gregog, it would probably eat them both.

"Oh, screw this. And screw you." He grabbed Havok's wing and slammed the two jagged bones back into alignment.

Havok screamed, then pounced, tackling Dante into the dirt, pinning him down with a knee between his legs, his hands on Dante's chest. He seethed, breaths sawing through his teeth. Hate and pain burned in his red eye. The gem shone too, eradiating with hurt.

Dante had a hand on Havok's heaving chest, holding him off. But even wounded, Havok was capable of breaking Dante's neck. He wouldn't do it, not even in his fury. Dante had to believe that. They breathed hard, waiting, watching, so close to violence that the air between them sizzled with threat.

Havok's sneer faded and the rage contorting his face subsided. The firm pressure of Havok's smooth tail encircled Dante's ankle, ensuring if he fled, he wouldn't get far.

Havok's breathing slowed. Something sparked in the monster's eye, some kind of... recognition? A memory, perhaps, of tousling with Dante in the summer's long grasses. Dante opened his mouth to ask, but Havok snarled and reared up onto his knees.

Still pinned, Dante kept his hands raised. On his back, unarmed, Havok had won this fight.

"I should have let you fall," the jailor muttered.

He could have. But Havok had saved him when the walls had collapsed. For all his rage and sniping comments, he'd protected Dante. He'd also told him to hide from the gregog and had hidden Dante from Reina. Why despise him, yet go to great lengths to keep him safe?

Dante might begin to believe Havok had a shred of good in him, if he hadn't stolen Dante from his life and stabbed him through the gut with his sword—now lost in the den's rubble, thank the powers.

Havok's tail tightened some more around Dante's ankle, not yet painful, but enough to remind him how that tail could choke the life from him as easily as Havok's hands. The jailor's eye narrowed, his gaze turning curious, then he snorted a dismissive grunt and crawled off, dragging his broken wing through the dirt alongside him. "Come. We cannot stay here."

Dante climbed to his feet and picked dead leaves from his clothes. The scent of smoke and blood lingered around him. His fingers snagged in his hair; he yanked at it, pulling out knots, and stumbled after Havok.

Havok's limp wing left a trail in the leaf litter. It was going to need a splint or he'd never be able to use it again, but according to Havok, his abundance of stubbornness would be enough to fix it.

They walked on, Dante following Havok's trail in the dirt. Havok appeared to know which direction they were heading in. Dante certainly had no clue. The wet trees and vibrant green bushes all looked the same and there was nothing above, no stars, just oppressive darkness. Animals hooted and chittered in the fog. Harmless animals, he hoped. Havok didn't seem bothered by them, but he was also distracted by hugging his middle and dragging his wing.

The third time Havok stumbled, Dante circled ahead and blocked his path. "We should stop."

Havok's permanent snarl rippled. "And where do you propose we do that?"

"Right here will do, before you fall down."

"As though you care." He shoved by Dante and stomped on.

"I don't, but I'm not going to pretend I don't need you." Dante hurried up behind him. "You're right. There's a lot I don't know. That gregog thing... that was just a tiny piece of your secrets, wasn't it?"

"We must keep moving."

"Where?" Dante dashed ahead a second time and spread his arms. "Where are we going?"

"I must speak with Reina—" He cut himself off and glanced over his shoulder, watching the fog for threats.

"Your master?"

Havok grunted. "She sent the gregog. She knew... She knew I hadn't killed you... *yet*." He snapped that last part. "I have to explain what's happening here."

"Good, while you're at it, explain it to me too."

"I could." He snorted, then caught a knotted root under his boot and tripped, falling to his knees. His wing twitched. He hissed and growled, clambering back to his feet, clearly in pain.

"I am done. With you, with this place." Dante dug his heels in and folded his arms. "We're staying right here until you splint that wing."

"Stay here and die." Havok plodded on between the trees. Within a few strides, the fog closed in, blurring his disappearing form, and after a few more steps, he was gone altogether.

Alone, the fog muffled everything but Dante's heartbeat.

He'd be damned if he was going to trudge behind Havok like a pet. All that was missing was the leash. No. Damn him. Damn all of it. He kicked at the dirt and leaned against the nearest tree. He'd done enough, gone far enough, suffered enough. He refused to go a single step more.

Thumping his head back against the tree's lumpy bark he closed his eyes. "By the powers, I'd sell my right arm for some ragvine." It had been cycles since he'd touched the poisonous plant, since he'd craved it, but the vine would make this nightmare a dream.

Something rustled in the bush to his right. Something... not small. Dante straightened. He'd lost his knife in the gregog's neck and his only means of defense had just stalked off without him.

It was probably a squirrel. The bush shivered and a creature snuffled out from under it. Long snout, four legs, covered in black fur. As big as a farm dog, it looked mostly harmless. Dante crouched. The thing's little whiskers twitched and its beady eyes blinked at Dante. He extended his hand...

Havok pounced from the fog, slammed his clawed hands down on the fluffy creature, and broke its neck with a grisly crack. "Dinner."

Dante blinked, somehow disgusted *and* impressed by Havok's stealth. "It's no surprise you don't have friends."

If Havok heard he didn't reply, just turned and started off again. "This way, there's a stream. We'll clean up, eat, and rest there."

Havok built an unlit fire beside the trickling brook in the divot made by a fallen tree, while Dante plunged his hands into the cool water and washed off the blood and dirt.

He dragged his fingers through the whiskers on his chin, dislodging grit and things he did not want to dwell on.

He cupped water in both palms and drank until Havok's rustling drew his eye. The jailor had gathered dry twigs and leaves from a sheltered spot under the fallen tree. He rippled his fingers over the pile of tinder, the little gem on its chain between his horns winked, and tiny flames burst into life.

"What the..." Not wishing to appear more a fool than Havok already believed him to be, he quietened himself and watched.

Havok fed the small fire, so engrossed in his task he hadn't notice Dante's gaze. He'd seen Havok do something similar when they were small, but back then he'd just assumed he'd had some kind of fire-lighting implement. But he had nothing now, just his hands, and that gem. Did the gem give him that power? Dante almost asked, but then remembered the rule: No questions.

Yet he had so many.

As boys, he'd asked Havok about his horns—where they'd come from, what they were for—but Havok hadn't known the answers. They'd just always been a part of him. The gem too, he'd always had it. It was just another part of him, like his tail.

Havok picked up the limp body of the critter, dug a claw in, ripped off its skin in one efficient tug, gutted it, and slung it on a spit over the flames.

"How far is Lenola?" Dante asked, taking up a spot by the fire.

"You can't ever go back," Havok replied without a shred of doubt. He knelt by the stream's edge and cupping water in his palms, washed his arms and chest down, cleaning off dried gregog blood and his own.

"It's my home."

"'Home'?" Havok winced and rolled his scabbed and bruised shoulder, then ran his hand over the firm bicep and down his veined forearm. "There is no such thing, just the illusion of one."

As he washed, his tail lay behind him, so close to Dante's boot he was tempted to poke it. "Illusion or not, there are people there I care for." Would Havok even know, if he just prodded the appendage? Would it move, like a snake?

"Who, this... lover of yours? You are dead to them. Move on." The pointed tip of Havok's tail twitched.

Dante folded his arms and turned away, resisting the urge to touch the tail. "Yes, him. But others too. Jean, she was a good friend. Ricard's death—" He cut himself off, not wanting to recall how Havok had knocked Ricard from the roof. He missed Calen. Missed his laugh, his lighthearted manner, how he made everything seem easy. Dante missed his old life, simple as it had been. At least it had been better than the horror he was living now.

"If you go back, you'll risk all their lives." Havok returned to the fireside, his silvery hair wet and swept back, away from his four horns, and his face clean. "Those who leave must never go back."

Nobody *left* Lenola. Nobody needed to. The mountains cradled them, and they had everything they needed within the city. "Why?"

Havok picked up a stick and poked the fire. "Ignorance is peace."

Beside the fire, muffled inside the fog with just the tinkling stream beside them, this moment was soft again, one of few he'd found when Havok lowered his guard. "Do you think you're protecting them?"

He didn't answer, just poked the fire. His tail flopped one way, then the next.

At times like this, Havok was open, and Dante guessed... *vulnerable*. He couldn't resist driving a verbal blade in. "The only thing they need protection from is you."

Havok stood so fast the fire spluttered and almost extinguished itself. He returned to the stream, scooped up handfuls of water, and began to wash his wings. Mottled bruises on his back showed just how much of a beating the gregog had given him. But if it was like before, he'd heal within hours.

"You should fix that wing," Dante said. "You heal fast. It will heal bent."

"I don't need your advice. It is fine."

"It's clearly not fine." One sharp twist, and it would split apart again. "I'll help you."

"Help me or hurt me? You don't even know your own mind. Am I your enemy or not, Dante?"

That was a good question. He wasn't sure he knew anymore. When he didn't reply, Havok glanced over. He rose, shifted his wing, and made his way back to the fireside. The campfire's light played over his scuffed chest. When Havok had pinned him earlier, and Dante had held him off with his hands on his chest, his skin had been warm, soft, his chest masculine and firm. Dante had expected him to be cold and hard, the same way he behaved and sounded.

Havok plucked the roasted critter from the spit, tore a leg off, and handed it to Dante. "Eat."

Dante tried not to snatch it and devour it in a few

bites, but he was starved. Surviving on just bread, vegetables, and some fruit had left him desperate to sink his teeth into something moist and meaty. He groaned. The critter had looked cute, but it tasted better. He caught Havok's long stare and swallowed his mouthful. "Whatever this is, it tastes divine."

Did a little heat warm Havok's cheeks? He smiled and took a bite of his roasted limb.

They ate side by side, and despite the swirling fog and the unknown waiting on the other side of it, Dante almost felt comfortable. Havok might have been the only thing *not* wanting to kill him. He accepted more meat from Havok, and ate heartily, sometimes watching Havok gnaw on the bone. His sharp teeth hadn't been so viciously sharp when he'd been smaller. The young Havok had bared them a few times in snarls, making Dante laugh. His claws were weapons now, but when they'd wrestled by the pond, those claws had tickled Dante's ribs. He hadn't laughed as hard or as freely since those days.

"What's the story behind the butterfly tattoo?"

Havok's brow furrowed. He glanced down at his hip, twisting at his waist to see the ink. "Ah, my companion."

Like an imaginary friend? But Havok made no further effort to explain. "You told me the butterflies spoke to you. I thought you mad."

"Oh, they talk." Havok nodded, chewing on his roasted limb. "At times, too much."

"You still hear them?"

Havok shook his head, dislodging bangs of damp hair that fell between his horns. "There are no butterflies here. Not in this place."

This might have been the most answers Dante had

ever gotten from him. "What do they say?" he asked, keen to keep going.

"They are fanciful. They talk of many things. Much of it is nonsense... like you." Havok huffed a laugh and Dante let a chuckle slip free.

"They like to tell stories," Havok went on. "Some are real, some are fiction, some a mixture of both, I think."

Storytelling butterflies. Only in Havok's world was something so insane possible. "You always did like stories."

"Truly?" Havok's eyebrow arched, his face curious.

"Your favorite was of a king who lost his marks. You'd have me read it over and over."

His icy smirk thawed and it almost seemed as though the smile he revealed was the first real smile Dante had seen on him. Strange, how that one small thing could change his whole appearance.

"Do you remember?" Dante asked, braving his wrath for daring to ask such a pertinent question.

Havok jerked his chin, sniffed, then lunged. His hand clamped over Dante's mouth. Dante tensed, assaulted by the surprise and the visceral feel of Havok slammed close. "Hush," Havok whispered, then pulled, urging Dante from the fireside. The last time Havok had warned him, he'd been too slow to react and almost gotten them killed. That wouldn't happen again. Dante nodded, and Havok removed his hand but led Dante to the divot in the ground, where the fallen tree's roots had made a depression in the earth.

Havok guided Dante down among the gnarled roots in silence, his gaze on the blanket of fog above them, and then he folded himself in close, pressed awkwardly alongside Dante, and hooked an arm around his waist. His surprising warmth coiled around Dante.

Havok's hand covered his mouth again, and now he had a whole lot of firm male plastered up his entire left side, and by the powers, it had been a while since anyone had held him close, since he'd felt the quiver of muscle and the flutter of another man's breath on his neck. Calen had been the last and that hadn't gone well, due to Dante's lack of interest.

Unexpected shivers teased down his spine. He squeezed his eyes closed and tried to focus on anything but Havok's skin sliding against his own, of the hand over his mouth, firm but not painful. He needed to get control of himself, to think of something else, something much less arousing.

A winged beast slammed to the ground. Its arrival slapped his runaway thoughts aside. The thing was huge, four legged, longer and thinner than the gregog, its movement quicker. It whipped its feathered head back and forth, sniffed, and gobbled up the remains of the critter they'd cooked.

Havok's steady breathing calmed Dante's racing heart. If Havok was calm, then they'd be all right.

The creature snuffled around the camp some more and when a cry sailed through the fog, it lifted its head and took off, leaving swirling fog behind.

Dante's heart thumped, racing too hard. Havok's hand slipped from his mouth and came to rest on his shoulder. His other arm was still looped around Dante's middle. By the powers, they hadn't been closer in cycles. Havok's breath teased the fine hairs against the nape of Dante's neck. He'd kissed Havok before, knew how he tasted, warm and spicy, of exotic things. Havok had once explored his body with his tail, using it to stroke over his hip and around his waist. Dante's cock warmed at the memory, and his breathing deepened, no longer from fear.

"You can move now," Havok's deep voice rumbled.

He jolted into motion, scrabbled out of the divot, and marched to the fire, careful to face away. "What was that *thing?*" Was his voice too high? It was definitely too high. He cleared his throat and glanced back to see if Havok was grinning.

"Everything down here is prey for everything up there." Havok pointed up. "That includes us." Some little spark of intrigue shone in Havok's eye. Was it curiosity or lust or laughter, or maybe all three?

Havok dropped his hand and adjusted the front of his scuffed and torn trousers. Oh damn. Was he... Did he.... Or maybe he'd just been uncomfortable for another reason that had nothing to do with getting hard *for Dante?*

This was madness. Dante had lost his mind. No man in his right mind would get hard for a mass-murdering, bone-collecting monster.

The jailor ate people, cut them up, and used their skin to make his clothes. And those were the things Dante *knew*. The things he *didn't* know were probably worse. He staggered to the stream and splashed cool water on his face. It didn't mean anything. He was just... frustrated. He and Calen had been struggling. They hadn't been intimate for a long time. His reaction was just... desperation. Havok was intriguing to watch. He moved like a predator, his every inch of muscle closely controlled. Poised, strong, but not brutish—qualities Dante had always admired.

If Havok knew his thoughts he'd laugh and wouldn't stop.

"We must move along before it returns," Havok said.

"Uh huh, yeah." One more splash. He sighed, willed his

heart to quit racing, and with his body back under control, he followed Havok from the camp.

He definitely did not *want* Havok. Like that. And even if he did, which he didn't, Havok wouldn't be interested. He'd made it clear where they both stood, with Havok holding Dante's leash.

CHAPTER 10

*D*ante sat on a patch of grass while Havok dozed nearby, propped against a leaning tree. He'd tried to get some rest, but too many chirps and rustles, clicks and caws, kept his nerves rattled.

So he sat, with his knees drawn to his chest, and considered all the things he thought he knew but probably didn't. The jailors took an offering from Lenola every cycle and had done so since before Dante was born. Calen wanted children. Dante had known family was important to him. It always had been. And he'd agreed they'd adopt, when the time was right. But he'd lied, said he wanted kids to keep Calen smiling. And Calen had begun to suspect the truth.

But Dante had been of the mind that what was the point of a family if the jailor could take them away?

By the powers, he'd made stupid mistakes. And for what?

Lifting his gaze, he peered into the mist. The rising sun revealed green vegetation, dotted with enormous trees full of thick, rubbery leaves. Grasses taller than Dante swayed.

The more the fog lifted, the more its absence revealed a strange land. Jagged black mountains jutted in the distance like teeth in a monster's jaws. On and on, they went. He'd rarely felt so small. The higher the sun rose, the more the strange new world came into view. In the distance, the trees vanished under purple-tinted skies with several dark shapes moving among distant clouds. More monsters, he presumed.

This land wasn't Lenola.

Although, if Havok was with him, did that mean Lenola was safe from its monster? It should, but there was too much Dante didn't know. What was stopping things like the gregog from descending on Lenola? What stopped things like that winged creature that had eaten the rest of the critter? What if the only thing stopping them *was* Havok?

Had that been why Havok had returned all cut up that day? He'd fought a beast, kept it at bay? He'd hinted at it. Said he *protected* Lenola. But why take people at all? And what did Reina have to do with... any of it? Why was it so damn important to her that Dante die?

And where the fuck were they now?

Everything was so different from his home, his city, his life. But one thing was clear. Dante did not belong.

As Dante mulled on the impossible, Havok awoke, rose, and approached, his wing still a hindrance. "We must cross this plain. Reina's palace is near the base of those mountains."

Dante didn't see a damn thing, certainly not a palace, just heat haze and a whole lot of barren nothingness. "You gonna tell me why you're keeping me around?"

Havok's eyebrow arched again, like it did whenever he queried Dante's apparent foolishness. "I already did."

"As your entertainment? Are you really that lonely that you'd keep someone you hate for company?"

"Hm."

"Hm?"

Havok didn't reply, just stared across at the plains. The soft breeze ruffled the silvery hair and the thin early morning sunlight glinted on the ring around his lower right horn.

"You know what would be useful to get across that?" Dante gestured at the expanse of nothing. Havok tilted his head. "Wings."

The jailor frowned at his broken wing. "I suspect it needs splinting."

"Does it?" Dante almost choked on a dry lump of laughter. "What a surprise."

"Will you help or are you going to sit there and stew in the foul mood you've woken in?"

"I already offered to help and you refused. So, the deal has changed. I'll help, but what do I get?"

Havok folded his arms. "Not to die."

He snorted. "That threat is wearing thin."

A little bit of secret amusement glinted in Havok's eye. "I'll answer three of your irritating questions."

"Just three? Make it five."

"No."

"Four?"

"No."

He wasn't going to budge. But he did arch an eyebrow and slant a glance at Dante that seemed to suggest further negotiation might be possible later.

"Three it is." Dante stood and met Havok's cool, thin gaze. "Such a shame we can't splint your delightful personality."

"There's little need to fix that which isn't broken, Dante."

Oh. He had a reply for everything. Although, Dante caught that same glimmer of mischief in his eye as he'd seen before. The jailor had a sense of humor, it just happened to be buried under layers of thorns.

Dante chuckled, heading back into the trees. "I'll find you a splint." Few branches yielded a limb large enough to brace Havok's wing, but he did eventually find the perfect one, although still attached to a tree.

Dante headed back and spotted Havok in the same place he'd left, standing with his back to the trees, one wing bent, hair ruffled by the breeze, gazing out at the expanse they'd soon have to cross. He hadn't noticed Dante's approach.

Havok raised a hand, and on the claw of his forefinger a tiny blue butterfly perched. It glittered in the sun, as though made of mist.

He'd said there weren't butterflies here, so what was this one...

Strange, how the butterfly was the same size and color of Havok's tattoo. Dante couldn't see the location on Havok's back, his wings obscured it, but this living version seemed almost identical.

Havok raised his hand, spread his fingers, and the butterfly danced around his claws. Watching Havok play with butterflies wasn't the surprise it should have been. The true surprise was his smile. Soft and true, it took Dante back to those days by the pond when Havok had listened to his storytelling, enthralled by every word, his tail looped around Dante's ankle, its tip tapping his leg. They'd laughed at the story's silly ending with the king trapped in ice for all eternity. What kind of ice could trap a king?

Havok suddenly stilled. His back straightened. He flicked his fingers and the butterfly vanished, evaporating in the sun. "Back so soon?" he said.

Dante cleared his throat, and the soft familiar feelings with it. "I found a branch, but you'll need to break it."

Havok plowed into the forest and under Dante's direction, tore the limb from its tree and stripped it of its leaves and twigs. With the splint prepared, Havok knelt, relaxed his wing, breathing through his teeth, and offered its broken length to Dante.

He'd expected the feathers to be wet, but they were smooth instead, and impossibly soft. So soft they invited Dante's touch. He may have stolen a few unnecessary strokes, drawn to their sheeny down. And carefully, he fixed the splint in place with strips from his torn and otherwise useless shirt.

Havok tested his wing. He wouldn't be able to fly, but at least the wing was fixed and wrapped out of the way.

Dante brushed his hands down and watched Havok roll his shoulders, testing out his balance. "At the rate you heal, it'll be fine in a few days."

"You are a practical man, Dante."

That almost sounded like a compliment. "I've had to be." The remains of his shirt weren't performing any function, so he unbuttoned it, pulled it free, and balled it up into a cloth to wipe dirt from his chest, while he considered how much to tell Havok about his past. "I was orphaned young. Shortly after we met. Since then, I've been alone."

Havok's keen-eyed glare narrowed. "Orphaned by my predecessor."

Of course he'd know. "Yes. Pah was chosen as an offering. Mah refused to leave him. They er... They locked me in my room." He rubbed at a stubborn bit of dirt but the damn smudge wouldn't come off. "I escaped—ran to the plaza."

"You saw it?"

"Everything." The memories were old but still barbed. He'd fought the crowds to see and climbed onto the old bank roof. "It didn't have to take her too." He'd never seen a jailor before that moment. But as it had swooped down and plucked the two people who mattered the most to Dante from his life, he realized he'd seen a creature *like* the jailor before: the boy with wings and claws that came to him by the pond.

"Did you tell me what had happened?" Havok asked, his tone curious.

"I was angry, for a long time. I vowed never to go back to the pond, to you. But I'd given you my word I'd return. Eventually, after several cycles, I did, and you were there. Bigger, older, but still the same." All the fear and hate had faded as soon as he'd seen Havok waiting for him by the pond. He'd clung to that memory through the cycles, using it as a beacon of hope that not everything in this world was bad. That boy was still inside Havok; he'd seen him moments ago when he'd played with the butterfly. That was the real Havok. But Havok had locked him away, like Dante had been locked away that day. Something had happened to him too, turned him sour, made him forget.

"No, I didn't tell you what had happened. You weren't anything like the jailor. I didn't want my shitty life touching you." *And what we had.* He'd said too much. He looked up, but Havok was already gazing across the plains.

He probably hadn't even heard the confession. "Never mind."

"We'll cross at dusk," Havok said.

Didn't he care about their past at all? Or did he still believe Dante was fabricating it all to pass the time. "I fixed your wing, so when do I get my questions?"

"When we cross. Until then, rest. You will need your strength. The next part of your journey will be an arduous one."

Dante half laughed. "Is it not your journey too?"

He cast his gaze away again and as he admired the plains, a muscle fluttered in his cheek. "We'll see."

DANTE TRIED to doze in the shade against one of the trees, but his thoughts chased themselves around his head. Havok had no trouble sleeping; propped against the tree next to Dante's, he'd fallen asleep in moments, then woke and shifted position to lie on the ground. He'd caught Dante watching him, bared his teeth, then fallen right back asleep again.

Somewhere across the rippling heat haze was a palace, and Reina, Havok's overseer. And whatever or whoever she was, she wanted Dante dead. Why? And why did Havok answer to her?

Dante must have dozed, or daydreamed, because the warm, firm weight of a touch on his ankle jolted his mind back into the present moment. Havok's tail had looped itself around Dante's leg. Its pointed tip twitched, snaking beneath the trouser's cuff. Havok snored, fast asleep—but his tail was set on wandering.

Dante gave his foot a shake. The tail clung on. If he

tried to pry it off, it would wake Havok. He scowled at the smooth, crimson appendage. The younger Havok's tail had often reached for him—sometimes for fun, sometimes to irritate him, and sometimes for comfort. So what was this?

Havok was asleep, he didn't know what he was doing.

The tail was as thick as Dante's wrist at its base, but it narrowed to a triangular point. There had been one time, by the pond, when Dante had grabbed it and dared to stroke it. Havok had yanked the thing back as though Dante had set it on fire. He'd sulked for the rest of their time together that day. If he touched it now, Havok would wake up, and he'd be furious. Dante grinned at the thought. Havok might throw a few insults, threaten to kill him, hiss at him, and probably strut off in a huff. But the death threats were empty, and they both knew it.

He was beginning to understand this Havok. He could be vicious, could kill in a blink, but he was curious too, and careful, and had a lot more happening inside his head than he let fall from his lips. He threw threats around like knives, and if they didn't work, he lashed out, but he also exercised restraint. If Havok had been a man, Dante would assume he'd been viciously attacked in the past. His myriad of scars suggested great physical pain, and his wariness might have stemmed from mental trauma. Havok, the boy, hadn't been so scarred.

Dante left the tail where it was and roamed his gaze along its length to Havok's leg, the curve of his ass, clad in scuffed leather pants, his bare chest and arms. He'd been so shy, revealing his wings, letting Dante touch his horns, and that time, when they'd kissed. *"You're my secret,"* he'd told him.

And later Dante, like a fool, had ruined it all. Dante had wanted to be liked, to be loved, to have something normal in his life, to have a friend. To not be alone anymore. So he'd told Calen he had a secret, one he hadn't visited in a while, and he'd taken him to the pond, thinking he'd be impressed. The idea was a stupid one, and a mistake. Dante made a lot of those.

But this one had cost Havok his eye, and maybe even his memory. What had happened to him in all those cycles since? What had turned him into the jailor?

So many damn questions, but he only had three chances to get his answers.

He'd have to be clever in what he asked. More clever than Havok. If such a thing were possible. And he had to find out why Havok was taking him to the one person they both knew wanted Dante dead.

CHAPTER 11

The sun dipped behind the mountains and the air cooled. Havok had woken as soon as the heat left the day and night approached.

Not wanting to get caught up in an awkward conversation about why his tail had claimed Dante's foot, Dante closed his eyes and pretended to sleep. Havok unlooped his tail without a word and its absence cooled Dante's leg.

"Come," Havok said. "The half-light is a good time to cross."

They began in earnest, leaving the tree cover and cutting through the tall, damp grass. Havok watched the skies and the widening expanse in all directions. There was no doubt they were exposed, but this was clearly familiar territory for him.

"If I give the word, you must take cover in the grass," he warned.

Dante nodded. "How many monsters are there out here?"

"Is that one of your questions?"

"No, I..." He chuckled at Havok's prickliness. "Forget I asked."

They'd made it a few more paces when Havok said, "What you call monsters are the sacha. I am one of them." He glanced behind him, eyebrow raised, looking for Dante's assessment.

"But you're..."

"Different?"

"Well, you're capable of talking, for one, and the beasts we've encountered don't appear to be."

"I am different. I was *made* different."

Dante waited for him to explain. But he strode on with no further details forthcoming. Made? Who made him? Dante pushed through the grass alongside him, drawing level so he could see Havok's face. "What does that mean? *Made*? Who made you?"

"Lenolians are born, yes? You breed and that's how you produce more of you. That's not how I came to be." He extended his hand, and ran a sharp claw across his wrist, over a fine pale line. Dante had seen similar scars on him. He'd assumed they were scars from old wounds. "I was made. Stitched together. Crafted from pieces."

"What?" Dante frowned. "Like a doll?"

"A doll?"

"Never mind." He wasn't born. He'd been made. "Who made you, Havok?"

"Reina."

Reina had stitched him together with what, spare parts? "If you were made then..." He trailed off as his thoughts derailed into disturbing territory. Havok had both man and monster parts. Where had the man parts come from? He recalled the bones beneath the floor, the way Havok had stitched himself a coat made of skin, and he didn't want to think anymore after that.

"What's wrong?" Havok enquired.

"Nothing."

"My origin disturbs you." He said it fact-like, unconcerned, just curious. Perhaps even amused. His smirk was back too. "Ask your questions, Dante."

"What does the gem do?" He gestured at his own forehead to mirror the placement of Havok's ruby gem.

"Ah, yes. My mark. You've seen how I have a small measure of power. I am able to kindle fire, for example." He raised his hand and a tiny flame hovered above his palm. But just as quickly as he showed it, he snuffed it out again. "Reina bestowed me with this mark. It is her gift to me and I am forever in her service. Your next question?"

But that one had produced so many more questions, such as what other powers did he have? Did all monsters have a mark? Did that mean all monsters were made by Reina? But he had to stay focused. He knew the questions that needed to be asked. The rest could wait.

"Why are you keeping me alive? And don't tell me it's for entertainment. It's more than that."

Havok's smirk bloomed into a smile. "The day I took you, I witnessed how you held that Lenolian female back in the plaza. I assume I was due to take her loved one as the offering. Your intervention caught my eye, but then your team attacked, and while they had weapons, you were the one in control. You were the most dangerous element in that plaza. I took you as a warning to those who remained. Standing against me is a futile exercise."

"Then you didn't take me because you recognized me?"

"Is that your third question, Dante?"

"Shit, no. Wait—"

"I've told you multiple times how I do not know you. Think carefully now, I'll not be this lenient with answers again."

He wanted to ask so many different things, but he'd decided long ago what his third question would be. He just wasn't sure if he was ready to hear the answer. They walked on, carving two adjacent paths through the grass. The sun had vanished behind the mountains now, taking its warmth and light with it. But ahead, hidden in the ripples of the heat-haze, jagged spires jutted from the ground, like the points on a crown. The palace. It had to be. And perhaps where Dante's journey ended.

"Will you kill me?" he asked.

Havok stopped so suddenly that Dante almost plowed into him. The jailor's smile had locked on his face, briefly frozen there as though he knew that anything else might reveal too much. "As much as I might wish it, I will not kill you, Dante."

His relief was almost palpable. He puffed out a sigh, and even laughed. "All right." This was good. Whatever happened, Havok wouldn't kill him, might even save him again like he had several times already.

Havok turned his back and marched on. "No more questions."

Bolstered by the good news, Dante hurried on. "An observation then? This Reina... You say she created you?"

"Yes."

"She lied. You had that gem when we were small. It's yours, she did not give it to you."

"I've had it since I was made," Havok said, matter-of-factly. "It's mine *and* hers. It belongs to me, and thus I belong to her." He skimmed his clawed fingers across the gem, making it sparkle. "I've revealed enough."

"Why are you taking me to her if she means to kill me?"

"No more questions."

"Will she kill me like her monster tried to do?"

"Not monster. Sacha."

"Like her fucking sacha tried to do?"

"She will not kill you."

"But it's your job, as the jailor, to kill the offering?"

"Harvest."

"What?"

"I do not kill them, I harvest them."

Dante stopped in the long grass, heart and guts sinking. He knew, suddenly. It was there all along. The people of Lenola, they lived their quaint little lives in the safety of the city. It wasn't perfect, but it was home, even in the shadow of the spire and the jailor. But they weren't free. They were being farmed. Havok had called Dante his pet. The monsters reigned above... the Lenolians lived below, and everything below was prey for the things above. The offerings were harvested for *spare parts*... to make Reina's monsters.

It was so awful, he almost couldn't withstand it. "By the powers..." He staggered to a stop. Nausea simmered in his gut.

Havok turned, frowning. "Come, we must not dally out in the open."

"'Dally'?" No, he couldn't do this. He couldn't walk to that monster's palace; he couldn't be a part of this insanity. His parents, after they'd been taken, had been stripped and dissected for parts?! Like the hundreds of innocent people before and after them. Dante was just meat, just pieces, destined to be made into something else...

"Dante..." Havok growled.

Dante turned. "No." He had to get back to Lenola, to tell them the truth. Somehow. Their lives were a lie. He bolted back through the trampled grass. Fuck Havok and his sacha. Fuck them all. It was wrong. Everything was wrong. They needed to know. He had to tell them!

Havok slammed into him, somehow kicking Dante's legs out at the same time as shoving him forward. He toppled, landed on his shoulder, and scrabbled forward, clawing at the grass and dirt. Havok scooped an arm under him and wrestled him onto his back. He had one wing raised, the other trapped in its splint, making him lopsided but no less powerful. His vicious snarl stilled Dante. His gem sparkled.

"Stop," Havok warned.

"I can't—I can't be a part of this." He shoved at Havok, wildly punching him.

Havok grabbed his wrists, pinching them together against Dante's chest. "You do not have a choice."

"Get off me, Havok."

"That is not my name." His sharp teeth gleamed.

"No, you're right, it's not. Get the fuck off me or I'll scream and bring every monster for miles down on us."

Havok's smirk somehow found its way behind the snarl. "Not even you would be fool enough—"

"Try. Me." Dante shoved at his hold; pinned, he had nowhere to go, but he could scream like a damned gregog if that meant Havok let him up.

Havok dropped forward, snarling an inch from Dante's mouth. "You are nothing. You are pieces of sacha yet to be made. Your life is insignificant. I am the only thing between you and your pitiful destiny and you are testing my patience—"

"You're a heartless beast. And to think I once cared for

you. I must have been out of my mind. *You disgust me.*" He spat in Havok's face

Havok recoiled. His snarls vanished with a hiss. He dropped his head, hovered his lips close to Dante's, his one good eye dazzling—a brilliant window into the monster's brittle soul—and then his mouth slammed over Dante's, and his tongue thrust in, his body surging, driving against Dante's. He tasted of spices, of warmth, how Dante remembered, and for the briefest of seconds he was beside the pond again, kissing Havok, hand sliding up Havok's chest as Havok's tail slid up his leg.

Havok had him pinned, his hands trapped between them, his mouth a scorching tease.

Dante swept his tongue with Havok's, sucked on his lip. Lust burned beneath his skin and down his back, but the rage was far more potent. Rage at the jailor and his lies. He bit, teeth sinking into Havok's lip. Havok tore free with a cry and spat blood to the side. "You fiend!"

Dante writhed, Havok fought to keep him pinned, and when Dante got a hand free, he swung his fist, catching Havok with a right hook in the jaw. Havok reeled just enough to tip his weight back. Dante bucked, kicked Havok off him, flipped onto his front and scrabbled through the grass.

Away... he had to get away!

The feathered sweep of a wing slapped Dante sideways. He rolled, tangled in grass, and then Havok was on Dante's back, his hot breath brushing his neck. "Hm... don't think I don't know how much you want me," he purred, pouring the words into Dante's ear. "You may have taken my eye but I am not blind." He hooked an arm around Dante's chest, hauling him up onto his knees and back into Havok's crushing embrace. "All the times you watched me, Dante. The lust in your gaze. I saw." Something rigid probed against Dante's lower back. Havok growled and thrust the rod harder—his cock, hard for this, for Dante. Dante knew he should hate it, should fear it, but his fierce strength, his rough handling, it peeled the wrong kind of moan from Dante's lips.

Dante writhed, but trapped in Havok's arms, he couldn't escape. "I'll kill you."

Havok chuckled, pouring more delicious shivers through Dante's traitorous body. He didn't *want* Havok, he couldn't, but by the powers, he *yearned* for his touch, for that tail to explore again, for his mouth to brand Dante's skin.

"Challenge accepted, little pet." Havok's thick, wet tongue swept up the back of Dante's neck and must have had some direct link to his cock, because the damn thing was as hard and hot as forged iron. And when Havok sucked on his ear, the resulting moan couldn't have been Dante's.

His tail... Its firm press looped up Dante's leg, around his thigh. And then its tip swept between his legs and stroked his cock, through his trousers. He gasped, and a demand for more almost fell off his tongue but he swallowed it.

Havok spun Dante in his arms, grabbed his chin, and tilted his head back. "We are not boys now." Sharp claws dug into Dante's cheek. He was too strong, too everywhere. Dante bared his teeth and panted through his nose.

This kiss was like the first, only Havok's tongue swept in, claiming, devouring, and Dante had no defense against it. He took it with his own, tasting Havok, drawing him inside, kissing him back as though Havok was his whole world. *By the powers, yes.* This was what Dante had wanted since he'd known who he was, since before then, when he'd ached for a touch that couldn't ever be Calen's. The sensation of having his soul set ablaze and his body burned up. He'd sought it elsewhere, paid to chase the high in the hands of strangers, drowned himself in ragvine, tried to summon it from other lovers, from Calen, but none had felt like this—like Havok was the *only* creature who could make him feel alive.

Havok broke the kiss, breathing hard. Dante searched his face for any sign that he remembered. He *had* to. If he remembered nothing else, he must remember the kiss?

Havok smiled and dragged a claw along Dante's bottom lip. "My butterfly boy."

That name... "You *do* remember."

Havok laughed, but the sound was fractured, pieces of it falling away. He shoved at Dante's chest with a hand, knocking him down. The wickedness Dante had seen in the spire's chamber shone in Havok's eye now. "How could I forget?" He flicked a hand at his missing eye and the scar left behind. His laughter cut off, sliced away, and he sneered. "When you left your mark so permanently."

The horrible, sickening sense of betrayal chilled Dante's blood. He'd known it to be a game, but he hadn't realized how thoroughly he'd been played. "You never forgot, did you."

Havok laughed. "So sweetly gullible butterfly boy."

A black-winged monster swooped down behind Havok. As magnificent as she was monstrous, she wore a crown of razor wire around two spiraling horns and a scarlet smile. Black stitches crisscrossed her milk-white arms and neck, but the rest of her was hidden inside a black patchwork gown, similar in design to Havok's coat. And as she folded her wings in, she approached Havok. He didn't react, not at first, but as soon as she stopped beside him, he knelt, bowing his head. "Reina."

"Beric, you've brought me an offering? Such good timing. Your previous gift has become quite the bore."

He raised his head, fixed Dante in his gaze, and grinned.

Behind the devastating pair, the black masses in the sky Dante had thought to be clouds shifted, swirled, and pooled together in one great wave. He heard them then, the beat of a thousand wings, and they were all coming for him.

"Will he run?" Reina asked, head tilted, finger tapping on her chin.

"He'll try," Havok replied.

Dante ran.

CHAPTER 12

He thrashed along the trail they'd made in the grass, legs and heart pumping. If he could make it to the tree line, he might have a chance.

But as the swarm of beasts descended from above, his hope faded. They spiraled in a storm of howls. Claws swiped through the air, hands shoved. Dante escaped some, but others dug in, cutting open his arms and chest. Fiery pain hissed with each new cut. He dropped and hugged himself small, but they buffeted him from every angle. They'd kill him. He knew it.

A heavy net fell over him, crushing him under its weight, and then scooped him up, as though a giant had grabbed him. He tumbled, caught in the net's lattice ropes. Howls and snapping teeth, lashing tongues and zipping claws. Some caught him, tearing at him. It was all too much. He curled in on himself and let the monsters whir and rage. It would be over soon. It had to be. Dead or alive, he couldn't do anything to stop them.

And Havok... Havok had betrayed him. He was worse than Dante had imagined. He'd lied about forgetting, lied about everything! Dante had been a fool to listen, to let Havok lead him along, to believe there had been some good inside of him. Any glimmer of kindness had been an act. A ruse.

A trap.

After too long, when he feared the maelstrom would never end, the net opened and Dante tumbled, reaching for the net's edges, but they slipped from his fingers. He fell and hit the ground hard enough to punch the air from his lungs. His thoughts flickered, his consciousness fracturing. He had to stay awake; if he closed his eyes he might never open them again.

He rolled onto his side and coughed around a spasm of pain. Everything spun, his guts heaved, his ribs burned again, old breaks refracturing, and a thousand cuts leaked blood.

But he breathed, he lived... And the raging monsters were gone.

The same black rock as the spire surrounded him, the walls curved inward. He spotted a wooden door and half crawled, half staggered to it. It didn't open when he pushed against it, and there was no handle on the inside to grasp.

A prison, a cell, a hole in the darkness. He shivered, sick with fear and shock.

"Dante," Havok's voice echoed from above.

The walls were curved in a perfect circle and when Dante staggered back to the center, he looked up, and at the top, at its edge, crouched the smirking Havok.

"Why are you doing this?"

"Darling Dante, you know why."

He didn't want to talk to him, not anymore. All he'd get back was lies.

"Don't worry. I have a surprise for you," Havok said. "I think you'll like it."

Dante slumped against the rock wall and examined his cuts, already caked in filth from the bottom of the well. If the monsters didn't get him, infection probably would. "Am I to be kept in this hole now?"

"I'm sure you will come to appreciate it."

He lifted his head and fixed Havok in his glare. He didn't know him at all. "Fuck. You."

Havok chuckled and stood. "Thank you for the kiss." He touched his lips. "It'll be our secret. But Dante, *you mustn't tell*. Oh, and don't worry, *I'll come back*."

He vanished before Dante could throw him a rude gesture. For him to quote Dante's old words back to him, clearly Havok remembered everything. Which suggested all of it, from the capture in the plaza to the kiss, boiled down to revenge.

And maybe Dante deserved it.

CHAPTER 13

avok

He should have killed Dante when he'd first seen him at the city plaza; he could have grabbed him, flown high above the city, dropped him from a great height, and had the matter over with. He could have allowed him to die of rancid wounds instead of stitching him up. Could have let the gregog devour him, could have stood back while multiple sacha tore him to pieces. In all the cycles he'd watched him go about his life from above, he could have killed him during any day or night.

Instead, he'd done none of those things and Dante remained alive. Which had not been the plan at all.

He strode the vast hallways, wing tips brushing the arches he passed through. Other sacha nodded at his passing, regulars to Reina's palace. But few of his kin had access like Havok did. Although, he wasn't Havok here and never had been. He was Beric, Reina's favorite and most beloved of creations.

Spiral stairs took him down to where torches spluttered, holding back the damp and the dark. He passed locked doors, behind which Reina's creations shuffled and moaned in the shadows. Those ones had failed Reina and were destined for a life of solitude and darkness. Some he knew watched him walk free with jealous eyes.

When he'd first seen the enormous door ahead of him, he'd been small and timid, and the ugly wooden door with its grotesque gargoyle carvings erupting from it had looked like the real faces of sacha trapped in the wood. Now, he swept it open, no more disturbed by it than the countless array of enormous jars and their writhing, twitching contents. Limbs of all kinds hung suspended in preservative. He passed racks of bottled hands and feet, passed the wall-to-ceiling panels, on which hung wings of all shapes and sizes. And on the walls of the central dome, where the main workbench sat like a centerpiece, were a thousand pinned butterflies, all dead, their iridescent wings frozen in place forever.

Reina stood at her magnificent workstation, needle and thread in one hand; the other she used to trace the chest of the partially complete sacha tied down in front of her. Naked, the new sacha had been stitched all over, pieces of him changed, crafted, made better. He breathed hard around a gag. His wide blue eyes swiveled straight to Havok's approach.

"How is our new pet?" Reina continued to run her hand over her project's chest. She'd begun at the bottom and crafted him upwards, leaving the details of the head, her favorite part, until last.

"Settling in." Havok stopped beside the workbench

and rolled his shoulders, ruffling his good wing—the other remained splinted and fixed rigid. He'd always admired Reina, and enjoyed watching her work, but today a strange sense of unease slithered down his spine.

His gaze landed on the wall of motionless butterflies. He turned his face away and admired the new sacha instead. The sacha's suffering was a necessary baptism after which he'd begin a new life in Reina's service.

Reina looked up. Her black horns and wings shone like ink spilled around milk-white skin. She was his queen, his creator, and all things began with her. She never failed to enthrall.

"I sense some frustration, Beric. Is it disappointing you?"

"No, I..." How to describe his thoughts about Dante? He didn't know where to begin and wasn't sure he could explain the strange feelings inside. She didn't know he'd met Dante before. That was Havok's secret. And he didn't like to keep secrets from her. If she knew, she might take him from Havok, and he wasn't finished with him. "It was slow to understand the way of things. But it will come to accept its fate."

"They always do." She stitched the flesh up the side of the silent project and its eyes darted. It had probably learned not to move. Moving prolonged the agony. "Such simple creatures. However, why did you have him hidden, Beric, when I visited you?

He formed a lie quickly enough. "As a surprise. He wasn't ready. He needs... work."

"I'm interested to see what you do with the new pet before you present it. It has strength, the new one?"

"Some." Dante *did* have strength. He'd almost finished off the gregog Reina had sent to test him. Dante had also tended Havok's wounds when a sacha had attempted to breach his territory and attack Lenola. The resulting battle had left Havok bleeding and weak. Another fact Reina did not need to know.

"I do like it when they fight." Reina's sharp teeth gleamed. "They're so entertaining, don't you agree?"

"The stronger are more interesting than the weak." For so many cycles, he'd dreamed of all the things he'd do to Dante, all the ways he'd make him suffer. How he'd torture him. There was still time. This was just the beginning. But Reina could not have him yet, and that was... a problem.

Reina smiled at the subject, having stitched up his side. "There now. Isn't it marvelous?"

Havok regarded the subject. They were all much the same these days. None as good as Havok, naturally. But this one had retained many Lenolian features like Havok's. Arms, legs, hands with five fingers. No claws. And two heartbeats. They all had two. Apart from Havok. He'd only been given one.

"Why two hearts?" he asked.

"One for life and one for love."

"'Love'?"

"Removing the heart of love produces unfavorable results."

Then why did Havok have the one heart? Was his single heart an error? He hurried on to another subject, fearing she might recall her mistake. "Will you give it wings?"

She smiled and her dark eyes gleamed. "Wings are reserved for only my most precious."

The subject's eyes widened. It heard everything. Good. Havok leaned closer and studied its face. Half was bone and weeping flesh, but half was untouched, remaining as it had been when he'd plucked the subject from its life and brought it to Reina. "You should be grateful," he told the subject. "It is an honor to be changed." It didn't look grateful. The wide swiveling eyes and heaving chest suggested terror. Those eyes could almost be pretty, with their long dark lashes and warm tarnished bronze color. Did it recognize Havok? Did it remember? He hoped so. "Take one of its eyes," Havok said.

Reina turned to a tray of jagged saws and implements and picked up a spoon-shaped pair of forceps. "This one had a name, you said?"

"Yes." Havok stepped back, giving Reina room to work. She brought the forceps close to its face and it whipped its head to the side, moaning behind the gag.

Havok grabbed its chin. "Be still." Its gaze fell to Havok and really saw—*remembered*. A kernel of satisfaction grew in Havok's chest. *Yes, see me. See what you did. And witness my revenge.*

Reina thrust the forceps into the subject's eye socket. The subject bucked, unable to remain still. Its hands clenched, its back arched, but Havok held it, and with a jerk, Reina plucked the eye free and raised it high in triumph.

"Its name," Havok said, "was Calen."

CHAPTER 14

ante

THE WOODEN DOOR rattled and groaned open. Havok's distinctive silhouette filled the doorway.

This was Dante's chance.

He charged, his fist connected with Havok's jaw, snapping Havok's head back, staggering him, but as Dante dashed for the open doorway, Havok caught his arm, yanked him off his feet, and threw him facefirst against the stone wall, bending his arm behind his back and holding him pinned.

"This will be easier for the both of us if you behave." His cold, hard words brushed Dante's ear. "Allow me to be clear. If you run, you will die. And it will not be a quick, merciful death. You are but a toy, and the sacha will treat you as such. Nod if you understand."

"You didn't bring me here just to lock me away in a hole," Dante growled. With his face pinned, getting the words out wasn't easy, but he'd damn well be heard. "Why am I here? Revenge? Is that it?" He couldn't see Havok's face and even if he'd been able to, he couldn't trust what he saw. Dante had believed he'd known him, even just a small part of him, but in truth, he perhaps never had.

"Nod, if you understand," Havok repeated.

He was going to die here.

Not now, but soon. He knew it. His life and the world he lived in was a lie too. He didn't know what was real anymore. Was this a nightmare? Was he unconscious somewhere, under Havok's needle?

But maybe there would be a chance to escape, and maybe he could flee the palace, and just maybe he'd be able to find his way back to Lenola. He had to hope, didn't he? Because if he didn't have hope, then he may as well lay down and die now. And he wasn't ready to give up.

Dante nodded.

"Good."

Havok's weight eased enough for Dante to turn. Havok carried two wrist shackles clipped to a length of leather. A leash.

"Put these on."

"No."

Havok sighed, more exasperated than angry. "Do you want to leave this hole, or have you grown so attached to it that you'll happily stay?"

He hated the hole. He'd probably only been inside of it for a day and a night, but it had felt like weeks. He hated how the damp gnawed on his skin, rubbing it raw, hated how he had to relieve himself into the drain in the middle, hated how pathetic it made him feel.

He threw on the shackles, and Havok gave the leash a tug. "Obedience is an asset." He walked ahead and led

Dante through the doorway and into a narrow, arched corridor with no windows, just a few spluttering torches. Havok's wing arches scraped the ceiling. He wasn't heavy, like some of the monsters Dante had seen, but he still almost filled the space. There would be no room for two like him to pass or for Dante to run.

"Where are you taking me?"

"No questions."

Dante trudged behind, his bound wrists slung in front of him. "I preferred you when you were nice, even if it was a lie."

"It was easier to have you walk here under the power of your own two legs than have to carry your unconscious weight."

"I fixed your wing for you, you ungrateful dick."

Havok stopped. He didn't turn, but his wings twitched —the fractured one still fixed in its splint. "You are naive." His head tilted. Rippling torchlight slid down his horns, making them gleam and his silver hair shine. "You will come to learn respect."

"I respect honor, bravery, and integrity. All the things you lack. Why would I respect a monster like you?"

Havok moved so fast, all Dante knew was that his feet were no longer on the ground and the air rushed by him, then his back struck a wall, the door slammed, and he was plunged back into the darkness of his rancid cell once more, but now with his wrists shackled.

"You're nothing!" he yelled at the opening above. "Just a rabid beast! Calen's arrow should have killed you that day at the pond!"

Perhaps insulting Havok was the wrong course of action, but maybe he was up there, listening, and maybe inside that cold heart of his, something hurt. Because, by the powers, he'd take any kind of victory he could get, even one so small.

HE WASN'T GOING to die in the hole.

Lenola was out there somewhere, its people unaware their lives were games for monsters. Dante had to escape, somehow. He'd find a way back and tell them everything. The people of Lenola were farmers by nature, not warriors, but they could be, with motivation. He'd built a resistance group, people who had *wanted* change. They'd failed in taking down the jailor, but if they knew the fight was far bigger, they'd pick up their bows and quivers, and they'd go to war. Jean, she'd fight. After losing her sister to the jailor, she'd despised its rule, and to know there were others like him, to know it was all for nothing—she'd stand beside Dante and fight to the bitter end.

But none of that could happen if they didn't know the truth.

He had to get away from the monsters, and the chances of that happening hinged on Havok making a mistake.

He picked up a pebble and tossed it at the far wall, watching it bounce and clatter down the drain.

He'd have to convince Havok he was obedient and had no intention of running. Havok, who was suspicious of everything and everyone, who seemed to be able to read Dante like an open book. It wasn't going to be easy.

He regretted teaching Havok to read. Regretted all of those days by the pond, being nice to him, playing with him...

Dante shuffled down the wall some more. The cold,

hard floor gnawed at his ass. His stomach hurt from hunger and his mouth was parched and sore from cracks.

No more smart-mouthing Havok. He couldn't afford to rot in the hole, making himself weak. He had to obey, to be smarter, to get out of the hole and to use Havok. This was his life now, trapped down a damned well and in the hands of monsters. Havok *was* the only way out.

He tossed another stone. It hit a far brick, dislodging a tiny roll of stained paper from between the grout and then bouncing down the drain. The roll of paper fell from its hidey-hole, unfurling, and inside it almost looked as though there was writing...

He crawled forward and picked up the slip of paper. Its edges turned to dust in his hands, but he managed to pry it open enough to read the tiny, jagged words: *the mark is a lie*.

What mark? And who had written this? Where were they now? He studied the faded handwriting, finding something familiar within its swirls, an itch he couldn't scratch at the back of his mind.

Someone had thought those five words important enough to tuck them away for safekeeping. *The mark is a lie*.

Whatever it meant, it couldn't help him now. Dante gently rolled the paper up and poked it back into its hole.

The only marks inside the well were scratches on the stone he assumed were made by animals or previous prisoners.

He sat back, hugged his knees, and mulled the words over, then considered his plan to lull Havok into thinking him tamed, and he waited for Havok to return.

The door groaned on its hinges for a second time and Havok stood in its opening, arms crossed, waiting. "Have you reconsidered your attitude?"

Dante hobbled to his feet on stiff legs and raised his shackled wrists. "I'm sorry. For before. I understand now."

"Do you?" Havok's eyebrow arched.

"I do, I won't fight you."

Havok attached the leash to the shackles and led Dante from the well again.

This time, Dante kept his thoughts inside his head, focusing instead on his surroundings. Being smarter began *now*. The corridor widened, then joined another, finished with plaster with windows blocked by closed drapes. The air was warmer too, and smelled perfumed, like a summer's breeze across a meadow. He chuckled and almost fell over his own feet, earning Havok's one-eyed glare.

Maybe he was delirious from hunger? *Focus*. He couldn't afford to fuck this up again.

When they came upon another monster, it was all Dante could do not to stare. She was female, in so much as she had curves where curves should be, but her tail was a thick stump and her legs bent like... goat legs. He tore his stare away and fixed it over Havok's shoulder, between his wings, but felt the crawl of the female's double-lidded eyes until they'd turned another corner and walked out of sight.

How many monsters were there? Did they all come from this place?

Havok led the way up some spiral stairs hewn from the same smooth rock as the spire, like hard black glass. Higher and higher they climbed, until reaching a landing and a carved oak door.

Havok pushed inside, revealing a luxurious chamber draped here and there with colorful patchwork fabrics.

The huge space, like the stairs, had been carved from rock, but rugs, cushions, cloths, and drapes softened its hard edges. It might have been the most comfortable and colorful sanctuary Dante had ever seen. His own living quarters in a two-room dwelling above the Lenolian bakery was a dull and functional box in comparison.

Havok latched the door behind them, unclipped the leash, then the shackles, and set them down on a chunky wooden sideboard.

"I'll draw you a bath," Havok said.

"A... what?"

"A bath. You need it."

Dante blinked. He did need a bath, but why was Havok being kind? He'd have believed his kindness before, but not this time. Havok wanted something.

Havok pushed through a veil of red-silk curtain. "I can hear your thoughts whirring. Don't fret. I'm not about to poison the bathwater. Behave, and I will reward you."

The curtain fell back into place behind him, leaving just a thin gap. Dante spotted a tin bath with what appeared to be a stove attached to one end and a stack rising through the rock ceiling. A *heated* bath. Clever. Had Havok created that, like he'd designed and stitched the soft furnishings and drapes?

This was his home, his *real* home.

Dante drifted toward the curtains, reaching to touch velvets and silks. He spotted a window, the drapes shifting in the breeze, checked Havok was still inside the bathing area, and hurried toward it.

Warped, hand-blown glass revealed the barren land they'd crossed to arrive at the palace. Nothing grew down there, nothing *lived*. He missed Lenola's verdant valleys, its serene blue skies, fields of waving barley, and flowing rivers. This wasteland didn't seem real, but it was more real than his life had been. His past had been the lie.

Even if he could open the window, which appeared to be fixed in place, the chamber was high inside a palace tower. Any attempt to climb out would likely result in a rapid drop to a dramatic ending.

"There is no escape," Havok said. He wiped his hands on a towel as he emerged between the bathing area's curtains.

"I was admiring your view."

Havok's smirk tilted his lips. He draped the towel over his forearm and flicked a hand toward the door. "The door is locked, the windows are barred, and we both know you cannot best me in a fight, so please, refrain from trying to escape and do as I order."

Havok's gaze returned to Dante, waiting for comment.

"I *have* bested you in fight, remember? When we first met." Dante smirked. "I know you recall it."

"I was distracted," he said, matter-of-factly.

Dante's heart fluttered. He did remember. "Yeah, by me." That day, by the pond, when Dante had sprung from the bushes and wrestled Havok to the ground, a knife at his throat. The day they'd first met, amidst butterflies and drifting lion fuzz. He could have killed Havok then—should have—but he hadn't seen a monster, just a boy, like him.

"Why are you doing this?"

"No more questions." Havok leaned against the sideboard and folded his arms. "Strip."

"Here?"

"Where else?"

His initial irritation sharpened to anger. "Just like that?"

DANTE'S END

"Unless you wish to bathe in your clothes?"

"Fine, then." He tore at his trouser fastenings, unlaced them, and shoved them down. He'd lost his shirt long ago. So there he stood, in boots and tatty underwear.

"All of it," Havok ordered.

Dante looked for the smirk but found no trace of it. He swallowed his protest, tucked his thumbs into his underwear, and yanked them down, exposing his ass and cock to cooler air, then knelt, undid his boots, and kicked them off. Straightening, he made sure to fix a blank expression on his face. His own pungent body odor reinforced the fact he did need the bath. He *was* filthy, bruised, and scarred from recent fights, but the rest of his body was fine enough. He carried strength, had always made sure to care for himself. His life demanded it. So when Havok studied him, he hoped some part of him liked what he saw, liked what he couldn't have. Right before he'd betrayed Dante, Dante knew Havok had been hard for him. So there had to be something in Dante that Havok liked.

He'd accused Dante of wanting him, and maybe some part of him did, but Dante wasn't the only one desiring what he couldn't have.

Havok's gaze remained cool, but Dante remembered, when they'd been boys, Havok would stare when he swam near-naked in the pond, like he stared now.

Gooseflesh scattered down his arms, and not from the cold. How long had he been standing on display?

"Your wounds have healed well," Havok said, his assessment over. "Now bathe, and be sure to clean yourself thoroughly."

Havok watched Dante's every step across the chamber, toward the bathing area curtains. At least, if he was watching his ass, then he wouldn't see how Dante's body had begun to betray how Havok's gaze tantalized him other ways, his cock filling.

When they'd been younger, he'd hidden his body's reaction in the pond, below the water, until the desires had passed.

His heart thumped as he climbed into the hot water, in fear that Havok would know, would see, how despite his treatment, or maybe because of it, Dante wanted to taste him again, to fix him in his painful grip and kiss him as though he despised him, because it was the only damn thing that had felt right in his broken life.

Havok lurked outside the thin red curtain, just a silhouette, a shadow, the jagged lines of his horns and wings distinctive.

Dante silently hoped he was hard and suffering. He ducked his shoulders beneath the warm water line and watched Havok's shadow move.

He seemed content to remain outside the curtain.

Dante dropped his hand and encircled his thickening dick, giving it a few encouraging strokes. A part of him wanted Havok to part those curtains and come inside. What would Havok do if he knew how Dante desired his rage? A shudder ran through him at the thought. What he really wanted to do was pump himself hard and come, knowing that Havok was just a few strides away, on the other side of that curtain, knowing the fiend was listening. Did he want that too?

Dante let go of himself, grasped the sides of the bath, and dunked his head below the water. He ruffled his hair, dislodging grit and mud, and broke the surface gasping.

Havok's shadow was gone, and with it, any urge Dante had to fuck his own hand with Havok watching. These wants had to be the result of a madness brought on by hunger and having his life destroyed.

The only reason he wanted to maybe taste Havok again, to fuck him even, was because he hated the beast. You could hate someone and want to fuck them.

He knew, because he'd been doing the same with Calen for countless cycles.

CHAPTER 15

A feast awaited him after he'd climbed from the bath and wrapped a towel around his middle. The eating area, curtained off earlier, was revealed behind hooked-up drapes. A long table overflowed with fruits, breads, and cold meats. He'd rarely seen such a bounty—only at joining ceremonies when families married and celebrated life.

He circled the table. It couldn't all be for him.

"Indulge," Havok said with a sweep of his hand. "But take it slowly. I have no patience for sickness brought on by overindulgence."

Dante needed to eat, but there had to be something else going on here too, didn't there? Where was the trap? Havok smirked as though this was a trick. He pulled out a chair, sprawled into it, one leg over its armrest, and he reached for an apple. Perhaps to prove the food wasn't poisoned.

Havok took a bite of apple, leaned back in the chair, and chewed with glee. "Not eating? Anyone would think you did not trust me." A laugh played on the jailor's lips. Dante clenched his hands, resisting the urge to punch his grin.

He grabbed an apple, sniffed it, and took a bite, proving he had no fear of Havok's games. An explosion of juicy sweetness hit his tongue. He moaned, stumbled into the nearest chair, and loaded a plate with breads, cheeses, meats, and fruit. He began slowly, but his gut was so starved, he soon plunged into the food with gusto, only slowing when Havok appeared beside him, glass of wine suspended between his thin fingers.

"Something to wash it down?"

Maybe it was the way his voice coiled around Dante, or how his closeness ignited his skin, or the mere fact he was somehow still alive, but his head spun, his thoughts woozy. Wait, *had* he been drugged? He stared at the plate of crumbs left behind. Havok hadn't eaten anything except that one apple.

"Did you—"

Havok laughed. "You're light-headed because Lenolians are weak. You're overstimulated. It will pass."

Dante grabbed the wine, intent on throwing it over Havok, but he caught a whiff of its bouquet and his mouth watered all over again. It would be a shame to waste it. He guzzled the glass and scowled at Havok's back as he moved away, still chuckling at Dante's expense.

So smug. He thought he knew everything. He sashayed away, hips rocking, tail rippling, wings relaxed, with one partially open, the other still strapped. "Now that you are fed and watered, you will do one thing for me."

Here it came. What awful thing was he going to demand? "Oh?"

Havok stopped, kept his back to Dante, and lowered himself to his knees. "My wing. Remove the splint."

He could have *asked* instead of ordered.

Dante eyed the jailor on his knees. His back was bare, his black wings rising from its pale expanse, and low on his hip lay the tiny blue butterfly.

This would be the perfect opportunity for Havok to see how Dante was no threat, that he could be accommodating, and helpful, and an asset. And not a prisoner preparing to flee.

Dante wiped his hands down, adjusted the towel around his waist so it didn't fall and expose him, and approached Havok from behind.

His wings and horns made him seem so much bigger than Dante. The tail lay still, with just its tip ticking against the floor. Dante would have to get in close to remove the splint. That tail was probably waiting for him to make one wrong move so it could strike.

"You know—" Dante took up a firm stance between Havok's shoulders. "—you once asked me what a friend was."

Havok's head tilted. He was listening, but he didn't reply. Dante reached up, laid his left hand on the thick, black-feathered arch, and ran his touch down the glossy fronds. By the powers, he'd forgotten how smooth and warm Havok's feathers were. There had been dreams, or memories, he wasn't sure, where he'd lain on the feathers and watched the stars crawl across the sky. A strange tightness knotted around his heart, almost like... grief for a lost friend.

"Is that what Calen was, your friend?" Havok asked.

"Calen? I..." The less they spoke about Calen the

better. "I suppose." Havok's wing dropped and Dante began loosening the strips of cotton holding the splint in place. "I didn't know he was going to hurt you..." No, he wasn't discussing it. He hadn't known Calen would react like he had and assault Havok. If he'd known, he wouldn't have taken him. He'd hated Calen afterward. In truth, he'd never stopped hating him for it. And he'd hated himself.

Havok had been nothing but kind and curious and fun-loving, with his butterflies and flirty tail and carefree laughter. It hadn't been a lie, not then.

"Friends help each other." Dante plucked at the cotton strips. "Not from fear or payment, but because they want to. You don't have to order me to help you, Havok. All you have to do is ask."

"Any friendship we've exhibited in the past has long been eroded away."

"I can't deny that you being a horrendous prick makes our friendship difficult." Dante laughed.

Havok's wings ruffled some, but he settled. "Enough discussion."

Dante leaned back and ran his gaze down Havok's spine to where the little blue butterfly tattoo should have been. It wasn't there. But he had seen it moments ago...

"It moves," Havok said.

Dante glanced up, over Havok's shoulder and straight into the mirror on the far wall, almost hidden between colored drapes. It reflected the scene they painted, one of Dante, bare-chested in a towel, standing behind Havok while he knelt, wings relaxed. Havok's bare chest expanded and contracted, his breathing heavy. His eye gleamed, and his smile said he'd been watching all along.

They looked good.

Havok lifted his right wing, revealing his hip in the reflection, and the tiny blue butterfly tattoo imprinted on his skin, just above his low-slung trouser line.

"You were searching for it. It moves," Havok explained.

A tattoo that moved? He'd never heard of such a thing.

Havok was a marvel, a wonder, a monster, and so much more. Would he allow Dante to tuck his silvery hair behind his horns, as he'd used to? Would he allow Dante to skim his fingers down his spine, just to hear him gasp?

With a huff, Dante tugged the last of the ties free and yanked off the splint. "There."

Havok's wing sprung open, dislodging a few feathers while the rest fanned wide. Dante retreated, needing space to clear his head of all the good Havok thoughts. He had to forget the notion he was anything but a lying fraud. To think him in any way good or desirable would just delay the hurt. But when Havok spread both wings, try as he might, Dante couldn't stop the good thoughts from filtering through. He couldn't *forget* who Havok had been once. And he didn't want to.

"Rest and get dressed," Havok said, folding his wings and heading for the door. "There are fresh clothes on the bed. Make sure you wear them."

"Where are you going?"

"No questions."

Was he supposed to rest in Havok's bed? "Wait—"

"Oh, and Dante..." Havok opened the door. When he turned, all traces of humor and softness vanished, leaving him as cold and hard as a sword's edge. "True friends never become enemies."

He closed the door with a resounding *bang*, and the sound of a metal lock clunked.

Dante stood alone, unshackled, naked except for the towel. He could still feel Havok's softness under his hands, still smell his warm spiciness, still feel how his closeness teased his blood and body. Havok was wrong. Sometimes friends did become enemies, and they were the most dangerous enemies of all.

CHAPTER 16

*A*fter trying the door and confirming it was locked, Dante padded about the sumptuous chamber, feet bare and towel hitched at his waist. He picked more food from the table and poked through Havok's belongings—finding simple sets of hand-stitched clothing. Only when he'd searched every corner and nook for a weapon and not found a thing, did he try the large bed. After the wastes and the spire, Havok's bed was bliss.

He laid his head down, and between one blink and the next, darkness had crept into the chamber. He'd fallen asleep; he could have been out for hours.

And he was no longer alone. Someone shuffled nearby.

If it was anyone but Havok, he'd run—

But the outline in the gloom of an angular silhouette and tipped horns was unmistakably Havok's.

Wait, was he about to climb into the bed *with* Dante? He froze. Had Havok forgotten he'd told Dante to rest? What if he hadn't meant rest in *his* bed?

In the darkness, Havok's face was hidden, but his

breathing sawed. His wings glittered, as though dipped in stardust.

Dante's sleepy mind scrabbled for an explanation. He opened his mouth to apologize, to say he'd move, but something in Havok's stuttering motion kept him silent.

Havok threw back the sheet and slid into bed, up close to Dante. And Havok *trembled*.

"Havok," Dante whispered.

Havok's icy breath chilled Dante's shoulder.

Dante stared at the bed's canopy draped above them, heart racing and mind picking at possible scenarios, but he feared Havok's ragged breaths weren't from rage. The opposite. Havok was *afraid*. He should reach for him, but then remembered Havok had lied and betrayed him. He was here as his prisoner, not a friend, despite what his foolish heart kept trying to tell him.

Havok's panting slowed and his tremors faded, until all Dante heard was the sound of Havok's steady breaths and his own thudding heart.

He turned his head and found his face adjacent to Havok's. So close that even in the gloom, he could make out his elegant black lashes, pale cheeks, and soft lips. The mark on its chain sparkled, but it had dulled, or so it seemed. No... not dulled. It was encased in something. The same glittering substance that coated Havok's wings...

Dante touched a feather with a fingertip. A drop of ice came away, instantly melting.

He was *freezing*.

Fuck his betrayal and the fact Havok was a wretched, lying, scheming piece of work— Dante eased an arm around Havok's waist and pulled him close. His stiff body shivered, cool and clammy where it touched Dante's, as though someone or something had sucked all the warmth from his bones. When Havok didn't stir, Dante pulled him closer still, wrapping his hunched body inside his arms. The horns made tucking his head under his chin too difficult, but Dante lifted his own head and rested his cheek on Havok's to chase the cold from as much of his skin as possible. Havok was still dressed. He'd come straight to the bed, straight to Dante.

"What is this?" Dante whispered.

No reply, and in many ways, he was glad Havok hadn't heard. Like this, they were young again, holding hands, fingers entwined, defying their differences as they lay in the grass. Back then, he'd have kept Havok safe from anything. The only thing he hadn't been able to keep him safe from was Dante himself.

The muscular press of Havok's tail spiraled around Dante's ankle—the touch so familiar that he closed his eyes and imagined they lay in the grass again, and Havok told him everything the butterflies said about him.

Havok had said there were no butterflies here. Just monsters. And Dante was beginning to realize, for all his threats and brutality, there was a chance Havok might not be one of them.

HE SNAPPED AWAKE, expecting to find Havok still in his arms, but the only evidence that remained he'd been there at all was the pile of crinkled sheets.

Sitting up, Dante searched for any moving shadows among the colorful drapes. "Havok?"

Nothing.

He padded from the bed, wet his face at the basin, and ran wet hands through his hair and beard. Havok hadn't been foolish enough to leave a shaving blade, although Dante ached to rid himself of the itching whiskers.

His old clothes had been taken and with no other option, he dressed in the plain leather pants and tunic left out for him. The mirror framed a picture of a stranger. He'd lost weight, but he'd been carrying enough to lose without much hardship. His eyes had darkened, it seemed, and his hair had grown some, while gaining a few wispy white locks. Even the beard was peppered with white. In black trousers and the tunic, its piping a deep purple, he couldn't recall ever appearing more handsome.

He almost forgot he was here to die.

But that wasn't going to happen. Havok had said he wasn't going to kill him.

So, what was the attire for? His would-be execution, or something else? Whatever the reason for the clothing and the impending event, it would hopefully give him more time to get closer to Havok. Last night they'd made huge progress. It hadn't been a dream. Havok *had* come to him. *Needed* him.

It was that softer Havok that Dante needed to manipulate into keeping him alive and convince him to let him go. Even if the thought of lying had guilt writhing in his gut.

The door clunked and Havok breezed in, wings up, horns sharp, lips pressed into a thin line. Even his customary smirk was absent. A swathe of black and purple leather lay folded over his arm. "Ready your shackles," he snapped.

Dante crossed to the sideboard and collected the shackles, keeping a watchful eye on Havok. He seemed agitated. More so than usual. Like this, he was unpredictable. Now was not the time to discuss last night.

Havok laid the leather on the sideboard and produced the leash to clip to Dante's shackles. But before attaching it, he pushed the leather garment across the sideboard. "Wear this."

"What is it?"

Havok's sharp glance cut to him, then sliced away again. "No questions."

Dante raised his hands, placating him. "All right." On closer inspection, the leather had been stitched, like the coat Havok had made in the spire chamber—the one that had been lost when the gregog attacked. Dante almost picked it up, instinctively wanting to touch its supple-looking sheen, but then he recalled the bones hidden under Havok's floor and pulled his hands back. "Do I have to?"

"What?"

"I don't want to."

Something fiery and sharp flashed across Havok's simmering glare. "This isn't a request."

What was he going to do, pin Dante down and try to force the coat on him like trying to dress an unruly doll? Dante glared back. "I'm not wearing it."

Havok growled. "Why not?"

"Did you make it?"

"Ah, always with the questions! Put it on!" He grabbed for Dante's neck. Dante danced back.

Havok rolled his eye so hard, his whole head lolled, making the golden ring on his horn glint. "I do not have the patience to play these games with you, Dante!" He folded his arms. "Yes, I made the coat. I made it specifically for you. Now put it on or I will be forced to sever a minor extremity from your person. That member between your legs will do just nicely. Is that what you want? To lose a piece of yourself over an item of clothing?"

Would he really cut his dick off over such a silly argument? Dante glanced at the coat again. The purple matched a thin purple leather strip running down Havok's leather pants.

Havok growled and in a flurry of feathers and muscle, he grabbed Dante's shoulder, shoved him against the sideboard, and flashed a blade in his right hand. He swept his hand *down*.

"No, wait!" The blade nudged his crotch. "Is it made from Lenolians?!"

Havok froze, dagger poised. He blinked and his red eye, always so fierce, flickered with something Dante couldn't read. A moment passed, then another, and then Havok backed away. "You believe I would insist you wear a coat made from the skin of your own people?"

"I... yes. That's what this is, isn't it?" Dante dropped his hand and covered his crotch, just in case. "You harvest us. You take our pieces and make... things."

Havok tilted his head, frowned, and tucked his knife away somewhere against his back, under his wing. "The coat is not made from Lenolian skin. Enough of this nonsense. I'd rather not lose another coat to blood and carnage, so will you please wear it?"

He'd *asked?* Dante almost spluttered his disbelief but if he made a point of it, Havok would turn vicious, and he liked this softer version who *asked*.

He put the shackles down and grabbed the coat. It was so soft it almost felt like cool silk in his rough fist. He lifted it, letting its length fall to the floor. The coat was marvelous, now that he could look at it without recoiling. Although it would have suited Havok's tall, thin frame far better than Dante's shorter, more muscular body. The coat was important, more important than just a piece of clothing. But he'd used up the number of questions he could slip through without losing a finger, or his dick.

He slid one arm into a sleeve, then the next, and shrugged the coat onto his shoulders. It should have been heavy, but its weight was no more cumbersome than a simple shirt. He had to admit the coat was a perfect fit, its tailor a skilled artisan.

"Before you compliment it, don't," Havok said, irritably. "Your approval is unnecessary."

As Havok turned his back and collected the shackles, Dante rolled his eyes. *Your approval is unnecessary.* That hadn't been the case in the spire, when Havok had clearly wanted Dante to admire him then.

"Until you gag me again, I'll speak, and I like the coat. If it's a gift, then thank you."

Havok snapped the shackles into place around Dante's wrists, grinning as they locked home. "It is a gift. But not for you." He reached for the sideboard again, snatching up what looked like a strip of cloth, and before Dante could react, Havok shoved the cloth between Dante's teeth and tied it off behind his head. "Thank you for reminding me to silence you." He patted Dante on the shoulder. "Trust me, Dante, where we're about to go, you'll be safer without your troublesome tongue."

A gag. *He'd been gagged?* Bound by the wrists and now silenced?! Was there no end to Havok's wickedness? "You fiend!" he growled, although the words didn't make it past the cloth.

He poked the gag with his tongue, trying to work it free as Havok clipped the leash to his shackles and tugged him along. "Come, pet. It's time you were formally introduced."

Whatever that meant, it couldn't be good. Havok walked ahead, guiding Dante behind him, and as they made for the door, Dante caught sight of tiny fluttering blue wings low on Havok's bare back, just above the rise of his pants and the drop of his feathers. The blue butterfly tattoo. For whatever reason, the sight of it calmed his heart and mind.

They descended the spiral staircase. The black rock walls glistened, as though wet, like Havok's feathers.

Dante stumbled on one uneven step and Havok glared. One more wrong step would see Dante lose his dick. They moved on, emerging into a corridor. Havok's fast pace left Dante breathing hard around the gag. The corridors widened and enormous statues of gargoyle creatures loomed in hewn alcoves. Torches lit the way, spluttering against the dark. The more they walked, the more a sense of dread hardened like stone in Dante's gut.

He knew, didn't he... He *knew* he was being taken to others like Havok. More monsters. And with every step, the illusion of his old life faded into a bizarre dream. The nights he'd spent at the local inn, laughing with Jean and the others. The times he'd taken Ricard on overnight guard duty, standing sentry over crops, watching for wolves, and how they'd admired the sun painting the morning skies red. Little things, things he'd loved, things that weren't real.

Havok approached a pair of double doors taller than most people's homes. He pushed them open and despite their size, they swung away silently. The noise struck Dante first, like a storm rolling down off the mountains. A wave of growls and snarls, but voices too. The cavernous hall brimmed with wings and horns and *monsters*. Havok tugged, pulling Dante forward.

It was clear Havok was not the largest of his kind, nor the most monstrous.

There were creatures here that made Havok look like a dragonfly next to a crocodile, huge and muscular, their horns elaborate spirals and claws like scythes. So many with wings, some feathered, some leathery, some made of velvet. With every step, Dante grew smaller among them. A tiny urge to laugh almost had him choking on the gag. With every step, his lie of a life crumbled to dust. There were hundreds here. So many, too many. And he couldn't deny the truth any longer or hold out any hope that somehow his people were free.

Havok whirled, locked his clawed fingers around Dante's throat, and sneered. "Calm yourself."

Dante breathed hard through his nose. How could he calm himself? They were standing in a chamber full of enormous beasts! His heart thumped harder, so hard it hurt. His lungs heaved, his body spiraling into panic.

"Look at me, look at my eye, damn you," Havok sneered. His eye shone its ruby red, entrancing *and* penetrating. As though he could drill into Dante's soul.

Havok tugged again on the leash. "Calm yourself or you will not leave this hall alive."

Dante's heart galloped. The nearest beasts turned their great horn-topped heads, looking over. Every single one towered over Dante. Their claws could gut him in seconds. Their teeth could crush his bones. He had nothing, *and* he was tied. By the powers, his legs were weakening, his guts turning over.

Havok pulled Dante's face close to his. "Look at me.

Remember this, repeat it in your mind. *You are invisible. You cannot be seen.* Do you understand?"

He was going to die here. One of the countless beasts was going to kill him.

"Dante, damn you." Havok pulled Dante cheek to cheek and his next words whispered over Dante's ear. "Remember our days by the pond, remember chasing butterflies. You went there to be invisible. Now, here, you are invisible again. Nothing here can hurt you if you do not exist."

His firm hand scorched Dante's hip, having slipped unnoticed under his shirt. The touch branded him, snapping him out of his downward spiral. He blinked, searching Havok's eye. For its fierceness, his eye held the truth, and a touch of fear.

He was invisible.

Nothing here could hurt what did not exist.

The words must have had some kind of power, because as Dante repeated them over and over, mental barriers came down, his heart slowed, and he detached from the moment, drifting through it like a ghost. Nothing here could hurt him. He did not exist. He wasn't real. None of this was real.

"Good." Havok nodded. "You're doing well."

And then he noticed the people.

He should have known, should have suspected he wouldn't be the only one on the end of a leash...

Lenolian people. Like him. Some were bound at the wrists, some at the neck. All were led along with leashes, like pets. Women, men, young boys and girls.

I am invisible. What cannot be seen, cannot be hurt.

His heart skipped. The more he looked, the more horrors he saw. Some of the people were missing fingers, limbs, ears, eyes. And that was what he could see. No doubt, some were missing more.

Harvested.

They were the offerings.

It became too much, and the final barrier slammed down, sealing Dante's heart and head away. Now the world was silent, and he was as impermeable as stone. He stared ahead, between where Havok's wings sprouted from his back. He watched muscles ripple, torchlight lick down Havok's pale skin, to where the butterfly...

It was gone. The tattoo had vanished.

Maybe Dante was losing his mind?

This was a nightmare. He was trapped in a never-ending nightmare. Yes, that was it.

He'd wake up and none of this would be real.

He couldn't see any more, couldn't witness what was being done, couldn't allow the awful images inside his mind where they would fester. *He was invisible. Nothing here could hurt him.* He lost himself instead in the gentle glide of Havok's glossy black feathers resting in the layers cascading down his wings. They were so black, they shone with purples and greens, like oil under the sun. There were others here with feathered wings, some grey, some golden, but none as perfect as Havok's.

Havok stopped suddenly, and Dante almost walked into him. A creature so pale he almost glowed stalked around Havok, coming into Dante's line of sight. Several feet taller than Havok, his whole body was mottled grey, as though he'd been covered head to toe in moondust.

Startling blue eyes fixed on Dante.

The beast smiled with pink, glossy lips. "Hm, Beric... What a prize you have in this one." His voice rumbled like thunder, trembling through Dante's chest.

Dante's leash tightened as Havok pulled its end, but Havok remained quiet, watching with an eyebrow raised as the pale one circled around Dante.

"Is it for Reina, this one, or for you?"

That voice... It shivered through Dante, tingling his spine, and other parts. He should have been terrified, and part of him was, but a much larger part wanted the pale one to talk again so he could *feel* the words shiver inside him.

"Reina, of course," Havok replied.

Wait, were they talking about Dante?

"Shame, the things I could do with that body." The pale one's blue-eyed gaze shimmered with hunger. "Hair of flame." A hand the size of Dante's head reached out and took a lock of Dante's hair between his finger and thumb, then he leaned in and raised the lock to his nose. *I am invisible. Nothing here can hurt me.* The creature was close now, so close it was as though the moon had fallen and filled Dante's vision. White on white, with blue eyes so piercing they cut all the way to his soul.

"Unhand him," Havok growled, "lest you incite Reina's wrath."

The pale one's chuckle licked down Dante's back, stroking lust with it, and to his detached awe, his body warmed, his cock filling.

"You'd begrudge me a touch," the pale one said. He freed the lock of hair and his huge hand cupped Dante's face. "Yes, see how willing he is. Hm, let me have him, Beric, she'll never know—"

Havok grabbed the pale one's arm and his black claws pressed in, depressing his skin. The pale one froze.

"Step away," Havok warned, "or it will be Reina you offend, Scarrow, not I."

Ice water spilled through Dante's veins, chasing out the lust. He stumbled back, coming to his senses like rising to the surface of a lake. He was hard, so damned hard it *hurt*. That wasn't him, he couldn't want *the pale one* like that? Oh, but he did. He wanted him so much he'd have begged him right there and then, if he hadn't been gagged.

Scarrow's pink smile stretched. "Fire in his heart too. It might almost be worth Reina's wrath, this one, your Fireheart."

Havok's wings opened, feathers splaying. Havok freed Scarrow's wrist but slotted himself between him and Dante. "Back away."

Scarrow's blue eyes drilled into Dante's soul, and there, the beast rummaged around, plucking on every little want and desire, teasing him. That monster, he'd have Dante on his back, his tongue around the hardest part of him, and he'd make him spill over and over, until Dante begged him to stop, but he would not stop.

Dante almost moaned aloud. He shook his head, breaking Scarrow's eye contact and panting around the gag. By the powers, Scarrow was in his head, doing something to his mind and body, slithering inside, violating him.

"The rules are clear, Scarrow. You shall not touch what is mine. Walk away, before you cross a line you cannot return from."

Scarrow's lips rippled in a snarl. He huffed at Havok and turned, and there, against his back, lay the mangled stumps of broken wings.

Dante staggered. His gut heaved. Sweat wet his face and neck.

It was all... too much.

I am invisible.

Nothing here... can hurt me.

A sizzling burn tingled his left hip, distracting him from the madness happening all around. He lifted his shirt, and there, etched onto his skin, was the blue butterfly.

The sight of its delicate design slapped panic from Dante's mind, leaving his head silent and his heart steady. Havok had put it there earlier, when he'd touched him. Dante was sure of it. Was it some kind of powerful talisman or something to make him compliant? Either way, he welcomed the sight of it.

"Dante." Havok yanked on the leash. "Come now. We have only just begun."

Begun?

Move. Yes. Moving he could do. One foot in front of the other. The painful, burning erection had softened, fading quickly now that Scarrow had turned his attention elsewhere. But that one... Dante glanced over his shoulder and saw the white beast among his kind, his stare still fixed on Dante's back... That one was deadly, not because of his strength, but because of the way he'd made Dante's body sing for him. If Havok hadn't been between them, Dante would have had no defense. He'd have fucked him right here. Or been fucked. He shivered, disgust overriding any other thought. Such coupling wouldn't end well for him.

Scarrow's gaze, along with dozens of others, all weighed on Dante, pinning him down, making it known he was among monsters, and each and every one of them would hunt him, probably fuck him, and tear him apart.

If they were all this terrifying, then the one who ruled over them would be a hundred times worse.

Reina.

CHAPTER 17

avok

DANTE HAD BEEN compliant all morning, a blessing since Havok was in no mood to argue. His presentation was nigh, and it would be better for them both if Dante did not resist. Reina enjoyed some resistance, but not open defiance. Defiance would not be tolerated.

This presentation needed to go well.

If Dante angered her, she'd kill him. And whatever else happened, Havok didn't want him dead. In truth, he didn't want any of this. But as Scarrow had suggested, Havok could no more defy Reina than any sacha here. They were all bound by her rules and desires.

Scarrow, the fiend. He should have known he'd try to manipulate Dante, but there was nothing to be done. All things considered, the altercation could have ended far worse, had Scarrow ignored Havok's threats.

There were others here who wanted to take from

Havok, others who would try to trip Havok up, try to sabotage him, but Scarrow's retreat would deter them. Dante was safe. For now.

Had Dante not been gagged, he'd have likely talked himself into a quick death already.

Havok glanced back at the man. Dante walked behind, eyes glazed over, his focus pinned to Havok's back, as it should be. He'd do well to remain obedient. This would be over soon, and they'd return to his chamber and Havok would think of a way to delay the gifting for as long as he could. Perhaps he could find another Lenolian with red hair and fire in his heart.

These thoughts were foolish. Reina would know a substitute. Dante was promised to her. Havok couldn't keep him. Although, if he asked her to relinquish her ownership temporarily, promised her he'd give her Dante when he'd been *improved*... Hm, yes, that idea had merit. Havok hadn't made his own pet before, but he'd watched her create so many of them that he could easily stitch one together.

Well, whatever it took, he'd do it. He wasn't ready to give up Dante. He wasn't finished. Havok glanced back again, admiring the coat on Dante's frame. The fit was perfect, better even than the lost original. And of course Dante liked it, although his opinion was irrelevant. The thin leather flowed around him, the purple marking him as owned. Since Havok had carried him from his old life, he'd changed in subtle ways. Grown less naive, more acute, but he still had a great deal of learning to undertake.

Dante's shirt had ridden up, revealing a tiny glimpse of Havok's butterfly. That would not do.

Havok turned and tugged Dante's shirt down. "You must keep it hidden at all times."

DANTE'S END

Dante's green eyes widened. So full of questions. If Havok answered them all, they'd leave him so ruined, making him useless to Havok. "You do not need to know."

Dante mumbled something around the gag, probably one of his infamous questions.

"Hush."

But his eyes remained haunted. Scarrow's invasive attention had likely left him feeling unsettled, perhaps even violated, depending on how much Scarrow had shown him. Dante had obviously been aroused, and Havok would have been lying if he wasn't intrigued by whatever ideas Scarrow might have planted inside Dante's mind. Of course, Scarrow could turn the most defiant of pets into pliable toys. Clearly Dante would have enjoyed himself in Scarrow's hands, until Scarrow consumed him after the act. All Scarrow's pets met the same end. He'd delight in devouring Dante, more so because he was Havok's, and Havok had been the one to brutalize Scarrow's wings—under Reina's orders—for breaking the rules.

Yes, he'd have to be careful to keep Dante away from the likes of Scarrow. But even he wasn't Havok's main concern.

The air thinned, the bubbling chatter faded, and a pair of vast wings sailed overhead, creating a veil of mist in her wake. Reina.

One by one, the sacha knelt, respect or fear driving them to bow their heads. Of course, Dante stood, gazing at Reina's downward spiral like the fool he was. Havok tugged on his leash, jolting him to his knees.

He bowed his head too late, but Reina hadn't noticed.

Wings flapped, blasting a wave of air overhead, and Reina settled among them, folding her wings in. She assessed her audience, her smile a slash of scarlet on her stitched face, and with a flick of her hand everyone rose and returned to their conversations, like puppets on her strings. That made Havok a puppet too, he supposed, but what else was there?

Reina's gaze fixed on Havok. She crooked a finger.

This was it. Everything had to be perfect. One wrong move, one misstep, and he'd lose Dante.

Havok tugged on the leash again and pulled Dante upright. There hadn't been much time to train him, but the gag would prevent any unfortunate accidents. All Dante had to do was nothing.

"Hm, this is the one." Reina purred as Havok approached. Her purr rumbled deep into Havok's bones and body, eliciting respect and devotion.

She circled around Havok, gaze fixed on Dante—a predator with her prey in her sights. What would she do with him? Mutilate him, bed him, parade him around like the others until she grew bored? Perhaps create in him something like Calen, or something more akin to the gregog? Would he keep his mind, or would she opt to take Dante's will as well as his body?

Such thoughts rested uneasily with Havok, squirming inside of him like worms on a hook. Dante was his. Dante had always been his. He did not want to give him up. But like most things in his life, he had no choice.

"A wonderful specimen." She rippled her claws near Dante's face. He just blinked. *Good, pet.*

"And the coat, what fine workmanship."

Pride bloomed in his chest. "A gift. For you."

Her smile grew for Havok. "Yes, this one will be perfect." She extended her hand for the leash.

Havok couldn't move. It was a simple act, to hand him over, and if Havok didn't comply in the next few moments, he'd pay for his defiance. But even so, he couldn't lift the leash. He couldn't give her what she wanted. "I wondered if I might modify him for you?"

A few sacha nearby heard and stared, wings ruffling.

What he was suggesting wasn't open defiance. He only sought to improve on her gift, to make Dante perfect for her.

Reina's smile fractured. She withdrew her empty hand.

"I will make him perfect," Havok continued, and sensing he'd perhaps overstepped, he knelt again and bowed his head. Dante didn't kneel, but this wasn't about him. Havok could only hope he hadn't gone too far, that he'd earned her respect over the cycles. He was, after all, her favorite creation.

Reina's hand skimmed his cheek. One of her claws ran the length of his jaw. She tilted his head up and bent low, so the moment became an intimate one. "Do not think I don't know your past with this one."

Havok's heart thumped. He fell into her eyes, pulled toward the hungry darkness inside her.

"Don't think I don't see you plotting."

"Plotting? Never—"

"Hush!" She snatched his jaw. "This one is mine. He's always been mine. Now take him away and prepare him *for me*. If he is anything but perfect, you will suffer, Beric. As you well know." She'd break his wings. Perhaps his limbs too. It couldn't come to that.

His voice fled. Perhaps she had taken it. He nodded and she freed him, turning away to greet the others in her congregation.

Havok remained on his knee, like a rock on a beach with time and tide moving around him. The others sent sidelong glances his way, judging, mocking, plotting to take his place as her most favorite after he was gone. He'd overstepped. If he didn't give her Dante, he'd lose her favor and there was nothing else in this world he cared more for than pleasing her.

Scarrow's snarling smirk was the last expression he saw before rising and hurrying Dante from the gathering hall. He walked with purpose, his head up. He hadn't lost anything yet. He was still her favorite. Nothing had changed. All he had to do was give her Dante, just as he'd promised all along.

He made it to his chamber and slammed the door behind Dante, then let his leash go and paced.

Hand him over. It was the only way. There would be others like Dante. Other Lenolians with flame-red hair, and stupid, soft smiles, and the relentless mind-numbing questions... But none would feel the way he did, none would make Havok's heart soar. He growled, cutting off his wretched thoughts.

Dante stood inside the closed door, and despite Havok having dropped the leash, he didn't move. With his wrists bound and his endless chattering gagged, he should have been easy to ignore, but his green eyes conveyed his thoughts, and those thoughts were right there for all to see. Fireheart. He was different than most, although finding those differences was an art all of its own.

Dante began mumbling. Havok paced again. Give him up, he had to. Give up his butterfly boy.

His plans had gone awry. All of this was to be his revenge.

But Havok had misjudged so much.

Dante was unique, from his scheming mind, capable of plotting to bring down the jailor, to his warrior physique, quick and efficient with a weapon. He wasn't even aware of how wonderful he was. He hid it behind bumbling idiocy, but Dante was so much more than he allowed the world to see.

Havok... cared, and by the powers, he hated Dante for that.

Dante mumbled some more, becoming agitated.

If Havok removed the gag all the questions would tumble out. They'd be endless and irritating and pointless. No question could change his fate.

"Hush, your mumbling is distracting."

Dante's face screwed up and his mumbling grew louder. He rattled his shackles.

He had no idea of the fate awaiting him. Or perhaps he did; he'd seen the bone chamber, he'd seen the other people as pets among the sacha. He knew by now there was no escape.

"You do not understand." Havok paced faster. He stretched his wings, needing to spread their width to release their tension. "Your position is a precarious one. I am trying... I am trying to fix this."

Dante mumbled some more, his green eyes now pleading. Havok almost freed his shackles just to make those sad eyes go away, but that was his own weakness bleeding through. He'd cared for him once before, and Dante had betrayed him. It was all his kind were good for.

Havok had everything: status, position, Reina's love. Was he truly thinking of sacrificing it all... He stopped pacing and looked at Dante—*that*.

Dante stepped forward, wrists raised, eyes still pleading. Havok all too easily recalled him laughing by the pond, remembered how the butterflies twirled around him. Why could he not shake these vicious memories? Why did they haunt him so?

With a snarl, Havok crossed the floor, tugged the gag from Dante's dry lips, and placed a finger there instead. "Quiet. I am thinking and your twittering is pointless."

"Ugh gahn 'elp," he said from behind Havok's finger.

Havok shook his head. "You cannot *help*. You are the cause of all this, not the solution."

Dante blinked, now quiet. As soon as Havok removed his finger from his lips, the nonsense would begin. With a sigh, he plucked his finger back.

"You're meant to give me up to her, but you won't," Dante said. "You've delayed this whole time, but there's no time left, is there?"

Ugh, Havok hated how right he was. "It's not because I care for you."

Dante's mouth twitched. "Sure. If you say so. The fact remains, you're caught between two choices, neither of which you can live with." Dante raised his wrists. "Unshackle me."

"No."

He rattled the shackles again. "I won't run. Trust me?"

"Oh, I did that once." Havok flicked his fingers at his scarred eye. "The mistake was permanent."

Dante sighed and dropped his wrists. "I am sorry, Havok." Dante's eyes were beautiful; they'd always been his best feature. His eyes revealed the truth, no matter the words falling from his lips. The honesty in his gaze made it clear he did want to help, but he wasn't helping for Havok. Dante hadn't given up on escaping. He didn't ever give up. And Havok had been burned before.

Dante was using him.

"Why did you give me this—" Dante lifted his shirt, revealing the butterfly tattoo. "—if you don't care what becomes of me? It protects me, no? Or does it control me?"

"A whim, a mistake." Havok reached out to swipe the tattoo back, but Dante jerked out of reach.

"We were friends once," he went on. "Let me help you. Unshackle me. Talk to me. We had a good thing, and I know I ruined it, I will forever be sorry for that, but if you give me up to her, I'll be gone. We both know you don't want that. And clearly, neither do I. We need to work together."

"Unshackling you changes nothing." Last night, Dante had been unshackled. And Havok hadn't forgotten what happened when he'd fled back to his chamber, wrapped in the terrible cold that sometimes came when he was alone... when he was *afraid*. Dante had wrapped him in his arms and Havok, for his shame, had ached to be held. He'd needed him, in those moments, and Dante had been there without a harsh word or judgment.

He owed him for that kindness. He pulled the key from his pocket and unlocked the shackles, slipping them off. "For last night," he said.

Dante rubbed his wrists and nodded. "About last night—"

Oh no. No questions on that. He pressed a finger to his lips again. "We never speak of *that*. Understand?" Dante nodded, and Havok removed his finger. "Then what are your solutions?"

"It seems simple enough to me. You either let me go, or we kill Reina."

Havok blinked, then freed a sudden burst of laughter. "I'd forgotten how mad you are."

"How so?"

"Dante, she will kill us both if you run, and if we try

and kill her?" Havok huffed. "Insanity. I should have kept you gagged."

"You think me naive, you think I'm just some Lenolian toy to be paraded around? Maybe I am, I don't even know anymore, but I can see who and what you are. I see the rest of them, the sacha—the monsters. Will I do anything to live? Yes. But I also know you don't want me dead. You think it's because of some twisted idea about me being your pet, but it's not. It's because we're friends, we've always been friends, and that's never changed, even if we have. We have a bond, Havok, and I'm not imagining it when I can feel it still." He touched his own chest, as though his heart spoke to him.

Havok almost laughed again. "What you feel is my leash and your own will to submit."

Dante rolled his eyes. "All right, let's call it that. At the end of the day, we make a great pair, you and I. And Reina knows it. She's afraid of you, afraid of *us*."

He really was insane. "Your head was always so full of dreams."

"Yes!" Dante laughed. "You remember that, then you must remember how good we are together?"

"'Good'?" Havok arched an eyebrow. "I remember a Lenolian boy whom I played with to pass the time, that is all. You meant little to me then and you mean less now." He strode away, tired of him and his ridiculous ideas of friendship. "You are my entertainment, my toy. Nothing more."

Dante chuckled and folded his arms, then tossed Havok a smirk of his own. "If I mean so little, let Reina have me."

Havok snarled. "Perhaps I should."

"Then do it."

Hm, he wasn't playing Havok's game. He'd feared Havok, until recently. But something had changed between them—or, not changed exactly, more *rekindled*. He shouldn't have given him the butterfly. A lapse in judgment. A mistake. But Dante had one thing right: if Havok couldn't hand him over, then his choices *were* limited. Reina would kill Dante if Havok refused to surrender him and there was nothing Havok could do to stop her. If he did gift him to her, she'd change him, remake him, turn him into something else, and as irritating and insignificant as Dante was, Havok would lose him that way too. Whichever way he turned, Dante ended.

By the powers, he should have left him in the city plaza. He could have continued to watch him from above until his dying day. He'd have been safe in his pathetic, meaningless life.

A knock sounded on the door.

Dante whirled, and Havok waved him back, pressing a finger to his own lips to suggest he stay quiet. As Havok approached the door, he freed his dagger from the sheath at his lower back, and ignoring Dante's questioning glare, he approached the door.

There were those who serviced the chambers, but today was not such a day. He'd tell them to leave, then re-shackle Dante so he could think.

Havok heaved open the door, and Scarrow filled the doorway, horns scraping the ceiling. The brute lunged, Havok dodged, but Scarrow's left fist swung in, slammed hard against Havok's jaw, and whirled him around. A thick, heavy hand grabbed Havok's right wing and twisted, threatening to re-break the bone. Fire lashed down Havok's back. He roared and spun, yanking his wing from

Scarrow's grip, and plunged the dagger downward, sinking its tip deep into Scarrow's arm.

The sacha bellowed, yanked the dagger out, and tackled Havok against a wall. Havok's head slammed against stone, and the rest was darkness.

CHAPTER 18

ante

Havok lay facedown, pinned by Scarrow's boot. His wings twitched, but he wasn't trying to rise from under Scarrow's boot.

Without Havok, Dante was prey.

He eyed the open door. If he stayed, this would not end well. But the palace was huge, its corridors a mass of tunnels, a monster around every corner. If he ran, he might collide with something worse.

He'd rather take his chances out there than with a beast who could turn his thoughts inside out.

Scarrow roared over Havok's now motionless body, and slowly turned his bulk toward Dante.

Dante bolted out of the door, along the short corridor, and down the spiral stairwell.

Would Havok be all right? Damn him. Havok cared for his pet project and coats, and he could protect himself.

He tripped down the last few steps but righted himself and launched along a corridor and *away*. Didn't matter where. The palace had a rhythm to it, a light and a dark, cold and warm spots. The monsters liked the warmth, and stayed near those areas, so Dante sought out the cold, turning toward frigid air, following the breeze in the hope it would take him outside. If he could get away from the palace, he might be able to make it to cover. Something out there might kill him too, but Havok had made it clear something *would* kill him if he stayed.

I am invisible, nothing here can hurt me.

He ran.

Freedom, he could smell it. It smelled like rain on dust, like the passing of a storm, and he was so very close. All he had to do was pass through the massive door ahead. It was three times as tall as Dante—a door meant for monsters. He flung himself at it, heaved the handle and managed to creak its cumbersome weight open, and then he was out, assaulted by the vast open space of the plains and its unfamiliar horizon. The expanse of nothingness staggered him. Which way? All around there was dust and dry earth. Silent lightning forked across a purple sky. *Run. Just run.* He veered right, keeping close to the black rock walls until he could find some means of crossing the plains without being seen—

Enormous wings kicked up clouds of dust, blocking his path. The beast landed in front of him, threw out its claws, opened its elongated snout, and roared.

He pivoted and ran. Another great hideous winged creature swooped down from above, cutting off his retreat.

No, no, no! He'd been so close.

He switched direction again, boots skidding on the loose dust, and ran into the open expanse of nothing.

CHAPTER 19

avok

Heat thumped down the back of his skull. He raised his head, gave it a shake, rattling the mark on its chain, and blinked into the room. Sluggish thoughts dripped through his mind. Scarrow... He'd been here.

He grabbed his head. Cool wetness ran down the back of his neck. Blood glistened on his fingers. Scarrow could have killed him, but Havok hadn't been his target.

"Dante—" Havok stumbled to his feet and staggered through the doorway. He had to find him. He was Havok's. He *belonged* with Havok.

If Scarrow had Dante, there'd be nothing left for Havok to find.

CHAPTER 20

ante

The monsters flew in thick and fast. Dante darted from left to right, dodging their swiping claws, but the skies were filling with flapping wings, and those already on the ground galloped after him. There was nowhere to go, no shelter, nothing in sight, just shifting black sands.

It was over, he just didn't know it.

He skidded to a stop.

Running wasn't going to save him.

He turned, chest burning with every breath. There were so many now. Some were like Havok, slimmer, faster. Some were heavier, like the gregog. They sneered and snarled. Claws gleamed. Wings fluttered. He couldn't fight them. No armor, no weapons, not even a bow or a dagger.

"Wait..." He held up his hands. "I'm promised. I'm a gift... for Reina."

Some of the beasts stumbled aside, and when Dante

saw the huge pale-white mass of muscle carving his way through their number toward him, his heart sank. Scarrow.

"All the more reason to enjoy you now," Scarrow drawled, inciting the monsters to jeer and howl.

There were too many. Just one would be a hard-fought match for Dante. His heart pounded, adrenaline coursing through his tightening veins. His heartbeat thudded in his head.

"Havok will not let this stand." He backed up, almost stepping into a purple-skinned female. She leered, flashing fangs, and shoved him toward the center of their circle, toward Scarrow.

"*Havok?*" Scarrow scowled.

"Beric—I mean Beric. I belong to him." Dante clutched at the coat. "See, I wear his colors."

"Out here? All alone?" Scarrow spread his hands. "All I see is a lost little pet. You don't belong to anyone, *little pet.*"

More hands shoved Dante forward, buffeting him inside the circle with Scarrow walking the crowd's edge.

"I saw him first." The thick tailed lizard-looking thing broke through the crowd and reached for Dante. Dante skipped back, narrowly avoiding the beast's reach. Scarrow plunged in, driving the creature to the ground, tossing up dust and grit.

A dagger glinted at Scarrow's hip. Dante rushed in, snatched it free, and backed off. Now, he had a weapon. It wasn't much, but it would cut.

Scarrow glanced at his hip, then at the blade in Dante's hand. "Save us all the trouble, pet, and come willingly. You cannot fight us all."

"No, but I can make you bleed." He pointed the dagger. Bone-handled, the curved blade gleamed with iridescent colors forged into the metal. More of a short sword in Dante's hand than a dagger, but lighter than any sword he'd held. He would cut Scarrow to ribbons and then his own throat, if it came to that.

"Hm," Scarrow purred, his blue eyes shining like Havok's gem. "I don't need to fight you, little Fireheart, when your flesh calls to me. I know your wants, know you want to submit under me, to be controlled. You like it, little pet."

"Try me." He swallowed and clutched the sword tighter. "Come on, let's see which one of us gets fucked first."

The audience jostled and snapped, fighting among themselves. Even if Dante did somehow win against Scarrow, there were dozens to take his place.

He'd fight them all, knowing he'd lose. He'd die here and take as many monsters with him as he could. He snarled, baring blunt teeth. "You want me?"

Scarrow's lips stretched wide. He stalked forward, arms open, claw-tipped fingers stretched. He'd be strong, but slow. Dante was fast, he had that advantage. He couldn't let him get a grip on him. If Scarrow caught him, it would be over.

Dante darted left, danced away from Scarrow's reaching paw, and burst forward. He grabbed one of Scarrow's wing stumps and swung onto his back. There, nestled between his broken wings, Dante sliced the dagger down, through pale flesh, freeing a burst of Scarrow's blood.

Scarrow roared and bucked, arms swinging. He tried to grab over his shoulder but Dante ducked, tucked between his wing stumps, and stabbed again and again.

Scarrow had to have a heart, didn't he? If Dante stabbed that, it would be over.

Scarrow dropped to his knees, jarring Dante from his back. Dante stumbled, his boot slipped on blood, and he fell.

A second monster launched herself into the fray, making a play for him. He swung the blade, sliced through her fingers, and a horrible scream erupted. Another dashed in. Dante ducked, brought the dagger up, and sliced open its middle, spilling hot, stinking innards. Then Scarrow's white hand swept in, scooping him off the ground, away from the wounded, writhing creatures, and trapped Dante against his chest, with Dante's arms pinned.

"Those with spirit are always the most enjoyable to break."

"Touch me," Dante seethed through his teeth, "and I'll gouge your eyes out with my powers-be-damned fingernails." He bucked and writhed, but the beast's arm clutched him tight, locking him close. Scarrow smelled of burned caramel and a horrible, sickly sweetness.

Scarrow's thick laughter rolled down his back and with it came the sickening sensation of the beast slithering inside and touching his mind, trying to pluck out his desires. Desires he hadn't even known he'd possessed and couldn't wrap his thoughts around.

Dante got his hand free, yanked the blade down, intent on stabbing Scarrow's gut, but Scarrow's hand shot out, dangling Dante midair at his arm's length. "I'm going to take you in every way, little Fireheart. It will be all the more sweeter knowing you belong to Beric."

The weight of the dagger still pulled at Dante's hand. He tried to swing it, but Scarrow held him off with ease.

"You smell like him." Scarrow chuckled, pinching a bit of the coat in his free hand. "Hm, I'll soon change that."

Dante's strength ebbed away. It was over. It had been over the moment Havok had stolen him from Lenola, he just hadn't known it then. He stopped fighting, surrendering.

With a triumphant smile, Scarrow plucked the blade from his tingling fingers.

"Whatever you do," Dante said, meeting the monster's satisfied glare, "I'll never give myself to you."

Scarrow's chuckle rumbled through Dante's body. "I don't need you to surrender. In fact, I prefer you don't. Oh, I'm going to enjoy you, Fireheart."

"Scarrow!"

Reina's cry rang across the plains like a bell. The gathered sacha dropped in a wave of submission, including Scarrow, who knelt with Dante awkwardly pinned at his side.

She flew down from the sky, her wings and gown both rippling like liquid darkness, and landed a few strides from Scarrow.

"Why do you claim what is clearly not yours?" Reina enquired, her voice lofty, but sharp with ice.

"This one was roaming free. How was I to know it's owned?"

"*Fool!*" The blow, when it came, launched Scarrow sideways. Dante knew little of it, only that Scarrow's grip vanished and he hit the ground, face scuffing on dirt. When he pushed up, Scarrow was righting himself too, but with his head and torso bent low.

"It clearly wears Beric's colors!"

"Beric fails to control his pets," Scarrow sneered, then lunged for Dante. "He is not worthy of your favor!"

Dante scrabbled sideways, away from Scarrow, straight into Reina's gown. She peered down and now that he was closer, he saw how her patchwork skin varied in color. She'd been stitched together from pieces, made by someone else.

"What an intriguing thing you are... all the way out here, hm." She cupped his chin in her hand, tilted his head. Her touch was cold, like the skin of the dead.

Dante should look away but couldn't. He blinked, and behind her, approaching from the palace's jagged black spires, a familiar winged outline revealed Havok's imminent arrival. Whatever he thought of Havok—feared him, despised him, cared for him—he needed him right now.

"Already the cause of so much trouble," Reina said, as Dante's attention flicked from Havok to her. Reina lifted her head and addressed the sacha. "This one was to be my gift, as you all are fully aware. Still, there is merit in competition."

Hurry, Havok! He still swooped in but was seconds away.

Reina cocked her head, thinking. Her next smile unfurled, turning cruel. "Run, little pet. The first to catch you shall have you for a single night."

"What?" Dante blinked.

"Run!" She snapped her teeth an inch from his face.

Dante staggered and glanced around him at the feverish sacha faces, their eyes full of hunger.

Run!

He spotted a gap in the mob and launched himself toward it.

CHAPTER 21

*H*avok

OF COURSE DANTE was the center of a riled crowd, with Scarrow on his knees and Reina presiding over them. He'd never known a Lenolian to find trouble as easily as Dante.

Bargain for him, beg... He had to find a solution that didn't see Reina slaughter them both.

Then Reina's barked, "Run!"

Every possible choice, every potential outcome became redundant. There was only one course of action: Save Dante.

Dante bolted and the sacha closed in after him like waves on a beach. He'd last a few minutes, but no more. They'd catch him and rip him apart.

Havok swooped over the top of Reina's horns, ignoring her command to land, and plunged after Dante. But soon the air was filled with sacha clawing their way toward their prey. Reina had made Dante their prize—even though she knew he was Havok's—breaking her own rules because she could.

Coming in fast, Havok plucked a sacha from the air and flung them aside. A few others whirled, startled at his appearance. He bared his teeth. If any of them touched Dante, they'd be feeling the jagged edge of Havok's wrath. He spotted Dante, still running, even breaking away from the cumbersome sacha. A strange little tic hiccupped Havok's heart, something like pride, and then Dante tripped.

The sacha surged.

Havok roared, slammed into one, knocking it off its feet, then grabbed another's wing, launching it sideways. He tore through them, desperate to reach Dante. They couldn't touch him; they couldn't have him. Dante was Havok's butterfly boy. He'd kill anyone who dared lay a finger on him.

A savage, ruthless streak loaned Havok a furious strength. He tore through his opponents one by one, slicing, shoving, roaring. They grabbed him, but he raked his claws through flesh, sank his teeth into muscle. Damn them all!

Dante let out a cry. One of the sacha had him by the leg. He tried to kick them off. The sacha leered, dragged Dante by the ankle, and dangled him in the air in triumph. His coat flopped down over his head, blinding him. He flailed, as desperate to get free as Havok was to have him.

Havok launched off his back foot and tackled the triumphant sacha to the ground, sending all three of them sprawling in the dirt. In the corner of Havok's eye, he saw Dante bolt, saw the others surge after him. Would it ever end? Havok slammed the writhing sacha's face into the ground and leaned into it, buckling bone, making his kin scream.

"He's mine, he will always be mine—nobody can take him from me." Havok growled. The sacha's eye swiveled, its lips moving, begging. Its skull buckled, and it moved no more.

Havok flung open his wings, burst into the sky, spotted Dante fleeing, coat flapping, arms and legs pumping, with the horde right on his tail. Damn them all. And damn Reina for sanctioning this madness.

Havok swooped in, slammed into Dante, and scooped him up under the arms. He screamed and bucked. "Hush. It's me." Havok pulled him close to his chest, trapping him inside his arms, and Dante's fight drained out of him. "It's Havok. It's me..." Havok repeated, over and over, too many times, with too much emotion. His heart hammered so hard behind his ribs that Dante must have felt it.

He carried him higher, faster than any other sacha could climb. Higher and higher, until the air thinned and churned with the metallic taste of lightning.

Dante was silent, motionless, tucked against Havok's chest. Havok had him now, and he'd find a way for them to survive this.

The mist closed in. The tips of the palace's black spires pierced the low-lying clouds. No sacha would follow them so close to the spires. With visibility so low, it was too dangerous.

The edge of one of the high hall roofs loomed from the mist, and Havok brought them down, wings spread, slowing their descent. He landed on a rooftop amidst churning fog and folded his wings, then freed Dante. The Lenolian staggered away. He appeared unhurt—a minor miracle all of its own. Had Havok arrived moments later, he dared not think about the outcome. They'd have taken him, his butterfly boy, and he'd have been gone, forever.

No, he couldn't think it.

He pressed a hand to his chest in an effort to slow his racing heart. Dante was safe now. The stupid fool. "What were you thinking?" Havok growled. "Any one of those sacha would have killed you had they caught you."

An impatient frown flashed across Dante's face. He stumbled again, turning on the spot. "Where are we?"

Havok folded his arms and clamped his wings closed. "I told you not to run. You run, you die. When will you listen?"

That impatience flared again, and Dante whirled. "You were out cold, and your sick friend was hunting me, so what should I have done, oh mighty Havok? Just fucking lay there and let him mind-fuck me while you were unconscious? I am done with you and them and this whole fucking nightmare. I am done with all of it. Where the fuck are we, Havok?!"

He'd rarely seen Dante so passionate. His flame-colored hair was a wild, damp mess, and his face flushed with rage. Seeing him like this, it tangled Havok's emotions in knots, confusing him. Havok's tail lashed, he knew it did, knew Dante suspected what that meant, but he couldn't stop it. He'd been so... afraid he'd lose him. "Back at the palace."

Dante's rage didn't abate. "Why?!" he snarled. "You could have flown us anywhere. Why come back to this wretched prison!"

His green eyes glowed with that fire Scarrow had been so quick to notice. Havok rather liked to see him come alive like this. He breathed hard, his body alert, wired. Even without a weapon, Dante had fought with a strength worthy of any sacha. And because of that, he answered him with the respect of one. "This is my home."

"Your home? With those... beasts?!" He scoffed, then laughed ironically. "Home. This is no more your home than the pond was. You aren't like them, can't you see that? They will kill you the second you lose Reina's favor. She poisons you."

Havok sighed. This wasn't helping their current predicament. Reina would now take Dante from him. He had to think of a way to keep him.

Dante paced into the swirling fog. "I cannot live like this." He thrust his hands into his hair. "I can't do this." The fog blurred between them.

Havok's heart tripped. "Mind the edge."

"What?" Dante froze.

"Mind the edge there. Fall off, and you'll meet an abrupt end."

Dante's face contorted with yet more rage. And when he paced back to Havok this time, his fists trembled at his sides. "Would that entertain you? Should I jump to my death, *master*? Or hang from your fucking leash?"

He didn't like his tone, didn't understand the hate in it. He'd just saved Dante, he should be grateful, but the hate was so powerful Havok backed up, then caught himself retreating and stood firm. He plastered a smirk onto his face. "If you do jump, will you remove the coat first? I'd rather not have to make another."

Dante's cheek twitched. "You wretched, selfish, vicious creature."

Havok arched an eyebrow.

"This is all your doing! Everything!" He jabbed a finger into Havok's chest. "You could fly us away any moment, but you won't because you're blind, and it has nothing to do with your missing eye!"

Havok backhanded the fool, surprising both of them. "Enough!"

Dante's hand flew to his face. He worked his tongue into his cheek, licked his lips, and spat blood to the side. "You wanna hit me again? Get it all out now. Blame me for whatever gods-awful life you've had after Calen attacked you. That is what this is about, right? So do it. Come on. Hit me again, you fuckin' monster."

He raised his hand and Dante, dashing in low, landed a punch to Havok's gut that stole the air from his lungs. He croaked, bent around the pain, and snarled as Dante skipped back, grinning.

Blood painted Dante's smiling lips. He beckoned. "Try and hit me again."

Havok straightened, rolled his shoulders, and flicked out his wings. "I fear you have regressed in your obedience training."

Dante's grin faded. His eyes narrowed, turning sly, and when he came for Havok this time, there was real intent behind his glare. If he'd held a blade, Havok might have believed he'd be about to use it. But instead, his hand reached for Havok's face.

Havok flinched, expecting a blow.

Dante's warm, snarling mouth sealed over Havok's in what must have been a kiss, although it didn't feel like one. Blood wet Havok's tongue, and then Dante thrust his in, leaning into Havok, while his touch on Havok's face captured all of Havok's thoughts, until there was nothing in his head but the push and pull of a kiss that shouldn't be happening, that he didn't want but couldn't stop.

The thrill of Dante's touch stoked a fire in Havok's

chest, lifted his wings, made his heart race, turned his thoughts to molasses and set his blood ablaze. Yes, it was forbidden, but yes, he wanted more of the boy from his dreams, from his past, who at times had seemed like a ghost or a fantasy Havok had created in a world he'd never felt he belonged in.

Dante shoved Havok away, ending the kiss, and swept his thumb across his own bottom lip. "I thought so," he said, although what he'd thought remained elusive.

Havok's own thoughts had abandoned him. He tasted Dante, but more than that, he felt him inside, in his racing heart and pumping veins, felt his body respond with need and desire.

Dante snorted a laugh. "You're as trapped here as I am, you just don't see it."

No, this would not do. Dante getting into Havok's head, using the kiss as a weapon against him, because that must have been the feeling he'd had—a weapon to unbalance him, make him doubt what he knew about himself, about the world. He'd underestimated Dante and his subtle abilities. He'd forgotten they were enemies.

He started toward Dante, intent on taking him back to the chamber to be bound and gagged anew, for his own good and his punishment.

Dante lifted a finger. "No."

Havok stopped. "You cannot say no."

"I just did."

"We must go back—"

"No."

"Dante, I do not negotiate."

"Do you hear any terms? I'm not going back." He folded his arms. "I am *never* going back."

"Then you leave me no choice but to resort to violence." He made a grab for him but Dante danced back.

"Come a step closer and I'll kiss you again." Dante's right eyebrow towered. "No? You don't want that? Oh wait, you do? Hm, what a dilemma."

Frustration with the fool's insolence boiled Havok's blood. "You're insufferable. And this is getting us nowhere. Reina will come—"

"Oh, I don't know, I've learned a great deal about you in the last few moments. A kiss is all it takes to make you soft, and hard... in other places."

Havok's patience snapped. He flew in, using his wings to push off the roof and plunge back down, dragging Dante into his arms, but the feel of him, shuddering with heat, panting hard—by the powers, it made Havok's body sing, made his cock ache, made him want to sink his teeth into Dante's neck and claim him in more ways than master and pet. In ways he hadn't even known were possible.

Havok gripped Dante's coat, hauling Dante almost off his feet, and thrust his tongue between his lips, seeking Dante's fury and winning it the moment Dante kissed him back, full of hate and fever and passion. What was this feeling consuming him, this need to taste and bite and stroke and lick and own a Lenolian?

He rubbed his filling cock against Dante's hip, more parts of him seeking and needing Dante's touch. He snaked his tail around his leg, feeding it upward, squeezing his thigh, and when its tip found his crotch and the heavy weight there, Dante groaned into the kiss, turning it messy and savage. He liked it. Havok stroked Dante's hardening arousal with his tail, summoning Dante's response, and plunged his hands down Dante's back, seeking skin and warmth and feeling.

This was more than a kiss.

This was some kind of magic, something Havok had no control over, some part of himself he didn't even know existed. And that part wanted to devour Dante.

He tore free, unraveled his tail, and backed away from the glassy-eyed Dante. "What is this sorcery? What are you doing to me?" By the powers, Havok's body was ablaze. He'd desired before, of course, mostly after the dreams of Dante, but not like this.

"Sorcery?" Dante's voice had dropped to a deep, honeyed drawl, and that too did something to Havok's self. "You mean a kiss?"

"*That* wasn't a kiss."

Dante touched his lips, then licked them, and Havok almost moaned. "Yeah... no, it was more than that. You felt it. You want me, Havok. You wanted me that day by the pool—wanted me ever since. Your body knows the truth, even when your head is full of lies."

"No, I don't... I can't."

"Lie to yourself all you like. You and your kind seem to do a lot of that." Dante's hand dropped to the bulge in his trousers and he adjusted himself, and now that bulge was all Havok could see. A proud, erect length that Havok's mouth watered to suck, that his fingers itched to stroke; his tail lashed, somehow aching to tease.

Dante's chuckle lit the fire of hurt and confusion inside Havok. Dante knew these things, these feelings, urges, and Havok did not. "If it's not sorcery, then what is it?"

"You truly don't know? Then I'm sorry for you. For this life that clearly isn't yours but you seem to be content to live the lie for whatever reason, probably for Reina's ease."

"Stop!" Havok growled. "Enough. You are Lenolian. You work the farms to feed our nation, and we harvest you. Your kind are beneath the sacha. Come now." He held out his hand. "I must ready you for Reina, or she'll kill us both."

"I said no." Dante backed up, the fog rolled around him, and the edge of the roof loomed. "I'm not going back, Havok."

"Dante, stop, the edge—"

Dante raised his trembling hand, holding Havok back. "I won't be passed between monsters. I can't live like this, in your world."

If Dante plunged through the mist, Havok wouldn't find him in time to stop him hitting the palace spires. And suddenly, perhaps for the first time, he knew he couldn't let him go. He'd dreamed of hurting him, but he'd also dreamed Dante was alive, and that one day he'd find him again. He had found him, watched him from the Lenolian spire, watched his life as he meandered with no real purpose, but it could not end like this.

If Dante was gone, what else was there for Havok?

Dante was right, Havok barely cared for the world he inhabited. He'd been alone in it for so long, he'd forgotten how to feel. But moments ago, Dante had reminded him. Like he'd shown him before, by the pond, his butterfly boy.

He cared for him, cared that he lived and that he was safe, that nobody could hurt him. He cared so much he'd do anything for him.

"Just take me home, Havok," Dante said, eyes begging.

"I can't do that." He could never go back to Lenola. His return would throw the balance of the harvests into chaos. His people could never know their fates.

"I just..." Dante sighed and glanced away. "I just want

to see Calen again, to tell him I'm sorry. I want to be who I was, Havok, before I knew it was all a lie."

Havok stepped closer, slowly, carefully, aware the edge was a single step behind Dante. "You cannot unknow the truth." Havok offered his hand. "Come with me, Dante, please. I was wrong, I think. I don't understand half of what you're doing to me or what's happening here, I just know... I don't want to lose you, and you're right, I've been lying, to you, to myself. But you must step away from the edge."

Dante swallowed hard. "How can I ever trust you?"

Havok's heart fluttered. He inched forward; just a little more and he'd have him. "Just... try?" It sounded feeble, and he hated himself for it, but it was all he had. "*Nothing happens without it.*" Dante's lips gave a little twitch of a smile as the sound of his own words echoed back to him. Perhaps Havok should have listened more, done more, been more... than the monster he was. "Give me another chance?"

"I want to, but what is there in this life for me? I can't be yours or theirs. I can't fear I'll be torn to shreds every day. Maybe you can, but I can't."

"I've known nothing else." By the powers, he sounded desperate and hated it, hated what this man was doing to him, but he needed him. "Dante...?"

Dante's heel skimmed the roof's edge. "If I am to die then it will be on my terms. All that's left to say is that I'm sorry I didn't save you. I never stopped wishing I had."

He stepped back and vanished into the mist.

CHAPTER 22

ante

Dante didn't expect to live, and that was all right. This world was not what he'd thought it to be, and there was no place within it for him. And so he fell, closed his eyes, and welcomed the sweet embrace of the end.

But the jolt, when it came, wasn't an end. Hands grasped his arm, dangling him midair, and the leathery swish of wings signaled he'd been caught, but not by Havok. Someone else had him. He peered up through the mist, his face wet and eyes burning, and there she was. The dark creature, her skin stitched with black thread: Reina.

He'd fallen into her hands.

He searched the mist, but there was nothing, no sign of Havok, just swirling greyness.

Reina carried him high, he felt that much in the press of damp air, and then she dropped, descending onto a large glossy black balcony, made of the same shining black rock as the rest of the palace. He struggled, but her hand remained locked onto his forearm as she led him through a pair of high arched doors and into a chamber larger than Havok's, decorated in black and grey silks and satins.

Everywhere he looked there were rooms divided by drapes. What did she mean to do with him? She dragged him toward a large domed structure with a silk sheet thrown over it. He could have asked where she was taking him, but it didn't matter. Nothing mattered. He was invisible. Nothing could hurt him. How else could he survive this? Survive *her*, them, this world?

Reina gripped the sheet and flung it off, revealing an iron cage with a sparkling blue gem nestled in an iron cradle at its top. The cage resembled a huge iron chest cavity. She unhooked the door's latch, flung it open, and shoved him inside, then clanged the door shut with enough strength to rattle the cage and him inside it.

Reina's perfect red lips curved into a thin smile. "Welcome to your end."

She threw the silk sheet back over the cage, plunging him into darkness.

THE SILENCE WAS TOO THICK, too unreal. His own thumping heart and jagged breaths were his only company —no sound came from the outside. He shivered, but he wasn't cold; he didn't feel much of anything. He was numb, invisible.

He could rage, bang on the cage bars, threaten her, but what good would it do? He had nothing left to fight with and if he somehow escaped the cage and ran, they'd catch him.

He sat, pulled his legs to his chest, and closed his eyes.

∼

Reina flung off the black sheet and light spilled in. He squinted at her, reading her narrow, pale face, her all-black eyes, the way each stitch tugged on her skin, stretching it.

She studied him, as he studied her.

"I expected more fire from you, Fireheart."

He stared back. Silent. Motionless. Invisible. His silence was all he could control, so he'd use it.

"This is your life now," she said with a hand flourish. "Accept it and begin anew."

He visually traced the curve of her lips, noting her sharp teeth and how her tongue worked around the words. She was beautiful in the worst ways, like a poisonous flower, or a venomous snake, its beauty a warning and a trap.

She approached the curved bars, and her jagged, leathery wings spread behind her, framing her in a canvas of darkness. "Within this cage, you will not hunger, you will not age, time cannot touch you. You will stay unchanged, my pretty pet, for as long as I wish it."

He stared back, cold and hard on the outside, screaming within, his mind already fracturing around this new reality.

"However," she purred. "Speak, and I will grant you one wish."

The temptation was to ask for freedom, but she'd never give it. So, no. He would not speak. His voice was all he had left that belonged to him. He'd given the monsters enough. She could not take that too. For as long as she kept him caged, he'd never say a word.

"Very well." Reina dipped her chin and threw the cover over his cage, plunging him into darkness and silence once again.

He sat still, sat quiet, and buried himself inside his mind, back to a time when he'd played with a monster boy beside an emerald pool, the only time when the world had made any sense.

CHAPTER 23

avok

IT HAD BEEN three days and nights since Dante had stepped from the edge and vanished. He was dead. Havok knew it, despite not finding his body. He'd searched, flown through and around the jagged, deadly spires, each one coated in mist, endlessly looking for his broken butterfly boy. But to no avail.

I'll come back.

But Havok knew, sometimes Dante didn't come back. And this was one of those times. He'd never come back again.

The kiss still burned on his lips. The touch on his cheek, so full of Dante's fire. He felt it still and didn't want to let it go.

He'd misjudged Dante. He hadn't understood him at all. Or his own feelings. He recalled those final moments again and again before Dante's parting words. *I'm sorry I didn't save you. I never stopped wishing I had.* Dante had *cared* for Havok, and despite everything that had happened, who and what Havok was, he perhaps still had cared. Wasn't the kiss proof of that?

Havok had been wrong about *everything*.

He touched his lips as he marched through the palace corridors, toward the gathering hall. He tasted him there, tasted him *inside*. It had been like before, by the pond, when things had seemed so much simpler. He'd thought Dante foolish, thought him weak and insignificant in the wider world because of where he'd come from. He'd been a game to Havok, a plaything, or so Havok had told himself. But in truth, Dante had been so much more. He'd been *everything*.

Havok had watched him from the spire, searched for him among the crowds during the offering day. Without realizing it. Havok had hung his dreams on his butterfly boy. He'd been a beacon in the darkness, a figure from his past that told him friendship could be real, and that it could be broken.

He'd hated him for taking that away when he'd brought Calen to their pool, hated that he continued to *care*.

And now he was gone.

He'd failed him. Failed himself. He'd wanted to please Reina, to make her see he was worthy, to give her a gift to thank her for raising him up beside her, but why? *Why...* Dante would ask. Why to everything. So full of questions. Questions Havok would never hear again.

He pushed through the gathering hall's huge doors and strode through the sacha. His sword hung heavy at his hip —the sword he'd retrieved from Lenola's ruined spire. A hungry, killing blade—his blade, not given to him by Reina, not a gift. He'd always had it, kept it buried near the hawthorn bush. Over time, its edge had dulled, but it would shine again, when it tasted blood.

Sacha knew to step aside, to clear a path, and that path led straight to his target.

"Scarrow!"

The wingless brute turned toward him and snorted a derogatory laugh. "Reina's favorite pet has finally come down off his perch?"

Havok raised the point of the sword. "You stole what was mine. By rights, I will have payment."

"Careful, Beric, Reina doesn't like it when you slip her leash."

A growl bubbled up from Havok's chest. "Choose your weapon."

"Has she sanctioned this little—" Scarrow waved his hand. "—outburst?" He huffed again. "So furious that I took your toy? It's almost as though you care for the creature."

"He's dead."

"They are so very good at dying." Scarrow laughed. "And I was so looking forward to devouring that one. How did it expire?"

"He took his own life." He wasn't sure why he bothered to explain anything to Scarrow, but hearing the words and the finality in them drove an invisible blade through Havok's chest and into his heart. His vision blurred and the sword wavered in his hand. Dante had ended his own life rather than live in Havok's. There was something profound in that, something that made Havok want to roar at the sky and rip every single star down, turning the world into darkness.

"And you failed to prevent it?" Scarrow folded his thick

arms. "Reina will be most displeased to hear how *you* killed her gift."

It was true. She'd be furious. But there was nothing to be done now. He'd deal with her, but for now, Scarrow was about to discover the sharpness of his blade's bite. Vengeance would be Havok's.

Havok lunged, clipping Scarrow's arm, drawing a line of blood across his flesh. Blood splattered across the floor. Scarrow roared and swung a massive fist, but Havok dashed aside and plunged in again, flicking the sword up Scarrow's leather-clad thigh. The leather split, as did the sacha's skin, and more blood streamed.

Havok thrust open his wings and sprang vertical, feathers keeping him aloft. Scarrow reached for him and Havok swung the blade, slicing off Scarrow's fingers. His roar turned vicious and rabid. With no wings of his own, he groped at the air, desperate to grab Havok, his failure enraging him. The whites of his eyes showed in their madness.

Havok whipped his tail around Scarrow's arm, and as Havok yanked up with his tail, he dove down, thrusting the sword deep into Scarrow's chest.

The sacha stumbled, dropped to his knees, and Havok leaned into the sword's hilt, driving it deeper still, wings flapping behind him, forcing it through blood and muscle, into flesh and through bone.

Blood bubbled from Scarrow's lips. His expression slackened as his rage faded.

Havok landed, kept one hand on the sword, and freed his dagger with the other, then punched it into Scarrow's side, where the sacha's second heart beat—the original gift from Reina.

Scarrow gulped and spluttered blood. Specks dashed

Havok's face. He clutched at Havok's arm, his strength still impressive, and his fingers dug in, as though he could drag Havok into death with him.

Havok leaned in close and watched his enemy's gaze cloud over. "Your death for Dante. You were a speck of dust against his raging flame, and I only wish he were here to witness this."

Scarrow spluttered some more, but his fingers loosened. He fell onto his fingerless hand, then buckled over onto his side and lay gasping. Havok yanked the sword free of Scarrow's chest with a savage jerk and kicked Scarrow onto his back.

The others observed, silent and wary.

Whoever said there was no victory in revenge did not know vengeance, because as Scarrow lay dying, satisfaction calmed Havok's thoughts and steadied his resolution.

He spread his wings and lifted his head, looking into the eyes of those gathered to watch the demise of one of their own. Some held their pets at the ends of leashes. Forgotten, forlorn men and women thrust into a nightmare not of their making. Each and every one had been taken, harvested; some had been changed, and it had seemed right because Reina was their sovereign and all must obey her. But why? Havok heard Dante's voice. *Why*, he would have asked. Why did Havok follow her, why did he answer to her, why entrap the Lenolian people for her? And why did Dante have to die for Havok to see his point?

By the powers, Havok was the fool, not Dante.

Havok bared his teeth at all of them. None had been his friend, not like Dante had been. He'd been alone among them. They glared back, some afraid, some defiant, some indifferent.

They were sacha, and so was Havok, but he longer recognized them as kin.

"Beric!" Reina's roar echoed through the hall.

The crowd flinched and dropped in a wave of submission.

Instincts tried to tug Havok to his knees, but he defied them. Blood dripped from his blade. He folded his wings in, but not completely. He might need them soon.

Reina landed a few strides away, her wings stirring a downdraft of cold, dusty wind.

He lifted his chin. Defiance felt good. He saw in his mind how Dante had stepped from the edge, defying them all.

Havok could be foolish. Perhaps this was, right now, as Reina came for him. But few things had felt as right as meeting Reina eye to eye.

"Bow down, Beric."

His tail lashed. "Why?"

Reina's fury came over her like a blast of fire. She reached up, plucked a blade from over her shoulder, between her wings—and swept it down so fast he had no time to react.

He didn't feel its cut, didn't register how it severed his arm clean from below the shoulder. He just saw the limb fall, knew it was his, but that didn't seem possible... because there was no pain.

Smoke sizzled from the shoulder stump, where his arm had once been.

Ice crackled up his legs, freezing him still. And then the horrible truth of what she'd done flooded in, pulling the pain with it. The pain of losing Dante, and losing his arm, and some part of him he'd been so sure of but no longer cared for, the part Reina had made. It all slammed into him, rocking his mind and body.

"Kneel!" Reina roared.

Ice pulled him down, encased his legs, his knees. It captured his tail too, then it trapped the sword, hanging limply in his right hand.

What was this?

He let the blade go—it stayed poised, stuck proudly in the ice. He reached for the mark dangling from his horns. The mark kept him together, kept him alive. Without it, he wouldn't exist. At least, that was what Reina had told him. But Dante had said he'd always had the mark, that it was a part of him, and if the mark was a part of him, then she had no control over him.

She did not rule him.

If he removed the mark, and he remained alive, heart beating, mind working, then the mark was a lie. And so was she.

Somehow, Dante had known, hadn't he?

He pulled on the mark's chain—Reina grabbed his hand. "You forget yourself, Beric."

Havok met Reina's furious glare and smiled. She had no power over him. "My name is not Beric." He pushed against her grip; his fingers closed on his mark, but she held him back, her efforts trembling against his. "My name is Havok."

"Have you lost your mind?" she seethed, her hold crushing his.

"No, I believe I've finally found it."

"What has you so possessed?" she hissed. "Come, kneel, or you shall be punished."

"Dante saw through our world, he saw the truth of me, of you. I didn't listen, until it was too late."

"Too late?" Her snarl softened and her slippery smile returned. "Beric, dear. Your pet is not gone."

His grip on his mark eased. "He lives?"

"Cease this madness," she said softly. "Let us talk some more, outside of prying eyes."

Dante wasn't dead? He lowered his hand and as he did, the ice encasing him receded, thawing in seconds. "There now." Her expression softened and her wings sagged. She glanced at the others in the gathering hall, all silent as they'd watched Havok's act of defiance and its outcome.

"He lives?" He didn't want her knowing how much he cared, but she knew of their past already, she'd said as much, and she likely saw the hope on his face in the moments before he'd slammed his expression down, guarding it.

"Oh yes." Her tone darkened. "But, Beric, you know your Fireheart is mine. He was always mine." A dagger flashed in her hand. Havok's dagger. She'd stolen it.

She plunged the tip down, thrusting it deep into Havok's chest until it struck something hard, with a jolt.

His breath lodged in his throat. He looked down at the handle, her hand wrapped around it.

"I only have one enemy, and that is defiance," she whispered against his cheek. "Perhaps it is time I gave you another heart. Yours has become unruly."

He couldn't stand, couldn't breathe. The blade had found his heart and he was falling into Reina's arms, into her trap. The smile that chased him into his nightmares told him he'd never be free of her. And that his world was about to change forever.

CHAPTER 24

ante

His coat smelled of warm leather, with a hint of winter spice, like Havok. If Dante closed his eyes, he could imagine him close. He'd say something bitter and snide, probably threaten to cut out Dante's tongue, or his dick, but Havok was all bark and no bite, at least when it came to Dante. Would he ever see him again?

The kiss... That hadn't all been hate. He'd thrown it at Havok in madness, already lost to the chaos of the world and his place in it. And then the kiss had struck like a match to the fuse. The heat it ignited between them was like nothing he'd encountered before.

That kiss had been a fitting farewell.

It had been days, weeks maybe, since he'd stepped off the roof. He wasn't sure anymore. Trapped in the cage of silence, there was no sense of time passing. He didn't hunger, didn't need to relieve himself. His dreams came with his eyes open, memories too. He welcomed them. They kept him company. Sometimes he dreamed of home —his first home on the farm before the jailor had taken his childhood. Sometimes he dreamed of Calen, or Jean and the others who'd tried to fight, dreamed of a life as meaningless as a fish's in a glass bowl. Other times, he thought of Havok, and sometimes he dreamed of butterflies.

One butterfly was very real. It fluttered around him now and came to rest on his hand. Little Blue. Occasionally, it played in his hair. He'd been afraid he'd bat it away and might crush it at first, but it was faster than him. It came from the tattoo Havok had branded into his skin. A gift. A secret. Never to be shown. *You are my secret.*

Dante was dead. He'd stepped off the palace roof and plunged to an abrupt end.

He wasn't sure who he was now. Invisible. Hidden. Forgotten. Or perhaps this was an opportunity to remake himself?

By the powers, his mind was breaking.

The butterfly danced. Havok would tell him what it said, if anything. They were foul-mouthed, vicious creatures, he'd told Dante once. But Dante had laughed, unsure if Havok was jesting. He couldn't imagine Little Blue was anything so crass.

Little Blue had to be magic, didn't she? For a tattoo to come to life.

Whatever fueled her, he was grateful for the company.

The silk cover withdrew suddenly. Dante swiped Blue from the air and placed her against his side once more, hiding her on his hip, beneath the coat. Squinting into the bright light, Reina's outline came into focus. She came often, like this, demanded he speak, luring him out with the promise of one wish, but he'd stayed silent. She'd been furious to begin with, but after time, her anger faded.

"I have a gift for you, Fireheart." She grasped his cage bars in both hands and peered inside. "I'll show you, if you speak."

He kept his lips sealed and drew his legs to his chest. The coat draped from his shoulders and pooled around him. He didn't get cold, or hot, didn't hunger, or tire, just as she'd said. But he grew *harder*. Changing himself into something—*someone* else, not Dante. Perhaps he *was* Fireheart now. A creature the monsters had made. But not the one Reina wanted. She wanted a pet to tease, to taunt and play with. Something that would quiver in her presence like the others on their leashes. That wasn't Fireheart.

Reina's quick smile widened. She waved behind her and a towering, modified man lurched into sight.

The bottom fell out of Dante's world. Even grotesquely changed, there was no mistaking Calen's blue eyes—but she'd taken one, mauled his face, replaced half his chest and hip with something *other* made of thick, scaled hide. His lips had been sewn shut and his one remaining eye swiveled, searching for an end.

"What do you think?"

He slammed down his barriers even as his thoughts raged at her, demanding he scream. He wanted to grab the bars and tear them apart, then tear her apart. The anger was so savage, so visceral, his body shook and his breathing sawed. But he kept his face as blank as stone.

"Beric brought him to me." Reina smirked. "A gift, before you. He seemed to have some personal distaste for this one. I do wonder why. Do you perhaps know?"

Havok had done this?

It was a lie. It had to be.

But Havok was capable. He was, after all, a monster just like Reina.

He couldn't let her see how the knowledge dug under his armor and threatened to crack it open. If he broke apart now, she'd win.

He was invisible.

Nothing here could hurt him.

Calen didn't deserve this.

Dante turned his face away. There was nothing he could do from inside the cage. But one day, she would open the door, and then she'd see what a monster she'd made of him.

CHAPTER 25

Havok

THE NEW HEART beat louder than his own—*thud-thud*—hot and heavy and alien. Its relentless rhythm pumped Reina's touch through his veins, stole his will and poisoned his mind so he became a passenger in his own flesh.

When Reina finished her surgery, she carried him away—cool air slid over him, her wings beat the air, like the beat of his new, wretched heart—and then she set him down on a flimsy wooden bed, the mattress made of straw, the night sky spread above him, stars twinkling. And she left him there, to mend, to die, whatever he wanted.

The new heart's poison slithered through muscle and flesh. With every breath, its strength grew and his identity crumbled. He'd lost a part of himself to, an arm... But the missing arm could be fixed... He knew how, he just...The chamber spun around him and sickness lined his gut.

He was Havok.

He'd begun life forgotten and alone, living on the fringes of a world he did not belong to, until he'd found the butterfly boy and realized there was more. Those days were dreamlike, and soon, they'd belong to somehow else, because the heart was consuming them too, beat by beat.

Thud-thud.

Another piece of him wilted and turned to dust, another memory snatched away.

He was losing himself.

Dante.

He was alive.

Reina had him.

Thud-thud, another memory, Dante's hand in his as they watched falling stars.

He had hair as red as a forge fire and eyes as green as the emerald pool, didn't he? Dante's face blurred, the details missing. Green eyes or... blue? Dante's hand wisped from his, turning to smoke.

He was losing him.

The heart was taking Dante, erasing him.

He had to stop it. He couldn't lose him again.

Havok clutched at his chest, where the new heart thumped. He dug his claws in, drawing five lines of thin blood, forcing his claws deeper. Stiches snapped, unraveling. Heat flared, but it was nothing compared to the agony of losing himself.

His ribs barred the way.

Rolling onto his side, he blinked through fogged vision toward his old workbench, strewn with rubble. He'd been returned to Lenola's spire, the jailor's sanctuary. It hadn't been destroyed, not completely. If he could reach that bench, reach his tools... he might be able to carve out the new heart.

He fell from the bed, twitching, bleeding and broken, then half crawled, half dragged his broken body across the floor.

She could not keep Dante; she could not take his butterfly boy. Havok would rather die than lose that piece of him, the only piece that mattered. His single, remaining hand slipped on blood. His blood. He heaved air into his lungs, forcing his body to move. The stump below his shoulder twitched, dripping thick blood, weeping for the missing limb. Pain was temporary. The heart would be permanent, if he didn't carve the damned thing out of him.

He staggered to his feet, fell against the workbench, grabbed a knife, and held its point over his chest. He'd need to make a pathway first, remove the skin, break the ribs, and slice out the heart.

Thud-thud.

His hand wavered, the knife's point wobbled.

He had to remain conscious. He climbed onto the workbench, breathless and wretched, then lay down, took a steeling breath, and began to cut.

Peeling off the rest of Reina's stitches was the easiest part. The top layer of patched skin went next. With the ribs exposed, he reached for a pair of tongs, bloody fingers slipping over cool metal. Reina had fused the ribs together. The break was already there, he just had to undo her work and pry himself apart once more.

With the tongs fixed in place, he yanked downward. Bone snapped. His vision swirled, head and alien heart thumping. Could the heart know he had come for it?

The next rib snapped in his grip. Then the next. With his chest cavity exposed, he plunged his hand into the warm, wet cavity, feeling for the alien heart's hungry arteries. Getting a finger on each, he sliced them off. *Thud-thud-*

thud. With the last cut made, he yanked the organ from its home and raised the beating, bloody muscle into the air.

Flailing arteries lashed, desperate to cling back on. The fleshy muscle was black like Reina's wings. With it gone, its poison had already begun to fade, his true heart working to cleanse his veins.

He glimpsed the fire in the corner of his eye. *Burn it. Turn it to ashes, gone for good...*

But first...

He set the thumping organ down and reassembled the pieces of himself, stapling and stitching, until the work was done, and he laid on the bench, blood-soaked, cold, trembling... but free of the black heart.

Now to burn the parasite.

He rolled off the workbench, fell, then stumbled across the floor. The heart thumped in his grip, arteries still writhing and knotting.

If he burned it, she'd sense its end.

No, if he was going to get Dante back, she had to believe Havok belonged to her, that he was devoted, obedient like he had been before.

He grabbed a jar of dirt he'd once gathered from Lenola's lands in a whimsical effort to grow a plant as company, dropped the heart inside, and sealed it tightly. The heart thumped and writhed, but the sand muffled it enough to be forgotten. After placing it under the workbench, he threw a cover over it and stumbled away.

His legs gave out. He dropped to his knees, his body heavy, his mind numbed. It was done. He sprawled on his side and closed his eyes.

His true heart beat within him. He let its sound carry him to sleep. And there, he dreamed of Dante.

As he healed, one thought was louder than all the others: Reina had Dante hidden away.

It had been many months, almost a cycle, long enough that Reina had reinstated his purpose as Lenola's jailor. But as he sat atop his lofty perch, watching the people below, his heart was filled with indifference. The only time he felt much of anything was when a sacha decided they would steal what Lenola offered. Those trespassers faced Havok's wrath. He killed them without mercy.

When the time for the offering came around again, he'd whisked the man away, taken his arm to replace his own, and dropped him at Reina's feet, to do with as she pleased. He didn't ask after Dante. He couldn't, not without raising her suspicions.

Havok stitched the man's arm to himself and clad it in leather. Within a few days, his body had adopted the limb as its own, but every time he clenched a fist he was reminded of Reina's harsh and swift punishment of his defiance.

To save Dante, he'd have to kill her.

He'd loved her once, or so he'd thought. But it had never been love. Infatuation. Misguided admiration. She'd been using him, just as Dante had said. He saw her now. And hate burned in his veins. But it was a good burn, the invigorating kind.

The wretched black heart sat in a jar beneath his workbench, still pumping. He'd come close to throwing it in the firepit, but instinct had held him back.

He couldn't fight her; she'd take his head. He had to trick her. But she was clever too, and no sacha would help him. There would be a way. Thoughts of her death consumed him, day and night, his inability to act festering like an open wound.

He couldn't stop her alone, and none of his own kind would help him... He had nowhere else to go but down among Dante's people, among the Lenolians. Among the people he'd been charged to protect, and to harvest.

Perhaps the time had come for them to learn the truth.

CHAPTER 26

ante

"You will speak!"

He'd learned a great deal inside the cage. Reina had tried to coax his voice out with false promises, then threatened him with Lenola's destruction, and when that hadn't worked, she'd raged like a storm.

She detested defiance. And his had worn thin.

"I will bring you Beric, if you'll speak." She didn't meet his gaze, not anymore. She'd only get a scathing glare back.

Havok had taken Calen and given him to Reina. Havok's petty jealousy had destroyed a man's life. Dante didn't *want* to see him. Or maybe he did, just to tell him how he despised him for what he'd done. Either way, it didn't matter. He wasn't speaking. He'd been quiet for so long, he wasn't sure he could speak.

He did wonder, as Reina paced and fumed, why she didn't remove him from the cage and torture him. She could have done to him what she'd done to Calen, but she hadn't dared open the door. Why?

That question again. Why? It circled around and around his mind.

Why was she doing all this? Why did she have a palace filled with monsters she'd made? What was she searching for in each creation? And perhaps the most important question of all, *who had made her?*

"He defied me." She stopped outside the cage and glared. "He *defied* me! So I took a piece of him." In a swirl of dark cloak, she pushed through a heavy curtain, forgetting to close it behind her.

Dante climbed to his feet, stretching stiff muscles, and approached the bars. Through a gap, where the curtains didn't meet, he saw some of her chamber. Drapes shifted as she moved behind them. A bed, large, cushion-covered chairs. He smelled rain, incense, and leather, and heard the creak of old stone. Small things, but he'd missed those background noises and smells, missed being *alive*.

Reina marched back into sight, carrying a severed arm. Blue fingers had curled in, like a spider's legs. The black claws were instantly recognizable as Havok's. Dante had held that hand. Havok had used it to touch Dante's cheek. Now it was cold and stiff. It didn't seem real.

If she'd taken his arm, what else had she done to him?!

He lifted his gaze and stared through the bars. He didn't speak, but she heard him anyway. One day, he'd be free and butcher her like she had Calen, like she had Havok and countless others. This world and its insanity wasn't Havok's creation, it was hers.

She cackled and glee sparkled in her dark eyes, making them shine. "Good. Yes. There's my Fireheart. Voice that hatred. Speak to me."

He stepped back from the bars, sat with his legs crossed, and waited.

Reina's wings snapped open. She screamed. The cage trembled, the air shook, all her monsters must have heard. And Dante smiled.

She threw the cover back over the cage, sealing him away from the outside world, taking the noises, the smells, the cool air, and signs of life.

Alone again, his thoughts churned. Why didn't she open the cage and torture him? Why had she taken Havok's arm, but not his? It didn't make any sense. Did he have some kind of power over her, something he wasn't aware of. His only power appeared to be silence. Unless there was something else, something he was missing.

They hadn't met before Havok had taken him. He'd lived in ignorance. She knew something he did not.

Blue danced in the air. He lifted his hand and let her settle on his fingertip. Havok had magic. Blue was proof of that. A magic that reached Dante, when nothing else could. Havok was different. Not just in his design, but he had a mark—the gem slung between his horns. A gift, he'd said, from Reina.

He recalled then, the note he'd found in the well. *The mark is a lie.*

He'd been ignorant his whole life, and while he knew more now, there was still much he didn't understand. His life had been a lie, so what else was *unreal?* That was the problem with secrets, they were unknown.

His old life had no real meaning. He'd been driven by menial tasks, paid for so he might afford to eat, to sleep with a roof over his head. Even his love had felt hollow. His life had never felt like his own, as though he'd been sleepwalking through someone else's dream. The ragvine had helped chase that emptiness away, but it always returned. Only Havok had made his heart race, made colors bloom, made each day feel as though it meant something, even when the prick had tugged him along on a leash.

Dante lifted his head. Atop the cage, where all the bars met in the center, a gem glistened. A mark, like Havok's. The source of the cage's magic, stopping time inside the bars. Havok had said Reina gave him his mark—a gift—but Reina didn't *give* anything freely. She took from Lenola, she took lives, she shattered families, and all to make her creations.

Havok believed she'd made him.

But that had the flavor of a lie too.

Blue fluttered her wings. Dante turned his hand over, letting the butterfly skip from finger to finger.

Perhaps it wasn't Dante Reina feared, but Havok?

CHAPTER 27

avok

THE LENOLIAN PEOPLE had proven themselves obedient during the offerings, until Dante's resistance. He'd assumed they'd look upon his arrival with the same quiet awe now. But as he landed atop one of the plaza columns, and the people scattered, screaming, to their homes, he'd obviously assumed wrongly.

The Jailor was a distant figure, a phantom, he supposed, but one bound by the rules of the offering, and not someone who arrived to terrorize them on a whim. Until today.

They'd get over it.

He watched the curious people flit here and there, finding them entertaining, until one got it in their mind to loose an arrow in his direction. He caught the projectile inches from his face and peered down at the assailant. A female, cropped brown hair, fierce expression. Ah yes, the woman was familiar. She had been a member of Dante's resistance group. It took impressive bravery to stand against a legend.

Havok snapped the arrow in two and let the pieces fall from his fingers. The woman's glare hardened. She reached over her shoulder, withdrew a second arrow, and nocked it in her bow, right in front of him, as though she didn't fear death.

He liked her.

Wings spread, he leapt from the pillar and landed as she pulled on the bow's string, about to let her arrow fly. He snatched the weapon from her hand and tossed it aside. "Allow me to be clear, if I was here to kill you, you'd be dead."

"Monster!" She plucked a knife from her belt but hesitated before swinging it. "Wait, you speak?"

By the powers, were they all so dramatic? He sighed. "For the sake of my sanity, listen and do not interrupt. I know Dante—"

"But he's dead?" Her killing glare softened.

Apparently, they were all incapable of following simple orders. He'd assumed it was just Dante who'd had trouble with obedience. Perhaps he'd judged him too harshly in the beginning. "He is not dead, no. Although, not from lack of trying. He's very much alive, and I need him back. I'm here to ask that you help with that?"

"I don't understand. This is a trick!" Waving the dagger, she backed away.

Around them, the Lenolian people still scattered, doors and shutters slammed. Someone's shoe lay on the ground nearby, abandoned in their hurry to flee. The sight of it had some unknown feeling squirming inside Havok. The lies would take some time to unravel. He pushed it aside and focused on the woman.

"Your name is Jean, yes?" When her eyes widened in shock, he lifted a hand. "My name is Havok. Don't fret. He told me of you."

"But... you're the jailor."

"Yes. Or I was. It's complicated. I'm also in need of assistance."

Her brow furrowed. "You take our kin and kill them, and now you're asking for my help?"

"Slightly more complicated than that, but also yes."

"Why shouldn't I kill you where you stand?"

He smiled. He liked this one; she was fierce and stupid. Like Dante. "Well, for one, I'm not so easy to kill that one of your arrows would suffice, and two, if I am dead, then you'll never learn the truth of your existence."

She lowered the dagger. "Dante is alive? You're sure?"

"Yes. I suspect he's trapped. I intend to free him."

"Why? To kill him?"

"You may find this hard to believe, but I made a promise never to kill him. Regardless of what you believe me to be, I am here to protect you and all these people." He swept a hand at the houses with their closed shutters and silent doorways, where all the people had fled.

Her barked laugh echoed around the empty plaza. "By killing us?"

An arrow twanged against the ground near Havok's tail, making it twitch. He whirled in time to see the line of foolish Lenolians, each one with a longbow already nocked. They let loose their arrows.

Havok spun, hooked Jean into his arms, and thrust his wings down, launching off the ground and into the air. Arrows zipped by, some so close he felt their kiss. Jean squirmed and writhed. She screamed too, but he'd clamped his leather-clad hand over her mouth, keeping her irritating noises muffled.

As they climbed higher, the air cooled, the wind picked up, and Havok worked harder, finally reaching the top of the spire.

He set Jean down on her feet and glided away, giving her space to breathe. Her gasping like a fish out of water suggested she was having trouble with it.

Taking up a spot by the workbench, he watched her study her surroundings, taking in the sparse, simple furnishings, the firepit, the workbench—a new one, as the previous one had been lost in the fight with the gregog. She was taller than Dante, but slimmer. Dante had spoken of her with high regard. They'd been... friends.

"Where is this?" she demanded. "Where am I? What are you going to do?"

"Take a moment to calm yourself."

"No, answer me. Is this a game?" She began to approach. "Did you bring me here to kill me like all the others? It's not offering day. Why are you doing all this?" She stopped a few strides away and waved her tiny dagger again. "Come near me and I'll open you up from your groin to your gills."

He'd forgotten how irritating Lenolians could be.

"Where's Dante?" she demanded.

That might have been the only question he'd answer. "With Reina, my... queen, I suppose."

Jean stilled. "There are others like you?"

Havok pulled a chair next to the firepit and reclined there, wings loose, one leg stretched out. "Let us begin with the simple fact that I do not like to answer questions, but for you, I will make an exception." She snorted, unimpressed. She was lucky he needed her, or he might have been forced to introduce the leash. "Are there others like me? I don't think so. But other sacha? Yes, many, and every single one wants a piece of you."

He told her of the sacha, of the harvest, and of how her people were playthings, their lives as insignificant as the flies she swatted. He told her of the jailors, who protected her world from sacha who would steal and take and consume with no thought for future harvests. Gradually, Jean's vehemence and fight drained away. She fell silent and pale. He suspected she would try to deny it, call him a liar, but eventually, hopefully sooner than Dante, she'd come to understand her place in the world.

When the firepit had burned low, Jean sat cross-legged at its edges, forgetting her terror of Havok, or forgoing it for a much wider fear—that of knowing her life would never be the same again.

"Why does she have Dante?" she asked quietly. "What is he to her?"

"He was due to be a gift from me to her. I am being punished. I made a mistake, and Dante is paying for it."

Jean absorbed the information. He liked that about her. She wasn't too quick to reply or rash in her own answers. "Why do you care?" she asked.

And that was the perfect question.

Havok leaned forward and clasped his hands together. The fire didn't hold the answer, but he searched its flames all the same. "You noticed I speak with the same inflections as you? When we were small, Dante and I met." Dante had been a friend, Havok's first and only friend. "He has taught me much. Although, like him, I lived in ignorance."

Jean didn't call him a liar this time. "He never said he'd met the jailor."

"No." A smile pulled on Havok's lips despite his efforts to keep it hidden. "I was his secret. And when he realized the sacha he'd met as a child had become the jailor, I can only assume he made himself forget those days, turned them into dreams." *He was always my dream, my butterfly boy.* Recalling it now hurt his heart in unexpected ways. He rubbed at his chest, trying to smooth the ache.

"He didn't forget. He knew, that's why he rallied us to kill you. He knew who you were."

That was also possible, he supposed. Dante had brought Calen to the pool, and the result had left Havok scarred and disadvantaged. It could be that whatever kindness they'd shared had been an act all along. Dante could have played the fool so well, Havok assumed he was one. But when it came to Dante, he was often wrong. "Perhaps."

"I don't know that I trust you." Jean frowned at the fire, then him. "Or anything you've said. If my life isn't real, then why should this be?" She gestured at the spire's sanctuary around them.

"I'd show you the wider world, but we do not have time, and eventually you will see it regardless."

She nodded and chewed on her thumbnail. "You want me to help you?"

He bowed his head. "For Dante."

"How can I trust you? Or any of this?"

"I do not know. I only ask that you try."

"Will you take me back, if I refuse?"

He'd told Dante he could never go back. Those were the rules he'd lived by. But Reina's rules were no more real than Jean's old life. "I will return you, unharmed, if you wish it."

"And then what? You'll still try and save him without my help?"

"I'll find a way, yes."

"You didn't really answer why you're doing this."

Perhaps because he did not know. He swallowed and tried to organize his thoughts around a reply. "Know that I tell you this and in doing so, I give you a piece of myself— Do not think I reveal my next words lightly. I care for Dante. I always have, probably from the moment we met. I didn't understand it then and truly, I don't now, either. Whatever he feels for me, or doesn't, is irrelevant. I must see him safe and Reina... she... She will hurt him, change him, and I cannot allow that to happen."

A small smile lightened her face. "I believe you, even if I believe little else." She extended her hand. "If I help you save Dante, Havok, will you give me your word you'll not harm another Lenolian?"

He was going to need her. The reaction to his arrival in the city had proven as much. As soon as Reina realized he'd torn out the heart she'd given him, his days as the jailor were over, along with his life. He'd have nowhere to go but down, where the people hated him only marginally more than the sacha did.

He looked at her hand. "My word?"

"Your promise. Whatever monsters—*sachas* declare when they vow something. Shake my hand and mean it from the heart. You do have a heart?"

"I do. Just one."

"Shake and it's binding."

Havok wrapped his clawed fingers around hers. "Agreed."

She freed his hand and her smile grew even brighter. "Is that a... tail?"

He grinned and flicked his tail between them. "It is." Her chuckle warmed his heart, similar to how Dante's used to, when he'd asked to see his wings.

"What is it you think I can do, Havok?"

"You will be the next offering."

Her smile vanished. "Oh."

CHAPTER 28

avok

ANOTHER CYCLE HAD PASSED since Reina had taken Dante, and Lenola's offering day had arrived once more. Jean sat on the spire's cot, wrists bound, head bowed, as they'd agreed.

He'd visited her multiple times in Lenola between their first meeting and now, sailed in on silent wings at night, to reaffirm her commitment to their agreement and to watch and learn of her life, learn of her. Now the moment to enact their plan had come.

Havok scooped the still-beating black heart from its jar, dropped it into a fresh bag of sand, and hung it from his hip. His newly crafted coat fell perfectly, hiding the bag. As long as it was on him, beating its rhythm, Reina wouldn't suspect he'd carved it out. The sand would muffle its sound too, fooling Reina into believing the heart was still lodged behind his ribs.

All he had to do was convince her he was once again her most loyal companion. If she trusted him, she'd tell him where Dante was.

Reina landed with her typical sweeping grace, folded her wings in, and raised an eyebrow at Jean, then Havok.

He knelt, forearm braced on his knee, and bowed his head. He couldn't afford to fail now. Dante was somewhere, probably beaten, likely changed, suffering, in pain. It had already been so long. This plan had to work.

Her leathery wings rustled as she moved.

He unclenched his fist, careful not to give his innermost thoughts away. He'd planned for this. Emotion could not betray him.

When Reina's hand didn't land on his head, as was usual, he looked up to find her inspecting Jean, her grip on the Lenolian's chin, turning Jean's head left and right as though inspecting her. Choosing which parts to keep and which to discard.

"What a shame it isn't more interesting."

Havok narrowed his glare on Reina's back. She *had* to take Jean. He couldn't afford to waste another cycle finding the right Lenolian who would be prepared to not only listen to the truth, but to help him save Dante.

"It is interesting enough," Havok said. "Perhaps not to look at, but in spirit."

Jean sneered. "I led the resistance against you and *that*." She twitched her head, indicating Havok. "We will rise up and kill you and all monsters like you."

Reina let her chin go, stepped back, and for a moment, silence fell. Havok's breath lodged in his throat. Reina was capable of ripping out Jean's throat long before he could attempt to stop her. She hadn't killed an offering for being too poor of quality in many cycles; he'd assumed Jean would meet her standards. Or perhaps Reina was still angry at Havok.

Reina's sudden laugh started small, then grew into hilarity. "Oh yes, you are right, Beric, this one will be most entertaining. How clever of you to find one with such passion. And aren't her eyes beautiful. The body is meager, but its eyes are gems."

At Reina's glance, he mustered a quick smile. "I'm glad you approve."

"Bring it to the palace." Her wings spread, as though she was about to take flight, but she hesitated and glanced over her shoulder. "And Beric, do not disappoint me."

"I exist to please you." He tipped his horns in respect and when he lifted his head, she blasted into the sky.

Jean's fraught gaze locked on to his. "Did we do it? Does she suspect anything?"

He rose and reached out to hold her close for the flight. "We're about to find out."

HE HADN'T BEEN BACK to the palace since Reina had butchered him, implanting the black heart. His wounds had healed from that, but the palace had never felt more foreboding.

Jean stayed tucked close but watched with wide eyes as the world she'd known fell further away, revealing her harsh reality.

Havok's days and nights by the emerald pool were from a different time and place too, a piece of another life, like Jean's, that he'd given up. Wondrous, but as fleeting as a short-lived butterfly.

He wanted that again, he realized. That simple life by the pond, chasing butterflies.

It wasn't possible. As he'd told Dante, the truth cannot be unknown. And there was no going back to that version of himself. The version before...

Reina had... *taken* him.

The memory struck him hard and fast, as vicious and sharp as an arrow to the eye. He landed abruptly, luckily in the palace grounds and near the corridor leading down to the creation rooms.

The net... He remembered. The weight of the latticed rope had dragged him out of the sky moments after fleeing Calen's attack. He'd flown wildly, erratically, afraid, furious, shamed, and the net had caught him, pulled him down to the ground—

Jean touched his shoulder. "Are you all right?"

"Fine. It's nothing." He brushed her off and shook the images from his head. Didn't matter... They had a plan to get Dante back. He had to focus on that.

"Can you do this?" Jean asked, her voice small and riddled with fear. "Because if you can't, take me back *right now*."

"Do not doubt me, Lenolian. You're safe and we will succeed. Hush now. It's not befitting of a pet to chastise its master."

Jean snorted. "Master my ass."

If he hadn't suffered Dante's spirited retorts, he might have punished her insolence. As it stood, he had other, more pressing matters to manage. "Come." He clipped a leash to the wrist shackles he'd furnished her with earlier, and pulled her along behind him, into the palace's sublevel doorways and corridors, toward Reina's creation rooms.

Jean had been warned of the world she'd be walking into, but her jittery stance and darting gaze suggested she teetered on the edge of raw panic.

All things considered, she was coping well.

They approached the huge door, with its array of leering faces. Havok pushed it open and swept inside. Racks of bottled body parts lined the shelves, a sight that was as normal to him as the sky above them. He hadn't thought to warn Jean.

Her scream filled the cavernous space. Havok yanked her into his arms and smothered her mouth with his hand. Her wide eyes darted. Her nostrils flared. "Hush. Do not anger her—"

"Ah, Beric. Over here with it," Reina called. "I cannot abide incessant howling."

Reina's wings came into sight first, their jagged arches rising over the shelves. Jean saw them too, and writhed in his grip, perhaps beginning to understand the magnitude of her new life. It was too late for second thoughts. She was here. This was happening. And there would be no escape.

"It's time you created your own plaything, don't you agree?" Reina swept a hand toward her long, weathered workbench, speckled with nicks and scrapes made by previous candidates. "Sew its mouth shut for now."

"Yes, of course."

Jean moaned behind his hand. She bucked, putting all her strength into struggling, but she was little match for Havok. Perhaps she realized her mistake in trusting him. A Lenolian's trust was their greatest weakness.

He hefted her up, slammed her down onto the workbench, and clipped her ankles into the rigid shackles. "No, no! You promised!" she screamed. "We had a deal! He's not here for you! He's here for—"

Havok grabbed her throat, choking off her next words. "Hush or lose your tongue."

Panicked eyes searched his. Betrayal simmered in those pretty blue orbs, along with her tears.

Reina sidled up to him and handed over her bone-handled cleaver. "Good, now let's begin."

All he had to do was carve Jean up and make it convincing, proving his devotion. Of course, that part of the plan he'd kept from Jean. She'd have fought him far earlier than this had she known her fate. And her ending was inevitable anyway.

He raised the cleaver. Jean's eyes blew wider still. She thrashed her head, mouth opening and closing.

Her life for Dante's. It seemed fair. He didn't care for her, she was only a means to an end, to having Dante back, but...

The cleaver remained raised, his hand beginning to tremble. If he didn't bring it down soon, Reina would see his hesitation.

Then Jean lay still. Tears leaked from her eyes.

Havok withdrew his hand.

"Don't," she whispered.

He had to. For Dante.

"Beric!" Reina screeched. "Tarry a moment more and it'll be you on that bench—"

He whirled and swung the cleaver down, embedding its edge in the side of Reina's neck, above her collarbone. She gasped—reeled. And Havok yanked the cleaver free, splashing an arc of blood far and wide. He hacked again, this time at the rise of her wing, over her shoulder. The cleaver bit into flesh and bone. Reina's scream pierced his thoughts, but it was happening, and he could not stop it now. Havok pulled the cleaver free, struck again, and again, into her side, her arm, her hand—when she raised it to stop him. Blood rained, and then she was kneeling, gasping, blood glistening on her pale skin like spilled rubies.

He raised the cleaver again. *"Where is Dante?"*

Reina's lips moved. Blood bubbled from their corner and dribbled down her chin.

"Tell me or I'll take *your* tongue and cleave *your* eyes. *Tell me!*"

"Tower," she croaked. "Easternmost tower."

He knew its location. Difficult to reach, a jagged spire among many, but not impossible to fly to. He could reach it, he'd have Dante back... Reina's eyes pleaded. He should kill her now, bring down the cleaver, but her eyes begged him not to.

"Beric, no..." she rasped. "I've given you everything. You'd be nothing without me. You owe me."

He pushed away. She caught his wrist and yanked, trying to keep him from leaving. He swung the cleaver, severed her arm above the elbow, and pried the still-gripping hand off, then flung it aside without a care.

"Come!" He unlatched Jean's ankles, freeing her, and dragged her, mute and trembling, behind him.

"I thought you were..." she spluttered. "I thought you meant to..."

She didn't need to know her instincts had been correct. He'd do anything to save Dante, including sacrifice her and a thousand others just like her, if it came to that. But now, all he had to do was find him.

Outside the palace, he hauled her into his arms and launched into the air, climbing higher, faster, with every strained wingbeat. Reina had fallen, but she'd recover. He did not have long. Spires jutted, like spears thrusting into the fog. The flight was dangerous, but at least Reina wouldn't be flying after him. Not for a while. He'd made sure of that when he'd sliced into her wing.

She'd kill him if she caught him, cut him to pieces, pull out his insides and make him watch. He should have killed her, wasn't sure why he hadn't. Loyalty, fear...

But it would be worth it. Dante was close. Finally, he'd free him. And they'd be together. As it should have been.

The eastern tower loomed, the balcony doors vast. He landed, abandoned Jean, and kicked the doors open. Reina's chamber shimmered with black silk and satin, ripples of darkness and shadow. The room was a maze of drapes and curtains.

"Dante?"

He was here. Somewhere. Havok dashed inside, searching behind layers of drapes and in rooms hidden behind silk. He *had* to be here. "Find him..." he barked at Jean. "He's here somewhere." With every curtain he revealed and every turn he made, his fear grew.

Dante could be long dead. Reina could have lied. She'd lied to him, lied about his life, where he came from. *The net plunging down... Stolen. Taken.* Madness chased the truth around his head. "Dante!" If he wasn't here, if he was lost, dead all this time, he might lose his mind.

"Here!" Jean cried out. "He's here!"

Havok tore down a wall of silk and there he was, inside an oval steel cage, captured inside a mark's seal. He hadn't changed at all, as though he'd been captured in time.

Flame-red hair, tossed messily. The same coat Havok had made for him.

Dante looked up. That was all. He didn't stand, or smile. He didn't speak, he just tilted his chin and *looked*. That gaze burned to Havok's core.

"Dante..." He grabbed the bars. There was no lock, no hinges. But there had to be a way to open the door. The mark. It shimmered atop the cage where all the bars curved in and met. That was the key. It had to be. What else would it be there for? "We have to shatter the mark," he told Jean. "Find something heavy."

Jean stared at Dante, her face a muddle of fear and relief.

"Hurry!" Havok snapped. "Something heavy, go!"

Dante still hadn't moved.

His eyes had hardened, but they were the same verdant green.

Havok had feared him dead all this time. Dead or changed. Why would Reina keep him alive? Why had she kept him like this, unchanged in a cage? What riddle was this? It didn't matter, Havok had found him, and soon, he'd be free. "Dante. I..." *I'm here. I'm sorry. For everything.* He hadn't known the truth; he hadn't wanted to. Reina had taken him from his life, a life he barely remembered but was his all the same. She'd taken him and somehow taken his memories. And Dante had tried to tell him.

There would be time for talk, once Dante was free.

Dante still hadn't spoken. Perhaps, he couldn't hear.

Where was Jean?!

"Hurry!"

The more he met Dante's gaze, the more his sense of unease grew. He hadn't even risen to his feet, hadn't reacted at all. Something was wrong.

"Here..." Jean handed him what appeared to be a chair leg.

"Is that the best thing you could find?"

"It's all there is."

Havok weighed the wooden club in his hand. It would have to do. "Step back."

CHAPTER 29

ante

He wasn't sure if Havok being here with Jean was real or a dream he'd summoned in madness. When the cover had been flung from his cage, he'd expected Reina. It was always Reina. But Jean had stared through the bars. It was a trick. Her being here didn't make any sense at all. And then Havok appeared, his eye haunted, the mark still on its chain between his horns. Dark streaks of blood had dried on Havok's chest and face. Splatters stained his arms too. One arm was clad in black leather, all the way from his shoulder to his fingers. A replacement for the one Reina had severed. There were fresher scars too, one jagged one over the right side of Havok's chest.

His lips held that permanent half smile that could mean anything, and a part of Dante's heart soared to see it again. But he quickly shut it down.

Havok wasn't who Dante had believed him to be. He'd lied, manipulated, killed. He'd brought Calen to Reina, had *butchered* him. Havok would use anyone and anything to get what he wanted. Including Jean. That was why she was here. Distraction, bait, another gift for Reina.

Havok climbed the cage bars and crouched at its top, where the bars met around the mark. He swung the chair leg down, struck the mark, but it didn't break. He swung again. The mark resisted. It wouldn't work. It wasn't enough. Dante didn't know what the marks were, or where they came from. He only knew they were a lie, and a mere chair leg wouldn't be enough to shatter one.

Havok growled. His tail looped around one of the bars, locking him in place, and he beat the mark with the club. When that didn't work, he tossed the splintered club away and tore at it with his claws.

Reina could open the cage.

Havok dropped back to the floor, wings spread, and tore at the draping silks, ripping them from their hooks in a frenzy.

He stalked back to the cage. Breathing hard, tail lashing, he held Dante's gaze. "How can I open it?" Havok's face fell. He gripped the bars in both hands. "What has she done to you?" He pressed close to the curved iron. "I couldn't find you. I searched..." He licked his lips. "Jean is here," he said softly. "She knows everything."

Should he be grateful that Havok had brought her into this nightmare too? Ignorance was a blessing he wished he could have back.

Jean approached the cage. "Dante?" She extended her trembling hand between the bars. "It's really you? We thought you dead." Tears shimmered in her eyes.

She was real. They both were. Dante got his feet under him and stood, then clasped her hand in his and yanked her close, pressed his face to the bars, his lips to her ear. "Havok will kill you." The words came out as a whispering rasp. "Whatever you agreed, it's a lie."

Jean turned her head and looked Dante in the eyes. "You think I don't know that? I came for you. We need you back. Tell me how to open the cage."

He freed her hand and stepped back. Havok's smile had turned into a snarl and anger made his single eye burn brighter. "You can't," Dante rasped.

"Reina has poisoned your mind against me," Havok growled.

"No." Dante sighed. "*You* did that."

"I came here to *save* you. Not a day has passed when I haven't thought of finding you, saving you—"

"You don't care. You never did. I'm an object she took and you want back. Nothing more."

The words staggered Havok, but not for long. "You were. That is true. But I didn't know. I thought... I was told that was the way of things. I don't know who or what I am. I don't know what was done to me to make me as I am. I know only that I need you in ways my head does not understand, but in my heart it feels right. I thought you dead, Dante. It broke open some part of me, the old part, the boy I was *before*."

"It's true," Jean urged. "He cares."

Dante shook his head and stepped back from them. "Nothing about him is true."

Havok threw out a snarl and pushed away from the cage. "She has driven him out of his mind!"

Everyone else was at fault, never Havok. Dante

watched as Havok paced, his anger receding. With Havok's mind elsewhere, Dante caught Jean's eye. "Listen, you have to get out of this place. Everything is a lie. I couldn't escape, but you can."

"Not without you," she said. "Ricard is alive. He needs you back. We all do. I told them everything, all of it. How our lives are for the sacha, the city, it's all for them. And the others want to fight."

For the first time in a long time, Dante's ragged heart raced. Ricard was tough. And Jean had told the others everything? But that knowledge was never supposed to filter down to Lenola. It was why Havok had said he could never return. Alone, he couldn't do anything, but with Jean, with the others... There was a chance they could change things. Fight back, even. "How do you know so much?"

"Havok told me."

Havok looked over and scowled. He'd folded his arms across his chest and clamped his wings shut, steeling himself, but his tail lashed, betraying his efforts to appear calm.

"Not for you," Dante whispered. "He did it for him."

"Does it matter why?"

"Yes. Because every gift they give, they take back."

"He said you knew him, you taught him our language. You cared for him once?"

Of course he did; he was using Dante's name to slither his way into Jean's trust. "He's not that boy anymore. And neither am I."

Havok lunged back to the cage. "What did I do that was so terrible for you to hate me now?!"

Ironic, that he should ask while covered in blood. Dante whispered one word. "Calen."

Havok blinked and huffed a dry laugh. "Calen? He deserved his fate."

"Calen?" Jean asked. "He vanished. Do you know where he is?"

Dante nodded at Havok. "Calen is Reina's *pet*. Given to her by him."

"And I'd do it again," Havok spat. "The wretched friend of yours mutilated me." He gestured toward his scarred eye.

"It was more than that. You knew he and I were lovers. You mutilated him out of spite."

Havok's smile soured. "'Lovers'? Is that what you call it? You no more cared for him than you did any part of your old life. You fucked him because he was there. Nothing has felt real for you, not since you took him to the pool and shattered *what we had!* And my life with it. I watched you—I watched the both of you and the lives you had. You drowned yourself in ragvine and he pined for a love you could never give him. It was sad and pathetic."

"You were jealous, so you took him! You butchered him and made him into a monster." Every word hooked into Dante's rage and heaved it to the surface. His voice trembled, weak as it was. "And for that alone, I'll kill you."

"Oh, do stop being dramatic. The last time we met you kissed me and meant it. That was probably the first time your weak heart had beat in almost twenty cycles."

"Stop it! Both of you!" Jean snapped. "What was done is done. Fight all you want once we're out of here!"

"Only Reina can open it," Dante said. "The mark is hers and responds only to her."

All three fell silent. Dante paced the inside of his cage, two steps one way and back again. Jean was here, Ricard was alive, the resistance knew the truth. He had to return to them.

"If you despise me so, why do you still wear my coat?" Havok folded his arms and arched an eyebrow, his smile so smug Dante wanted to punch it off his face. Instead, Dante tore the coat off and flung it to the floor.

"I don't want or need anything of yours!"

"By the powers, both of you! That horrible bitch will be coming here right now. We need a plan to open this cage or she'll kill us."

"But not Dante—" Havok approached the cage, his gaze turning methodical. "She didn't kill you. Why is that? Why has she kept you alive all this time? Deliberately unchanged?"

Dante snarled back. "You sound disappointed."

"I didn't come here to see a corpse. I can see plenty of those in my basement."

How had he ever cared for Havok? *Desired* him, even. "You enjoy being wretched."

Joy sparkled in Havok's eye. "I enjoy what it does to you."

"I despise you."

"Hm," Havok purred. He closed his fingers around the bars again. "I'll take your hate, if that's all you're willing to give." Havok studied him, raking his intense gaze from head to toe. "But the question remains, why didn't she touch you?"

Dante studied him in return. His body bore the scars of his changes through the cycles. Inside, he'd changed too, and it all went back to that day by the pond when Calen had attacked him. Their paths had diverged, like stars colliding, ricocheting into different directions. That moment had violently split them apart. But was there more to it? Dante hated him, but he couldn't deny Havok's closeness rattled his heart and made his breath race.

"What is it about you..." Havok murmured, eye narrowing. His mark shimmered. "Why can I not let you go?"

The vast chamber door creaked open.

Havok turned, stepping forward in front of Jean, and through his feathers, Dante saw Reina. Her beauty had been shredded. Her stitched skin ran with blood. She limped into the chamber, dragging one broken wing behind her. Blood dripped from the cleaver in her hand.

The blood painting Havok? It was hers. He should have killed her.

Her furious glare fixed on Havok. "How dare you defy me!"

Havok glanced over his shoulder, temporarily meeting Dante's gaze. He wasn't smirking now. His smile vanished. His expression cooled, turning hard. "Remember me," he whispered, one corner of his mouth ticking up.

Those two words sounded like goodbye and Dante's heart plunged. "Wait—"

Havok strode toward her. "Open the cage."

"Your pet is mine forever." Reina's wet chuckle spluttered. "He will never leave that cage."

"Open the cage or I'll finish what I began and carve every piece of you apart. You know I can." His feathers began to fan, each frond spreading wide. "Did you fear this day, Reina? Do you fear your end?"

Her eyes narrowed. Despite Havok's words, she didn't appear afraid. "Kill me and your Fireheart will remain in that cage for all eternity, never changing, trapped outside of time."

"He is nothing to you. Open the cage, set him free, and I'll take his place within its bars."

"Havok!" Dante yelled, but the name fell from his lips as no more than a whisper. He gripped the cold bars in his hands. "Don't!"

"It speaks *for you*!? Of course it does." She cackled. "The Ice Prince and his Lenolian Pet."

"Enough, Reina," Havok growled. "End this now!"

Prince? An old story flashed in Dante's memory, of the book he'd read Havok by the pond. The King's Lost Marks. The mythical king's power over ice and fire had fled when his marks had been taken, and the ice had closed in, swallowing him forever. Ice... Havok had returned to his chamber that night, sparkling with ice. Dante had assumed he'd been hurt, but what if the ice *was his*? What if there was more to the myth, more to the story, and more to Havok than the forgotten sacha boy Dante had found beside the pond?

Two more monsters stalked through the doorway. Great winged beasts, with long snouts and four legs. They flanked the queen. Both her creations, and her weapons.

Jean eased a small dagger from up her sleeve. It would do little to save her, but it might slow them down. She caught Dante's gaze and smiled. "If I'm going to die, let it be fighting monsters."

"Jean, no. It can't end here."

The tips of Havok's wings sparkled like they always had, but now Dante knew why. Ice. He'd once told Dante he'd been forgotten, but wasn't lost the same thing? What if the king hadn't lost his marks, what if he'd lost *his sons*? Reina had said *prince*. Was Havok one of them? "Havok..." He reached through the bars, but Havok was too far away, and Dante's fractured voice soon became lost in the fray.

The pieces of that old tale and fragments of other myths fell into place inside his mind. The legend of the jailor told of how it sat atop a throne of bone. He wore a crown of spiked wire, those stories said. A crown. The king from the story had lost his marks, his sons, two princes. Havok didn't know who or what he was. The pieces of the past shuffled inside Dante's head.

The mark was a lie.

"Jean," Dante growled, his voice failing, "Take Havok's mark."

"What?"

"Havok's gem. You see it, on the chain between his horns? He has to remove it."

"I don't think now is the time."

"Now is the *perfect* time. Listen to me. Havok believes he was forgotten. His whole life he's been searching for the truth but it's inside of him. The mark hides the truth."

Yes, it made sense, all of it. The marks were a lie. They hid the truth behind illusions, behind lies. That was their power. Reina had spun the lie to control Havok.

Even the mark holding Dante inside the cage crafted a lie.

He looked up, saw the gem sparkling atop his cage, and for the first time, saw it for what it truly was. Nothing but a pebble found on a beach, just another weather-worn stone made to glitter and shine by illusion. He saw its truth now.

The gem's sparkle faded and snuffed out, revealing just a dull river stone in its place. The cage clunked, the door dislodged and fell open. Its resounding clang turned everyone toward him.

"No!" Reina gasped. "How—" Her shock turned to fury. Behind her, a new monster swaggered into the chamber, its body a patchwork of ill-fitting limbs, its arms tipped with savage talons, its mouth sewn shut. One unblinking eye fixed on Dante.

Calen.

Horror burned a sickness at the back of Dante's throat.

"Kill them," Reina ordered. "Kill them all!"

CHAPTER 30

avok

Dante must live. There was a simplicity to that thought. It spurred Havok on in what could be his final moments.

The sacha beside Reina surged, Havok thrust his wings down, pushing against air, and leaped for Reina. She'd expected it and slashed the bloody cleaver in a wide arc towards his arm, clanging against a metal plate he'd sewn inside, protecting it. Reina stumbled at the sound, while Havok grinned. She'd taken his arm, so he'd made himself a better one.

Her moment's hesitation gave Havok an opening. He thrust his horns down, clashing with hers. She reeled and screamed her rage. Her claws raked his face. He tackled her already broken body backward, driving her off her feet, and slammed her into the hard, jagged black rock of her chamber wall. One hand fixed around her neck, the other he locked against her chest. He'd kill her, rip out her heart and crush it with her watching.

"Havok!"

Jean's cry swung him around. He glanced over, to where Calen had Dante pinned against the outside of the cage bars. Reina's pair of sacha had Jean cornered. Jean waved her tiny dagger. It shouldn't matter that she was already lost. She was a tool. She'd die and the world wouldn't change. But when he tried to dismiss her cry for help, his heart stuttered.

He couldn't abandon her.

Life would have been so much easier if he did not care.

Reina's backhand staggered him and lit his face on fire. She stalked forward. "I am your queen, I created you. You will kneel to me!"

Her threats were just air. Havok spun, sprang onto Calen's back, and flapped his wings, dragging the mutilated Lenolian off Dante. Calen released Dante, but he bucked and writhed in Havok's grip, trying to wriggle free and reclaim his prize.

Dante coughed, choking on air. When he looked up, his eyes streamed. "Don't hurt him! Havok, please— He's suffered enough."

There was nothing left of Dante's lover to save. And even if it was Havok's fault, the truth could not undo what had been done. Better to have the new sacha's suffering over with.

He locked stares with Dante, saw the fear there, perhaps even love too. And Havok hated that. Dante was his. Calen did not deserve him. Never had. Calen had *taken* him. And yes, Havok was jealous. Dante had said he'd come back, he'd promised. Havok had waited by that pond for so long. And when he had returned, he'd brought another, brought a replacement, a Lenolian like him. Someone not Havok. The betrayal stung to this day. Havok couldn't deny his jealousy, or his spite.

He snapped Calen's head sideways, jerking the spine. Quick. Clean. A mercy, really. Calen slumped, hit the floor, and huffed his last breath.

"You selfish beast!" Dante wailed, his face contorting with rage.

Jean's scream tore Dante toward her. One of the sachas held her aloft. Its huge jaws opened, about to snap her middle in two. She stabbed uselessly at its arm.

Dante would never reach her in time.

Dante raised his hand and blew, launching a blue butterfly into the air.

"Khandra!" Havok growled the butterfly's name, but she did not listen. He'd have been more surprised if she had. Khandra had remained with Dante all this time?

The tiny blue insect flitted its way to the sacha holding Jean and danced in front of its eyes. With a growl, the sacha swiped at the butterfly. Khandra danced higher still and the sacha lowered Jean, needing both hands to grab for the darting butterfly.

Dante turned on his heel. "Your mark!" He flicked his fingers toward his own forehead. "Havok, remove your mark!"

His mark?

"Trust me!" Dante rasped. "It's the only way."

He *did* trust him. Reluctantly. Impossibly. There was more than just hate between them. So much more that it hurt to think on, but trust was one of those things. At least, from Havok. Any trust Dante had in Havok had long ago been scorched to dust.

He reached for his mark, and froze—

Fire engulfed his chest and soared through his veins. Agony choked him. The chamber spun, screaming erupted, and then Reina's wet, bubbling laughter simmered through the chaos.

He gasped, fighting for air that wouldn't come. Reina's laugh rolled on and on. Havok's vision fogged. His chest... The fire boiled from there. He clutched at it, dug his nails in. The heart... But he'd removed it! Staggering, he dropped his hand to his hip, searching for the wretched thing. But the bag of sand was gone.

Reina....

He blinked, clearing his sight as Reina lifted her hand, and clutched inside, she held the bag and its beating heart.

"Did you think you could carve me out of your life so easily?" Her bloody smile curved over sharp teeth. She strode forward, her strides jagged. She snapped her shoulder back, flicking her broken wing into place, and flared both wings wide, oblivious to any pain. "For as long as this heart beats, it binds me to you. And make no mistake, Beric, you are mine."

He should have thrown the heart into the fire when he'd had the chance. Now that damned thing would be his undoing.

Weakness washed through him.

Reina's claws dug into the pouch, piercing its sides, freeing sand, and sinking into the beating heart inside. As each of her claws pierced the heart, fierce agony plunged into his chest. He fell, choking on pain. Not even his wings could carry him away; they hung limp and useless on either side of him.

"Your insolence persists, but that is to be expected. The king was the same, before he was slain, fleeing his destiny. Such a tragedy, he never knew your fate. But your brother knew." Her smile grew. And a cruel knowing shone in her dark eyes.

Kings and brothers? Her words didn't make any sense.

His true heart thumped inside his chest, desperate to keep him alive, but the black heart thumped too, somehow still connected, driving him to his knees, where she'd always had him.

Reina loomed. She pressed a claw beneath his chin and tilted his head up. "You are my secret, Prince of Ice. It was a joy to have you so easily submit, but now the time has come to silence you forever." Her claws pinched into his cheek, piercing his skin, while her right hand held the pulsing bag aloft.

Khandra flitted in front of Havok's vision, her fragile wings glittering with... ice.

Reina snarled at the dancing butterfly, taking her eye off the room.

A sacha rammed them both, reaching for the playful butterfly. Reina screeched, let go, and Havok dropped. He clawed at his chest, even knowing the heart wasn't there to rip out. His mind had fogged and his body burned. There had to be another way.

His mark.

Dante had said to trust him. And he did.

He curled his fingers around the chain, faced Reina as she shoved the sacha away. She saw his hand on the chain, saw the intent on his face, and her eyes widened.

"No!"

He tore the chain and its mark free.

CHAPTER 31

*D*ante

A FLASH of white light flooded the chamber, bleaching color from Dante's eyes. The air cracked where it touched Dante's lips, then plunged down his throat, into his lungs, so cold it tried to choke him. He stumbled, reaching blindly for anything to hold him up.

An enraged roar erupted, shattering the crushing ice, allowing Dante to at least draw breath again, even as ice crawled over his skin, crushing around him. The ice was *hungry*. It consumed everything it touched. He knew that, in the same way he knew that if he didn't somehow escape it, he'd be dead in moments.

Jagged crystals of blue-white ice blasted over Jean, freezing her as she fled. Ice encased Reina, capturing the moment she reached for Havok, to stop him from removing the mark.

A frozen mist descended, crushing him. But as he

searched for a way out, he caught sight of his coat on the cage floor, untouched by the fans of advancing ice. He lurched toward it. Ice grabbed his boots, climbed his legs, snapped up his thighs—

Then it stopped, and like a receding tide, it withdrew from around Dante and lofted from the air, recoiling back into itself, back into Havok's splintered, crystalized form.

Dante's skin burned from the cold. He grabbed the coat and threw it on, He shivered so hard he could barely see, but he saw enough to watch how the ice crawled back to Havok's frozen body and melted down his spread wings. With a sudden gasp, Havok shattered free, exploding outward. He stumbled, tripped, almost fell, and then spun, his face so full of horror that Dante dismissed any thought that Havok might have had control of the ice.

Reina remained trapped in ice, and so did the sacha she'd brought with her.

"Jean..." Dante croaked, shivering and stumbling toward her statuesque form.

The crystal ice had captured the horror on her face. "Save h-her, Havok," Dante whispered.

Havok turned, wings sweeping, feathers raining snow as his ice thawed. He was terrifying and beautiful. Somehow both.

Havok's eye widened. Blue. His eye was blue, not its usual fiery red. So blue it dazzled, blue like his butterfly.

Dante staggered to his feet. "H-help her!"

Havok dashed to Jean's side, raised both hands, and hesitated.

"Quickly!"

"I don't—" He cut himself off and laid both hands on her. At first, nothing changed, but as they watched, the ice shifted, melting away, vanishing almost as quickly as it had come. Free, Jean fell to her knees, gasping, shivering.

Dante pulled off his coat and threw it around her.

"A way out?" he asked Havok.

Havok stared at his hands. Ice made his claws sparkle. It shimmered across his skin. Air misted around him, blurring his edges. He still had the mark hanging from the chain wrapped around his fingers. He lifted it with a panicked look and looped it back around a horn. A shudder ran through him, and when he next opened his eye, it was red again, the same as the mark, and the ice misted away as though it had never existed.

The lie was back in place.

Reina however, remained frozen, as did her creations. But the ice dripped, melting. Once it weakened enough, she'd come for them, and she'd bring her army of monsters.

"Havok, get us out of here."

He blinked, coming around from whatever spiral his thoughts had been locked in.

"An exit, a way out..." Dante prompted.

"Yes. Come—"

Blue danced between them. The butterfly landed on the back of Dante's hand, spread its wings, and was absorbed by his skin, tingling as it settled and turned into a fresh tattoo.

"Traitor," Havok grumbled at the creature. "Follow."

A seemingly never-ending spiral staircase funneled them into colder, thinner air. Dante stayed close to Havok's flicking tail and kept Jean tucked under his arm. Her trembling began to ease, but the cold was the least of their concerns. The palace was rife with monsters. They were far from safe.

Havok grabbed a flaming torch from its sconce and pushed down a narrow tunnel hewn from black rock. "Come now. Do not stop unless I order it..." He strode on, wings tucked close, as he guided them deep into a damp tunnel, its rocky edges rough and unfinished.

THEY WALKED FOR SO LONG, Dante's legs ached and feet burned. Occasionally, a bark or growl sounded far behind them, pushing them on. Jean stumbled, and then collapsed. Dante scooped her into his arms and carried her. Still, Havok plowed on, until the torch burned low. If it snuffed out altogether, they'd be walking in darkness.

"What happened back there?" Dante whispered. "With the ice?"

"Hush."

Dante didn't have the energy to argue; besides, he wasn't sure if Havok knew any more than he did. But one thing was clear. Havok had been lied to for most of his life. And Dante knew exactly how that felt.

THE TUNNEL SPAT them out deep into strange, giant, leafless and barren undergrowth. Perhaps a jungle once, but it had died long ago. Havok snuffed his torch out on the ground and led them deeper into the barren jungle's depths.

After he'd carried Jean for what must have been miles, Dante's legs gave out and he dropped, tumbling to the ground with her in his arms. "By the powers, stop, Havok."

"She will come," Havok snapped, his red eye aglow in

the near perfect darkness. "The others *will come*." He stalked to the rooted end of a fallen tree, tail knotting and unknotting. His wings pulsed with his every breath. "They will comb these lands and they will not stop until we are found."

He was afraid. Any fool could see it. But Dante was done.

"I can't..." He slumped against the fallen tree, propping Jean against his side. "Leave us, if you want. I can't take another step." His every word was a raspy growl.

"I didn't save you from Reina to lose you now."

Save him? Dante distinctly recalled saving himself from that cage. "You're a real piece of work, Havok, you know that?" He dropped his head back, folded Jean closer, and closed his eyes, just to rest them a while and block out Havok.

"I am. This is true."

Dante smiled with his eyes still closed, enjoying Havok's misinterpretation of his words. He couldn't think about the cage, about Reina thawing out and coming for them, about Havok's revelations or how he'd snapped Calen's neck out of spite. Jean was safe, he was safe, and that had to be enough for a few moments.

When he opened his eyes, a small fire burned in the clearing, its light muffled by the thick brush they'd sheltered in. He pushed upright, careful not to disturb Jean as she slept in the folds of Dante's coat.

"Havok?"

He wasn't by the fire, or nearby. Perhaps he *had* abandoned them.

Dante got to his feet, stretched stiff muscles, and stoked the fire, bringing it back to life. He collected a few more sticks and built up the flames but kept an eye on the nearby bushes. He'd seen the things that lived out here and unlike wolves, a fire wouldn't keep them away.

A bush rustled. Dante grabbed a flaming stick and swung it through the dark, armed and by the powers, damned ready to defend them.

Havok stepped from the knotted weeds, his expression irritated, carrying a small, skinned carcass. He swiftly made a triangular spit out of sticks and hung the carcass above the flames to roast it, all the while side-eyeing Dante and his stick.

"I didn't know it was you," Dante said, tossing the stick away.

Havok settled beside the fire, one leg drawn up, and eyed their roasting dinner. "A burning stick will not stop a sacha."

"It was all I could lay my hands on." His voice still sounded gruff, like rocks rolling down a stream. Maybe it wouldn't ever right itself. He rubbed at this throat, prompting Havok to hand over a small leather pouch of water.

Dante took it with a nod and drank. It had been a long time since he'd needed to drink, to eat.

Havok's gaze lingered, but when Dante caught him looking, it skipped to Jean, still asleep, then back to the fire. He seemed troubled, even for him. They had much to be troubled by. Not least the fact Havok had a terrifying power hidden inside of him. A power he hadn't known existed.

But Reina had.

"She took you from your life," Dante said softly. He was sure of it. Sometime between the pond and when Havok had become the jailor, Reina had taken him.

"She *was* my life."

Dante bowed his head. He regretted his part in Havok's broken past. But that didn't absolve Havok for what he'd done to Calen. Or how Reina had carved pieces off him. By the powers, rage and sickness surged whenever he remembered. But his heart was too battered for the hate to linger.

"Are you well?" Havok asked.

"What?"

"She didn't—" He blinked. "—harm you in any way?"

"No."

"Your voice? It's changed."

"Because I wouldn't give it to her."

"You didn't speak?"

He shook his head.

"And you still have Khandra, I see."

"Khandra?"

Havok touched the back of his own hand. "The butterfly. She refuses to return to me. So I suppose she's yours now. Butterflies are fickle creatures."

Dante raised his hand and admired the tattoo. "I named her Blue. She er... She was good company. Khandra? I like it, and her."

Havok's smile softened a little more every time he gave it to Dante. "It means sky-dancer. And you're right, she is good company."

That was more befitting a name than Blue. "Do you mind that she's with me?"

"They always did like you more." He sighed. "Telling a butterfly what to do or where to go is a fruitless task. They are unruly at best, chaotic at worst. Rather like you." His smile brightened some, then faded again. "Sleep, if you wish. I'll wake you to eat and then we must move on. The smoke and smell of cooked meat will bring the otherlings out of hiding."

Dante nodded and shuffled back against the tree. Jean mumbled when he accidentally nudged her, but she didn't wake. Havok had already taken one friend. Dante would be damned if Havok took another in Jean. He folded his arms and sighed the weight from his shoulders.

"Dante?" Havok asked, so soft it was almost a whisper.

"Hm."

"I had no wish to hurt you."

"Yet you did." He opened his eyes and found Havok focused on tending the roasting carcass. "And you're not sorry. If you were, you'd say the words."

Havok winced but didn't deny it. And he didn't apologize either. Dante needed Havok to get away from the monsters, but after that, it was over. As it should have been over between them long ago, their shared past lost to memories and dreams.

He dozed, half dreaming, half awake to watch for threats.

Havok's hand slammed over his mouth and his lips brushed his ear. "Hush, we're not alone."

The nearby brush shivered around the weight of some large beast, but in Dante's half-dreaming state, it wasn't the approaching beast that occupied his thoughts. It was how Havok's weight pressed against his side, how his warmth soaked into Dante's skin, how his thick tail pulsed with warmth.

Jean still slept against Dante's other side. He needed to think about her, about the beast snuffling through the bushes, and not how Havok's proximity burned though him. He could have guarded against it if he hadn't been half asleep, but he'd spent so long lost to silence, cut off from the world, and now he felt everything so sharply that, by the powers, having Havok close felt *good*.

The beast loomed—a creature made of six armored limbs. It found the tiny roasted meal, chomped it down with one bite, and stomped off, kicking over their campfire in its wake. The embers still glowed among the dirt, Jean still slept, and Havok remained pressed against Dante's side. He'd move soon, wouldn't he? Because his breath on Dante's cheek had all rational thought fleeing and his body coming alive.

Havok's tail loosened around Dante's leg but didn't let go. What would it feel like to have it roam higher, seeking out the hardening parts of him?

Havok's breathing slowed, his weight softened, and as Dante turned his head, he saw Havok's eye was closed, his lashes fluttering. Was he *asleep*? Dante tried to inch out from under him, but the tail tightened, sensing his retreat.

He was trapped with Jean on one side, Havok on the other, and his cock a raging rod of want for a monster he couldn't have and most definitely did not desire.

He hated the winged selfish prick. But with Havok tucked close, his every breath tickling Dante's neck, his hot tail a pulsing muscle around Dante's leg, Dante quit fighting the obvious and allowed himself to wonder what it might be like to have Havok in the way his body demanded. To have him under him, or better yet, to have Havok poised over him, buried inside, his tail looped around Dante's erection as Havok thrust inside him.

To have him so close, skin against skin, sharing breaths, touching him without fear...

Dante bit his lip to keep the moan at bay, but his cock throbbed, aching and painful.

He couldn't escape the need, not after so long being

caged and isolated. All he had to do was turn his head a little more, meet Havok's lips with his own, tease his tongue in, and he knew Havok would wake, and he'd respond. He'd wanted Dante on the palace roof. He'd wanted Dante when they were boys on the pebble bank. Dante hated him, but he wanted to take him, kiss him breathless, and fuck him stupid.

Desire didn't lie. *Feelings* didn't lie.

By the powers, if he could drag his hand from under Havok, he'd take himself in hand and pump his cock to relief.

He gritted his teeth, closed his eyes, and counted down from one hundred.

He could never have Havok, not least because he had to kill him.

CHAPTER 32

avok

Dante dozed, sandwiched between Jean and Havok.

Havok hadn't meant to fall asleep on him but being close to Dante had always softened his heart, made him feel at ease, as though he'd come home. He'd never reveal as much. Especially as now they were enemies again.

He'd hoped, like a fool, that Dante would have been grateful to be saved, that he'd have wanted to see Havok. But he'd been wrong.

The hate had grown stronger, not waned. Perhaps because Havok had almost killed them all in Reina's chamber, after removing the mark. The world had split open and ice had poured out. Where it had come from, what it was, he couldn't answer. But the mark had held it back.

How had Dante known the mark's secret? Had Reina told him?

He watched the man sleep and traced the fine line of

his bristled jaw with a finger, careful not to wake him. His red hair had fallen over his face in scruffy locks. Havok ached to place a kiss on his neck, to feel *his* kiss again. He'd always been... fascinating. And forbidden. And Dante was further away now than at any time before.

"Havok?" Jean croaked.

Havok blinked as she rose, sleepy-eyed. Hopefully, she hadn't seen him gazing at Dante.

By the powers, his tail was coiled around Dante's leg.

Dante stirred too, and Havok uncoiled his tail, flipping it away. If Dante knew how he sought to touch him, he'd accuse him of having some wicked ulterior motive. Havok climbed to his feet, ruffled dust and leaf litter off his wings, and moved away from the pair. "Our dinner was devoured. We've lost too much time. We must keep moving."

"To where?" Jean asked. She rubbed her face and frowned at their surroundings. "Where can we possibly go?"

"Lenola."

It was safer to travel on foot. Havok couldn't carry both for any great distance, and on the ground, they were hidden from airborne threats. For once, Dante didn't argue.

They trekked through valleys—great fissures in the earth—and up hillsides, but heavy undergrowth and their slow progress reduced what should have been a day's flight to three days. Havok caught and prepared food, while keeping an eye on the skies and his charges.

Dante said little, and when he did speak, it was to Jean.

A few times, as they'd sat at the fireside, quietly chewing on a piece of roasted critter, Havok had almost asked Dante how he knew about the mark, and what else he'd learned in the past cycle, but then Dante would catch Havok's gaze and frown. And the moment passed.

If there had been any bridges left between them, it appeared Havok had burned them all.

He wished he *didn't* care. Everything would have been easier. He'd still have the problem of who he really was, but not the burden of two Lenolians to carry.

He cared enough to take them home, to see them safe, and to leave Dante forever—to let him have his life back. But that would not be the end of it. Reina would come for them out of spite. And she wouldn't be alone. Returning Jean and Dante to Lenola would leave them and the city vulnerable, but what other choice was there? Lenolians did not have claws or wings. They were little more than lumbering prey and wouldn't survive the otherlings' lands for long.

They were both better off among their own kind. But as for Havok's place in it all? He wasn't sure he had one. He likely never had.

Lenola's vast ring of mountains resembled a crater from above, as though a huge powerful entity had scooped out a chunk of earth. He'd always thought it pretty—how the city lights sparkled around the base of the spire, like water at the bottom of a bowl.

The rocky outcrop Havok stood on had been a favorite perch of his over the cycles. It offered the most amazing views. The central spire rose needle-like from Lenola, and the city shone.

He'd carry Jean and Dante down there, back to their people, a people Havok had protected and terrorized.

All that was about to change.

If Reina suspected the Lenolians knew the truth, she'd wipe them out as a *mercy*. He'd been taught how they must live in ignorance, to have any life at all. But he couldn't trust Reina's truths.

Dante emerged from the bushes and approached the outcrop's edge. He'd have been fearful to step onto the outcrop before, but he'd changed during his time in the cage. He didn't even glance at the drop now, just met Havok's gaze with a nod. "Shall we go?"

Havok checked the top of the spire again. There didn't appear to be any activity. However, a new jailor could have flown ahead. They were not yet safe. He turned and brushed past Dante, heading back to where Jean would be waiting.

"What changed?" Dante asked.

Havok turned to find Dante standing in the spot he'd just left, gazing at the spire. His coat flapped in the breeze. He made a startling silhouette.

"What do you mean?"

"You said you'd never bring me back." His voice remained gruff. It might never return to its smooth resonance. "So what changed?"

"The rules I lived by were lies," Havok admitted. "I know less now than I did then, just that Reina is wrong. Besides, Jean has already told them about you, and their place in things. There is no unknowing the truth. I cannot undo what is done."

Dante didn't reply. He stood near the outcrop's edge

gazing into the basin from above, at his home, a prison he didn't know he'd been trapped in. The breeze rippled his hair too. "Are we putting them in danger, going back?" he finally asked.

"They were always in danger, they just did not know it."

Dante turned his back on the view and approached Havok. He stopped close and seemed as though he'd been about to speak, but whatever the thought was, he kept it to himself and nodded. "Let's go."

Perhaps it was too soon, but Havok feared some of the fire had left Dante's heart. A quenched blade must lose its heat to become stronger. Reina *had* changed Dante. Havok could only hope Dante survived those changes. Most did not.

IN THE MOON'S pale glow, he carried them down to Lenola's outskirts, where the city edges touched rivers and fields and farms.

"We have to get you out of sight," Dante said to Havok. "I know somewhere." He strode through the long grass into the dark with Jean behind him and Havok trailing them both. The air smelled fresh and... green, if such a thing were possible.

A stream burbled. Havok stroked his hand over the grass heads, collecting dew. It felt so soft, so true, that he had to force his feet forward so as not to fall behind. A bank of thorns loomed, and with it, a memory flashed. The thorn wall. He'd known this place when he was young. The thorn wall had been the edge of his world. He'd known never to go beyond it.

"What is this place?" he asked, closing the distance between himself and Dante again.

"You'll see." Dante trampled through the overgrown brush, opening a path ahead, to a river's edge, a meadow of sleeping flowers, and an old farmhouse, its window frames sagging, as though the building slept. All of it reminded Havok of a dream he used to have night after night. It had faded through the cycles, and then he'd forgotten it altogether. Until now.

They pushed on, through the wild meadow toward an old, overgrown farmhouse. Ivy clawed at its windows and grass had consumed a cobbled pathway.

This was... Dante's home.

Which meant they'd met, right over—

"Let's get inside." Dante tore down a curtain of ivy and forced the half-rotten door open.

"You know this house?" Jean asked, her boots crunching over the dried leaves scattered on a moth-eaten rug.

"My home. A long time ago." Dante gave a little laugh. "As you can tell."

Havok ducked his head and wings, squeezing through the door. He'd never followed Dante back down the winding path to his life. He'd known it was wrong to leave the pond, the thorn wall, and the hawthorn bush.

The pond was close. If Havok listened hard, he could almost hear the chirp of crickets and croaking frogs.

Jean asked some more questions about the house and farm, but Havok only half listened to his replies. This was Dante's life, his home. A framed painting above the old fireplace drew him closer. The art depicted Dante's parents, and Dante as a boy, standing in front of them. It must have been painted not long after they'd met, as

Dante's face was well-rounded from youth. The paint had faded, and in some places beetles had eaten the canvas, but there was no mistaking Dante's keen green eyes.

"They were good people," Dante said, appearing beside Havok.

"No doubt." In truth, Havok hadn't spared a moment to admire them. Their boy was far more fascinating, but as he lifted his gaze and laid eyes upon Dante's parents, familiarity tugged at the corners of his mind. Dante had his mother's red hair and his father's startling eyes. But this wasn't the first time he'd seen those people. "I know them."

Dante regarded the painting, as though he'd find the answers in it. "You do?"

"Yet I don't recall ever meeting them." He even knew the sound of Dante's father's laugh, its deep, honeyed chuckle, and his mother's smile, soft and friendly. He *must* have met them before...

Havok glanced around the inside of the house. Paper peeled from the walls, the ceiling sagged, old oil lamps had been eaten by undergrowth. Nothing here sparked any memories, but people made a home, not possessions.

He drifted toward the window, and while it was overgrown now, the way the house was oriented meant it faced down the hill, toward the emerald pond. So close, so tantalizing, with its singing butterflies and waters shimmering in the sun.

"I did not know them, I think," Havok said quietly. "But I saw them in this window, and they saw me." It didn't make any sense, but it felt like more than watching, it felt like knowing, as though he owed these people a debt, but couldn't recall why.

"That can't be right." Dante snorted, stopping at his

side again to peer through the filthy window. "They'd have told me."

"Would they? You were young."

Dante huffed and strode away, back through the room, righting old, toppled chairs that were far too gone rotten to sit on. "Regardless, they're gone. And this is the only place you can stay out of sight."

"I'm not afraid of your people."

"You should be," Dante said, like a throwaway line. He crossed the floor to Jean. "Take me to Ricard and the others."

"Now?" Jean blinked heavy-lidded eyes. "It's late."

"My arrival will draw too much attention in daylight, and Reina could launch an attack any time. We must be ready."

"All right... Is he coming?" She glanced at Havok.

"Havok is staying here," Dante said, as though he believed his words were fact.

"Havok will do as he pleases," Havok countered, folding his arms, but Dante either didn't hear or didn't want to. He left through the wonky door, and Jean nodded before following Dante outside.

Alone, Havok frowned at the damp, dark room. He didn't even have Khandra for company; Dante had taken her too. He'd kept them safe, brought them home, and they abandoned him as thanks?

Havok hushed his petty thoughts and sighed at the miserable room. Most of it should have been ripped out and burned cycles ago. He wasn't staying within its walls a moment longer. He needed to scout the area for threats and check again on the spire. While dark, he could move unseen and silently for a lot farther than Dante knew. He'd been doing exactly that for a lifetime.

CHAPTER 33

ante

DANTE'S BOOTS struck Lenola's familiar cobbled streets. Gas lamps flickered, lighting each corner and store doorway. Almost everyone was asleep, their window shutters closed. The night was peaceful, disturbed only by his and Jean's passing.

"I didn't think I'd ever see this place again," he whispered.

Jean smiled and squeezed his shoulder. "It must feel good, being back."

"It does." But it didn't feel like before. Before he'd had jobs, commitments, Calen, and the resistance. Back then, he'd been foolish enough to believe that if they killed the jailor, the monster's reign would have ended. He hadn't considered there'd be many more ready to take Havok's place. He'd been naive, kept that way by the monsters reigning over them.

"Do you think we can stop her?" Jean asked.

The streets narrowed into the old residential areas, where Ricard and many of the others in the resistance lived. Dante had stayed here too after abandoning the farm, in his loft apartment above the bakery. Luxury, compared to his recent lodgings.

"Yes," Dante said. "Reina has a weakness."

"Which is?"

"Havok."

"How so?"

"She's been nurturing him, keeping him close, controlling him. Some things she said in her tower, his power, and the fact she kept me alive. She wants him, maybe even needs him—I don't know—but he's our leverage."

"Does *he* know that?"

"With Havok, there's no telling what he knows."

"He didn't know about the mark."

"No. But Reina did."

Ricard's lodgings were up ahead. He rented a room, one of several tenants, in the old tannery. Dante's heart raced a little faster. He needed to see him, to know not all was lost, to know who and what he fought for, to live his true purpose in all of this—to protect, to fight for Lenola and its people.

"Do you have a plan, Dante? Because what I saw in their world... As strong as we are together, we can't beat them with arrows."

"We have Havok." He knocked at the old tannery's door and smiled at Jean's concerned expression under the glow of the gas lamps. "He's the bait."

The door opened and a bleary-eyed woman scowled. "Maud," Jean said. "It's me... and Dante."

"Dante! We thought you dead!" She ushered them

inside. "Let me get a look at you, Dante." Maud owned and ran many of the rented properties, including Dante's. She'd been a stalwart mother figure to many of the resistance, always providing sanctuary and tea. Dante hugged her, kissed her on the forehead, and told her he'd stop by for tea at a more favorable hour.

Ricard answered his door, as sleep-addled and confused as the landlady, until he saw Dante. The kid—not so small now, almost as tall and full of muscle as Dante had been before his recent ordeals—threw himself into Dante's arms. "You're alive!"

"So are you." Dante's heart soared. He hugged him back. Ricard had lost both his parents to sickness. Dante had tried to be there for him, knowing all too well what it felt like to be alone. In truth, he'd probably needed Ricard more than Ricard had needed him.

Jean stepped in. "Can we come in? We may not have much time."

"Why? What's going on? Is this about the monsters?" Black bangs fell over his big brown eyes. He swept them back and gestured for them to enter his small one-room lodgings.

Jean took the lead and told Ricard what she'd seen, condensing it all down to the important revelations. Reina was in charge of the monsters, and she was coming to Lenola. Dante suggested she gather the rest of the resistance at the nearby inn, for a meeting at sunup, and she left, saying she'd meet him there.

"The jailor saved you, huh?" Ricard asked. He poured them both some hot, herby tea he'd set on the stove. His mother's recipe, he'd told Dante once.

"And condemned me." Dante accepted a steaming cup and settled in the chair by the window, overlooking Lenola's rooftops and the approaching red rays of morning. "Havok can't be trusted."

"Does he really protect us from other monsters?"

"Yes, but they're like vultures squabbling over scraps. They serve only themselves. Ricard, listen, Havok is easy to warm to, when you begin to get to know him. And that's what makes him so dangerous."

"You survived with them for over a cycle." Ricard gazed at him as though he was a returning hero, but all Dante had done was survive. He hadn't changed anything; he hadn't killed any monsters. He'd just... not died. And he wasn't sure he was worth the admiration in Ricard's eyes.

"I'm glad you're well," Dante said, grinning as he sipped his tea.

"Yeah, I'm hard to kill." He laughed. "Like you. I did get this vicious scar though. Wanna see?" He yanked up his trouser leg, revealing a pale slice up his skin.

They laughed and joked some more. Ricard told him of a girl he liked but didn't yet have the courage to court. The normalcy of it all seemed dreamlike. Dante had forgotten what *normal* felt like. He envied Ricard his naivety. But he wouldn't go back to those days, that time, adrift without purpose, knowing his life was rudderless, and failing to fix it.

This simple existence—a city they called home, with neighbors, friends, choices, some good, some bad—he wished the truth didn't have to take it away from them. Perhaps, if his plan worked, he could save them from the worst of the monsters.

DANTE MET the resistance at the inn, at dawn, and while his survival was met with elation, the mood quickly darkened. He told them of his plan. And by the time the sun had set on another Lenolian day, the faces of all those around him were grim but determined.

Dante left as the sun set, all too aware of time filtering away. Jean walked alongside him, back down the cobbled streets and out into the unkept grasslands, toward the old farmstead.

"Are you sure you want to do this?" she asked, speaking for the first time since leaving the meeting.

He'd known the question had been coming. Whatever had happened between Havok and her, for all his threats and viciousness, Havok had a way about him, a slyness that seduced. Jean was no more immune than Dante had been. "He butchered and killed Calen. His arm is taken from a Lenolian, and I sincerely doubt he asked them to hand it over. He talks as though he's changed, but he needs us. He has nothing now. He'll say anything..." He hated that it had come to this, but Havok was a liability.

Jean's face betrayed some of her concerns. "Of course." She didn't sound convinced. But she hadn't seen what they did, the sacha, she hadn't seen the mutilated people pulled along by leashes, or Havok's basement of bones.

He stopped on the path, jolting Jean to a stop beside him. "Whatever he told you, whatever you saw in him, it's a lie. He makes it easy to forget the monster he is. We aren't people to them, we're possessions. Never forget that because Havok won't."

"I know, Dante." She gripped his arm. "I'm with you. All the way. We will end this."

"If he suspects anything—"

"Not from me, he won't."

"Good."

They walked on, determination growing in Dante with his every step. Any lingering guilt, he swept aside. The cycle he'd spent in silence had taught him how to shut that part of him away, the part inclined to forgive. He couldn't forgive Havok; Lenola's survival relied on it.

The moon had risen by the time they arrived back at the old farmhouse. Jean veered off down the path to the farmhouse, with its candle-lit windows and smoke rising from the chimney—it seemed Havok had been busy—but Dante hesitated at the fork, lingering to gather his thoughts before the lies set in.

Havok was intelligent, he'd know a trap. Dante had to be careful.

He took the left path and trudged through the grass, down to the overgrown pond. Shrubs he'd skipped around as a boy had grown unruly with age. Saplings had sprawled into vast, leaning trees. But even at night, magic sweetened the air. Fireflies danced, a breeze swept over the grass heads. And if he closed his eyes, he could almost imagine the last twenty cycles hadn't happened. He'd come to the pool to skip stones, and to see...

Havok.

The jailor stood waist-deep in the pool, his broad wings lifted high, each feather spread, and each frond laced with moonlight, making them shine silver. Havok faced away, and Dante ducked into the grass, scolding himself for behaving like a fool. He should have said good night to him, not hidden. But he'd been so surprised by Havok's nakedness, his thoughts had fogged.

Dante parted the grass and peered through.

Moonlight stroked over Havok's bare back, outlining him. Havok cupped water in one hand and poured it over his opposite shoulder. His horns jutted, the single ring glinting. His face was thrown into profile, lean and sharp. He *should* be monstrous. But it wasn't fear making Dante's heart race. Havok's beauty was a savage song of masculinity and monster. The first time Dante had laid eyes on him, at this pool, he'd thought Havok beautiful, and that hadn't changed. If anything, his feelings for Havok had been forged into something permanent and thrust through Dante's heart, because there was no denying how a part of him had always ached for Havok, and no denying how, when Reina came, Havok's life would be the price Lenola paid for freedom.

Moths fluttered in the moonlight. Havok raised a hand, and one landed on his black claw. Havok tilted his head and the way the light settled on him, how he stood waist-deep in the magical pool, it made Dante wish he'd never brought Calen here, made him wish Havok were still his secret.

"Did you lose something in the grass, Dante?"

Dante swore under his breath. "Yes, I was...just..." He stood and gestured aimlessly back down the path. "Just passing by. I didn't see you there." He sighed and propped his hand on his hip, wincing at his own mistake—hiding in the grass, as though they were boys again. Idiot. Of course, Havok had known he'd been there. "Did the moths tell you?"

Havok flicked his fingers and the moth darted into the air. "Moths speak in riddles."

Of course they did, because nothing around Havok was straightforward.

Dante waded through the grass, approached the pebble bank, and crouched. He picked up a smooth pebble, turning it over in his hand. In the moonlight, he could make out the old hawthorn bush on the opposite bank, where Havok would hide to watch Dante skip stones.

"Join me, if you like," he said. "The water is warm. The frogs are... vocal."

"Er... no." The last thing he needed was to get close to a naked and wet Havok. *Was* he naked? Dante scanned the bank and spotted a pile of leather next to Havok's boots. By the powers, he *was* naked beneath the surface. "I should—" He stood again and thumbed over his shoulder. "—get back."

"Don't leave on my account." Havok cupped more water and sloshed it over his arms. When he turned, keeping his wings high and dry, Dante darted his gaze away, but it soon stuttered back to Havok. He couldn't see all of him, just hints in monochrome, but the scars marring Havok's chest were so pale, they almost glowed. Havok removed the leather wrap around his arm. The crisscross stitching scars above his bicep stood out starkly against his skin. A metal plate gleamed. That was how he'd stopped Reina's blow with the cleaver. He'd modified himself.

All the talk of Reina making him, Dante didn't believe it. She made monsters, but not even she could craft a creature like Havok. He was too unique.

But he had to come from somewhere. She'd said some things about him, called him a prince, and the stories of old, coupled with Havok's suppressed power... There was more to him that nobody saw, not even Havok himself. Dante shouldn't pry. It would do no good to know more of him, when it all had to end soon. But he couldn't resist. "What's your earliest memory?"

"You," Havok replied. "Here." He strode through the water, toward Dante, creating a wave in the water that rode over his hips. He was lean, like a farm laborer, but strong with it. He'd felt Havok's arms around him, held him close—

Dante turned his head away and swallowed hard. Water sloshed as Havok left the pool and padded away to gather his trousers. Havok didn't care what he displayed, or perhaps he did, and he was tormenting Dante?

Dante glanced up and caught a moonlit glimpse of Havok's ass he was sure poets would be able to describe in lavish detail.

All he could do was clear his throat and look away, finding the hawthorn bush fascinating. "You know... you could cover up?"

"Cover what?"

"Never mind." He wasn't explaining how Havok's bare ass was so fine it rendered Dante's thoughts numb and his body hard

"Why would I cover such fine gifts?" Havok chuckled, and that dirty chuckle said he knew exactly what Dante was referring to.

Dante snorted. "You always did strut around as though you were the most beautiful thing out here."

Havok hesitated a beat and when he next spoke, the tone was softer, and closer. "You only had to say you didn't like it."

Didn't like it? Havok's body had been imprinted on his mind, branded into his dreams. "That wasn't..." He'd liked it, liked it too much, loved watching him move, watching him run and leap, wings flapping, catching butterflies, how his tail danced. After they'd shared that first kiss, he'd imagined tumbling in the summer's grass with Havok, kissing him again, making him moan, tasting him—

With a growl, Dante threw the pebble down. Why did his thoughts always turn to Havok, and what he could never have with him? This wasn't helping anyone or anything. "Get dressed." He turned and stalked up the path.

"Dante?"

"Yes." He didn't dare look back, knowing he'd find Havok dripping wet and naked.

"How does it feel to be home?"

"Like I never left." It was an easy, careless answer, and a lie. He walked on, stomping through the grass, anger growing. *Nothing* felt the same. *He* didn't feel the same. The world had changed around him, the rug pulled from under his feet, and nothing would be the same again. There was no Calen here to greet him, no simple life to return to, and the skies were full of threats, his head full of monsters. It was Havok's fault. All of it. Havok had to pay... He had to, even if the thought of what was to come turned Dante's stomach and squeezed his heart.

The jailor would pay for his crimes.

CHAPTER 34

ante

DREAMS PLAGUED HIM, dreams of Havok trapped in ice, reaching for Dante, his one eye crystal blue and full of horrors. Dante woke gasping, clutching at the coat he'd thrown over himself, the coat Havok had made. He shoved it off, planted his feet beside the bed, and dragged a hand down his face and chin, over rough whiskers.

He wasn't sure he could do what needed to be done.

But it was too late. The plan was already in motion.

He scratched at the beard, glanced at the dusty window and the heavy darkness outside, then lit a candle from the fireplace's glowing embers and set about cleaning the old shaving tools found inside a rotten cupboard. He soaped his chin and shaved off the beard. With the beard gone, he stroked his smooth chin and stared at the man looking back from the mirror. He'd expected to see his old naive self there, but that man was a ghost. And he was never coming back.

Who was Dante now?

He couldn't be sure. Was Havok changed too? Had events of the last cycle changed him?

If Dante could change, then perhaps so could monsters...

Dante had made mistakes, often the same ones again and again. That was his old self. A weaker, lost man. He didn't have to go back to how he'd been before. He was stronger now, different, he could change his fate. And that change began with not repeating the same mistake he'd made all those cycles ago.

He could not betray Havok.

The plan had to be stopped...

He grabbed his coat, tugged it on, and carrying his boots, so as not to wake Jean and Havok, he hurried down the stairs, through the farmhouse, and out of the front door into the cool night.

Stars winked, their silence as crisp as the cool night air.

Khandra stirred, perhaps hearing his racing heart, and broke from her tattoo. "I know," he told the butterfly, unable to hear if she replied. "It won't happen. I can't do it. I thought I could, but I can't... I hate him, but... It would be wrong. I'll stop it. I'll find another way."

"Find another way for what?" Havok stepped from the darkness into his path, wings clamped, horns upright, his mark a crimson wink in the dark.

Dante froze. If Havok was outside, then... He'd known.

Of course he had. He'd probably followed Dante into the town, hidden on the roof, and overheard some of their plotting. By the powers, Dante should never have tried to outsmart him.

Dante raised a hand, holding him back. "Listen, they're coming for you."

"Oh, I know." Havok's half smile turned sly. He began to approach. "You made it very clear we are not friends, and perhaps we never were. You intend to trap me, to offer me up to Reina, to bargain for the city's freedom. I am to be your last ever offering in exchange for her jailors leaving your precious city and its people alone. I am your bait." As he said that last word, soft starlight made his sharp teeth shine.

It was true. All of it. Havok deserved it. The jailor deserved it. But Dante couldn't see it through. "I'm going to stop it. Right now. I'll find another way, Havok."

"On the contrary," he purred. "It's a solid plan. She might even accept it."

Dante knew that smile, it was the predator's grin when it had caught its prey. Havok stopped a single step away from Dante. Eye to eye, Havok didn't blink. "All you had to do was ask."

Dante's guilt squirmed. "I'm sorry."

"Sorry?" Irony laced Havok's laugh. "I thought you different to the rest of your kind. Even after your lover took my eye, a part of me still fostered that thought. *Dante is good.* I sensed that about you. I clung to it, all this time. Hoping... But at every turn, you prove me wrong."

Was he so wrong? Was it all Dante's fault? "Havok, you take our people, you murder us for entertainment, you harvest us. And you killed Calen out of spite. It's not like you're fuckin' innocent!"

"Calen was an unworthy fool whose suffering I ended as a kindness. Forget him—"

Dante swung a fist, but Havok's hand clamped down, catching Dante's wrist, holding his hand in midair. Dante yanked, but Havok's grip held. Dante leaned close, so even in the dark, he saw all of Havok's snarl and the way his eye burned. "You gifted Calen to Reina because that's all we are to you, possessions. I'll never forgive you for what you did to him and to hundreds of others."

"Why would I seek forgiveness from a creature like you?"

Dante tore from his hold. "Leave then. Fly away, like you always do. Because when my people catch you, it's over."

He flicked his wings and growled. "We could have devised a plan *together*. But instead you plot my demise behind my back—"

"How can I trust you when you lie with your every breath?"

"I don't—"

"The mark is a lie. All of you is a lie! I found a note in the well you threw me in, it said *the mark is a lie*. That person, whoever left that note, they knew the marks aren't what they appear to be." Havok scowled, both angry and confused, but he had to know. How could he not? "The mark you wear," Dante continued, "it's a lie, like you. I don't know who or what you are, but that mark is a mask *you* hide behind. And you know it."

"Hide? You know so much, then what do I hide from?"

Dante almost laughed. Did he truly not see? "Yourself. Do you still not know? Havok, you are not the monster Reina made you. That mark is her control over you. She's afraid of you. You are something—someone else. But you refuse to see it."

Havok clutched the mark in his hand but stopped short of yanking it free. The fear Dante had seen in him haunted his face now. He didn't want to know the truth.

Knowing it changed everything. And once known, it could not be unknown. It could not be forgotten.

"Take it off," Dante urged. "Unleash who and what you really are."

Fear widened Havok's eye. He couldn't do it.

"Havok, listen... None of this changes the fact you're in danger. My people..." Dante wet his lips and glanced around them. There was still time to have him flee. "If you stay—"

Havok's body jerked. His wings flew open, but he didn't take flight. Blood dashed Dante's face, startling the rest of his words away. Havok staggered and peered down at the tip of the blade protruding from his chest.

"No!" Dante heard himself cry out. He rushed forward, but people surged from the covering brush and grabbed him, hauling him back. "Wait—let me go. I was wrong. It's a mistake. Don't!"

Havok dropped to his knees. His wings sagged. He continued to stare at the tip of the blade, shocked, incredulous, then lifted his head and met Dante's gaze. The shock vanished, turning to resignation. He'd expected this and by the powers, that hurt even more.

"Don't!" Dante bucked against those holding him. People he knew, people he'd ordered to do this. "Just... wait... Not like this. I was wrong. Please—"

Jean swept in from behind and hooked her arm around Havok's neck. She pressed a blade to his throat. "I'm sorry, but it has to be this way. Be still now, Havok. The blade was dipped in henbane to soften your suffering. Give it time to work. Don't fight it. Just rest."

No, this was so very wrong, powers be damned, he should never have done this. "Please, stop. Let him go. He said he'll help—"

"Hold Dante," Jean ordered, and more men loomed in the corner of his vision. Ricard among them, his face so disappointed that it hurt to look upon him.

Dante slumped in their grip. "Jean, why?"

"Why?" Jean shook her head. "*Never trust the jailor*, those are your words. And this is the only way."

Havok swayed. His eyelashes fluttered, his focus wavering. The blade Jean had driven through his back... He'd heal, but slowly, thanks to the poison. Dante had tried to stop this but in doing so, he'd lured Havok right into their path—and they'd all known.

Havok would think he'd been betrayed. Again.

He slumped onto a hand, then collapsed onto his side, eye closed. Jean yanked the blade from his back. "He's down! Quickly! Bind his wings!"

He'd heal, Dante knew that, he'd healed almost everything, but that didn't make it right. And as Dante saw him there, as he heard Jean issuing the orders, saw them throw a net over Havok, bands of guilt squeezed Dante's heart. He'd made a terrible mistake. And again, Havok was going to be the one who paid. Just as Dante had foolishly planned.

CHAPTER 35

avok

WEAKNESS TURNED his limbs to stone and fogged his head. They'd kept him drifting, not awake nor asleep, somewhere between where dreams and reality mingled. He might have called the Lenolians ingenious, if he hadn't come around strung by the wrists between two timber uprights in the city plaza. An offering to Reina. A jailor... as an offering. There was poetic irony in that, although he was in no mood to appreciate it.

Some citizens made up a small crowd, curiosity driving them to see the jailor up close. When he lifted his head to fix them in his sights, his vision blurred and fire raged down his back. He couldn't summon enough strength to keep his wings off the ground, and they hung limp and useless behind him.

None of this was a surprise. Havok didn't feel much of

anything, except perhaps disappointment. He'd have rather approached all this voluntarily, but he'd clearly thought too highly of Lenola and its people. Perhaps the only surprise was that they hadn't killed him outright and slung his carcass from the timbers.

Reina might even laugh when she came, moments before she tore out his true heart and replaced it with the black thing—she would have surely found it by now. He'd be her puppet forever.

He'd prefer to die.

He shook his head, trying to clear his vision enough to see the faces of those who came to witness his end. Dante wasn't here, at least not in the open. Was he hiding nearby, ready to spring the trap and take Reina down? Dante had no intention of negotiating with her; Havok admired that tactic, at least. In fact, he admired much about these foolish people, even if he despised their idiocy.

Which made him an idiot as well, he supposed. He was strung up like one.

Dante was right.

He should have taken to the air while he could and left them all to bow down under a new jailor or perish under Reina's wrath. Except, he never would have left them. He was their jailor, and their protector. He had been for many cycles. He cared for these wretched people from above. More the fool him.

Shaking his head again dislodged the mark on its chain. He couldn't take it off. He couldn't face the truth. That life, the one he'd had before meeting Dante at the pool, that was forgotten for a reason. He knew that much. And to tread there was forbidden. Even as fragments had begun to find their way inside his memories. He recalled Dante's parents—suspected they *knew* him. They'd watched him from the farmhouse window, knowing he was out there. *Never cross the thorn wall, never enter their world,* Dante's father had told Havok, so long ago. But Dante had broken that rule when he'd skipped his stones over Havok's pond.

There was still so much he didn't remember. And now it seemed as though he might never know his true self.

The sacha were coming. He could hear their wings, like distant rolling thunder. Reina would be at their point, and she'd kill him for this. There would be no remaking, no second chances, no forgiveness.

What had he done that was so wrong?

A growl bubbled from his lips. He shifted his wings, trying to get the blood flowing again. "She'll kill you..." he told the people staring. The words were clear in his head but fell from his lips as growls. These people wouldn't listen anyway. They'd all come to see the monster squirm and beg and howl, like an offering would. Perhaps see him weep for his life. He was about to disappoint them. Havok did not weep, and he did not beg. Not for them, and not for Reina.

His only wish was that Dante was here to witness the fruition of his great betrayal. He studied the faces in the crowd, men and women, but some children too. None gazed upon him kindly. "I protected you," he growled out. "I am all that stands between you and the truth."

They huddled closer to each other like lost little birds.

"Go," Havok snarled. None moved. *"Run, fools!"* He yanked on the ropes binding him. The timber uprights groaned, and some in the crowd hurried away, fearful he might escape and gobble them all. He almost laughed, and he watched some flee. More Lenolian faces watched from windows, terraces, and rooftops. All of them low-hanging fruit for Reina.

"You believe these ropes will hold me?!" he howled. "Run now, before I am free to plow you down like the useless crop you are!" They all fled now, scurrying like rats. Good. And just in time as the sky above filled with the sound of thunderous wings.

CHAPTER 36

ante

"No, no..." Dante pulled again at the ropes around his wrists, binding him to a chair. "You can stop this."

Jean stood at the window and watched the plaza, her back to Dante. She could see Havok out there, tied up like a gift for Reina, but Dante saw only last night—Havok on the ground, a blade through his chest, betrayal through his heart once more. Sometimes right and wrong were so closely intertwined that there was no unraveling them, but giving Havok to Reina *felt* wrong in a way that few things ever had.

"Dante, your plan is sound," Jean said. "Let this happen."

She'd always been the voice of reason, the stalwart one, and she wasn't even wrong now, but... how could he make her see that Havok needed to be saved. "I was wrong about him. Not in everything, he's a prick, and infuriating, and selfish, and he will and has done terrible things. He'll do them again. I'm not saying he's good." He looked up and Jean raised an eyebrow. "He's really not good, but who is? I'm just saying he's changed, and this is wrong."

"You've been through so much. Let us handle this now." She turned to face the window again. "He's terrorizing them. Even tied up, we run from him—from the sacha. It has to end."

"Damnit, you've seen them, like I have. This isn't just one or two monsters, there's a whole world of them out there. We don't have weapons, we're not an army, Havok is our best chance at understanding them. He's our only way in. If we lose him now, we have nothing left to fight with."

Jean sighed and glanced over her shoulder again. "In that tower, when he removed the gem he wears, he turned the world to ice. He almost killed us. You said he can't be trusted, you said he'll use us, you said we're nothing to him, and you had all that right. He's a monster, Dante, and you've been among them so long that you can no longer see the truth."

"It's *because of him* I see the truth, it's because of him that we're even alive to have this conversation." He tugged at the ropes again. "He's protected Lenola since we were young and yes, he took one of us each cycle—by the powers, I know what that's like—but that was the price for freedom and ignorance. I don't think it's right, but I understand why he's like he is." Hearing it aloud reaffirmed it and made what they were doing even worse. "Please, untie me. I can still stop this."

"If I let you go, you'll go out there and untie him." She shook her head. "No. We wait, and when his queen arrives, we'll be ready."

Slumped in the chair, he dropped his head back and stared at the ceiling. "What happened to you, Jean?"

"The jailor killed my friend."

When he lowered his gaze, she smiled sadly. She meant him.

"But I'm right here."

"No, you're not. Not like you were. They changed you. I won't let them make more victims of us."

"I get it. I want to help. So does he!"

"He is helping, by being out there, and so are you, by staying out of this. He has his claws in you, so I can't trust you right now. We will not be swayed in this. It must be done."

She wasn't going to relent.

And that left him no choice. He had to make it right before they lost Havok and their only advantage against the monsters forever.

He studied the room. The house they'd camped in wasn't anything remarkable. He'd been tied to a dining room chair and left there so the resistance could take up their positions around the plaza. The chair was a creaking, wooden thing. If he forced it, it would eventually break, if he put some muscle into it. But Jean had a knife on her, maybe two. As soon as he struggled, would she draw a blade?

Dante rested his head back and sighed. Was he going to risk hurting Jean to save a creature who had threatened to cut off his dick, a creature who had enjoyed tormenting him, walked him around like a pet on the end of leash, treated him like dirt?

Fuck.

He hated Havok. And if those crimes were all he was, he'd have gladly left him strung to the uprights. But Havok was more than his crimes. He was the boy who'd talked to butterflies, who had whittled little wooden animals for company, who had protected Lenola for much of his life. A boy caught in the net of someone else's lies.

Was he going to save Havok?

Yes, yes he was.

CHAPTER 37

avok

Reina cut a startling figure in her jagged clothing of stitched black patches and razor-wire crown. As the rest of the sacha landed inside the plaza, she approached Havok, smiling with every step. The bloody cleaver gleamed at her hip.

"This could have all been avoided, Beric, had you contained your insolence."

"I believe I did."

Her eyes narrowed. "Such a sharp tongue."

There were worse outcomes than dying, such as losing his tongue, thus his voice. He clamped his teeth together and bowed his head. His position, strung between the uprights, was already a subservient one, but there was still room to swallow his pride.

"You'd always been obedient. My favorite. What changed in you?"

What changed? He wasn't sure it was any one thing, just a drip-drip of lies gradually bleeding away. Beginning when he'd captured Dante. Something about the man and changed Havok's world, turning it inside out. "I saw through your lies."

"My lies." She laughed. "*My* lies?"

"If you're going to kill me, tell me of the mark, tell me the truth of it. Give me that, in honor of the cycles I've served you."

"Ah, the mark." Her smile tilted sideways, losing some of its shine. "Still afraid to remove it? Afraid of what it's covering up? You should be, Beric." She gripped his chin and lifted his head. "If you remove it, the world you see will crumble to dust. Everything you believe you know will vanish."

He didn't want to believe her, but the words rang true. It was the reason he'd continued to wear it, continued to *hide* behind it. Because he knew, deep inside, whatever the mark hid, it was somehow *worse*.

"Reina!" a Lenolian voice called. Dante's friend—Jean—approached from one of the houses. He'd rather liked her, until she'd stabbed a blade through his back.

Irritation narrowed Reina's brow but she didn't avert her gaze from Havok. She leaned close, and her sweet, acidic smell laced his tongue. "Watch," she whispered, "as I raze this city to rubble."

No. These people, this place, it didn't deserve that ending. If it hadn't been for Havok, they'd never have known their existence was a game. They were innocent. "Don't."

"Oh, sweet Beric." She ran a claw down his cheek. "You care for them. How pathetic."

He tore his head away. "Leave them. They are no threat to you. Take me, do with me as you wish, but leave them to their fantasy."

"And how long will they last without a jailor? Is it not crueler for them to suffer in slaughter when the sacha come, than to perish quickly by my hand?"

By the powers, *he* was their jailor, and their only savior. "Unleash me. I will be yours in all things, for as long as you wish it. Cleave me in two, carve out my heart, render me mute, if you so desire, but leave them as they are."

"Havok, no!" Dante.

He was here. Havok ached to look, to see him, in these, his final moments.

Was Dante here to watch Havok perish, to watch the monster get his dues? Dante couldn't stop Reina; he couldn't stop any of this. Perhaps nobody could. But Havok could... He had to try.

He locked his glare on Reina. "Ignore the Lenolian fools. This is between you and I."

"You protect them until the very end, in your duty you are true." She raised her hand and gently cupped his mark on its chain. Its crimson shimmer reflected in her dark eyes. "What hides within you that makes a lord tremble?"

Her words made little sense, but there was truth in them. If she pulled the mark free, it might free him too, or it might condemn them and every single Lenolian in the city. When the ice came, he couldn't control it. But what if it was their only chance?

"The thing that I am, the power we both know I contain, I'll surrender it," he said. "It too will be yours. Just leave Lenola untouched. Let them have their pathetic lives. With me, you can have so much more."

Her lips lifted in a smile. "You always did have a silver tongue, Beric." She skimmed her fingers along his jaw, then stroked over his bottom lip. "Without it, you'll be the perfect ornament." She pinched his tongue and her dagger flashed.

CHAPTER 38

 ante

"Now!" Jean bellowed.

The swish of countless arrows being nocked filled the air. Dante saw movement high on the rooftops, windows thrown open and countless bows being drawn. So many, just as he'd planned. Those arrows would rain down on the plaza and kill everything in sight, including Havok.

He bolted, ropes swinging from his wrists where he'd pulled from the broken chair. Jean hadn't stopped him then, and she wouldn't now. She thought him too late.

On the stage, Reina had a dagger raised, with Havok on his knees, strung from the uprights in front of her. He couldn't see what she had planned, but if she brought that dagger down, Havok would suffer.

Arrows stabbed the ground. Dante skidded, veered around the strumming shafts, and vaulted onto the stage. Reina roared. Her leathery wings flared. Arrows slammed into her wing membranes and torn through them. But the victory was short-lived. She screamed at the sacha to attack and all around the plaza, great winged and clawed beasts boiled into motion.

Her gaze speared into Dante a heartbeat before he slammed into her, driving her back against one of the timber uprights. Her wings flared, she danced, then her backhand struck him, flinging him aside. He hit the stage and rolled. A second wave of arrows slammed to the ground. Reina spread her wings and roared.

Havok...

He hung limp, his head down, messy silver hair obscuring his face. Why wasn't he moving? Reina wouldn't kill him. She'd torture him, butcher him, but she wouldn't kill him. She *couldn't*. He'd watched her from inside the endless cage, had her order him time and time again to speak. She'd kept Dante because she knew it hurt Havok. But *why*.

It didn't matter now. He had to get to Havok.

More arrows slammed into the ground, more finding their target in Reina's great wings. She beat those wings hard, sweeping up dust, and took to the air.

Now, it had to be now... Dante scurried to Havok and tilted his head up. "Havok?"

Havok's brow pinched in. Tears glistened in his eye, the dark pupil blown wide. Dante had never seen him so vulnerable. The sight plucked at the same feelings he had for the old Havok, made him want to hold him and protect him. *I'll come back*. Promises made and broken. Dante regretted so much.

"I'm getting you out of here." He picked at the knots holding Havok to the uprights.

"You saved my tongue, my voice," Havok croaked. "Why help me when you hate me so?"

Dante laughed. "I'll tell you when I know the answer myself."

Arrows rained. Blades clashed. Roars and screams barreled through the air. Dante could only hope the resistance's surprise attack had been enough to catch the sacha unawares and tip the battle in their favor. But they needed Havok. Lenola always had. "We need you," he said.

Havok blinked, coming around slowly. "Yes, you do. Had you *asked* me, I'd have stood beside you. Fool."

Dante gave a snort. "Lecture me later." The first knot gave, freeing Havok's left arm, and Dante scooted across to begin untying the right. Fire zipped up his side. The culprit arrow slammed into the stage beside his boot. "Damnit." They weren't aiming at Dante. They aimed their bows at Havok.

"They're dying," Havok croaked. "She'll kill everyone."

Dante glanced away from the knot toward the battle around them. The wounded lay bleeding and moaning. Some bodies lay motionless. A few sacha were among those who had fallen, but most were Lenolian. The more Dante looked, the more he saw how the monsters cleaved through the people as though they were nothing but air. Havok was right. They were all dying. Arrows and blades weren't enough. They couldn't win.

Reina's cackle erupted above. She circled, and in her hand, she dangled a severed head.

"Dante, untie me—" Havok urged.

Dante blinked at the vexing knot. So much death. Had Dante done this, brought this down upon them all?

"I can stop this." Havok tugged at the rope. "I can save them. Hurry."

The knot eased and Havok tore free, grabbed his mark, and ripped the gem from its chain.

A strange kind of silence fell over them both, isolating them from the raging chaos. The red of Havok's eye faded behind a shining, icy blue. "Dante, I remember...some, not all." His voice cracked. "There's a tunnel. To the east. Look for it at the bottom of the deepest ravine. Take it."

"What? I can't leave them—I won't leave you, not again." He reached for Havok, but ice sparkled around his horns and in his hair, frosting him in armor, building a barrier between them.

"The tunnel." Havok's blue eye widened, filled with fear. "You must."

"Why? How... How do you even know it's there?"

The fear in his eye softened to a knowing, the same knowing Dante had seen in his dreams. "It's where I came from," Havok said. The intensity of the ice in his gaze hardened. Jagged ice climbed over his feathered wings, encasing them in crystal. "I remember pieces. There's so much—" His gaze speared Dante. His wings flared, revealing a thousand daggers of ice nestled among black feathers. "Beware the Crimson Lord." He blasted skyward and slammed into Reina, tearing her from the sky. They plunged, tangled together, and smashed through a nearby roof, disappearing inside in a hail of shattered timbers and tiles.

Dante couldn't leave the city, not in the midst of battle. He was no coward. He dropped off the stage, grabbed a discarded short sword from the ground, and pinned the nearest sacha in his sights.

The ground lurched sideways. He staggered, reached out to shift his weight, when an enormous, jagged crack split the street, climbed the facade of a nearby building, and tore the house in two. More rumbles trembled from below, as though a storm had awoken beneath the city. Another split opened on the far side of the plaza. The air and ground quaked, and in the distance, the jagged black spire split with a sundering groan. Enormous chunks broke from its edges and plummeted toward rooftops.

The sacha launched from the plaza like a flock of spooked birds.

The corner of a nearby building dislodged, shifting sideways. "Look out!" Dante bolted toward the man in its path. But the brick and stone slammed down, blasting a wave of rubble and dust. As the cloud cleared, the man was gone, buried and lost. The fallen bricks glistened, as though wet...

Ice.

It snapped and sparked from the cracks in the ground, growing and reaching as though alive and hungry. People who had stood and fought monsters moments before began to run, but the ice, somehow sensing them, lurched up and over—trapping them inside its crystal folds.

Was this... Havok's doing?

"Dante!" Jean waved him toward a fallen column. "It's Ricard, help me!"

Ricard lay sprawled on his back, clutching his leg trapped beneath the heavy stone column. Dante sprinted toward them, ignoring the fallen who no longer moved. He couldn't help them. Houses crumbled in the corner of his vision. Black rocks rained from above, blasting through houses, killing sacha and people alike. The city was being pulled asunder.

He plunged the sword beneath the stone column and levered it up, off Ricard.

Ricard scrambled back, and Jean scooped him against her. "Dante, what's happening?"

Whatever the ice was, wherever it had come from, it wasn't saving Lenola... it was destroying it. "Leave. Take Ricard to the farm. I'll meet you there."

Dante bolted back toward the plaza and the house where Havok had brought Reina down. On the ground, winking quietly in the dirt, laid Havok's ruby-red mark.

"What are you going to do?" Jean called.

Dante scooped up the mark. "Save Havok."

CHAPTER 39

avok

"Foolish creature!" Reina's claws raked down the scarred side of Havok's face. "You think you're saving them? You've condemned them all!"

He didn't care. He had her pinned under him, her throat pinched inside his hands, and nothing had ever felt as right. "You knew! You knew all this time what I was."

Reina choked on a laugh. "And I reveled in it, *Prince*. I took you and made you mine. You'd be nothing but a forgotten little orphan runt without me!"

Ice cracked and snarled around the broken house they'd fallen into. It climbed walls, snapping and jerking from the ceiling, reaching closer with every beat of Havok's heart. It was a part of him, the part kept hidden by the mark—the true monster he'd been all along. He couldn't stop it and didn't want to. Fierce memories poured in, like nightmares, only he knew they were real. He came from a different land, a different people, and everything he'd been since then had been a masterfully crafted lie. His life with Reina, his place among the sacha, all lies!

He pried a hand free of Reina's neck and smothered her face, pushing her head down. He'd crush her to dust. "I was forgotten!"

Reina choked and gagged. It wasn't enough for her to die, he needed to *destroy* her, to taste her death, to swallow her final moments so they were forever a part of him.

"They forgot me."

"No..." Reina rasped. "He *made* them forget. He wiped all traces of you from existence."

Flashes blinded him. Memories exploded in his mind like fireworks. A sacha, like him, bathed in fire. His wings made of flame. His eyes like rubies, like Havok's mark. Havok reeled and clutched his head, trying to squeeze the invader out. His laugh... it hurt to hear. It sounded so like his own. Havok howled, and the ice lurched forward. He couldn't contain it all, couldn't think around it. It was too much. The world and his place inside it rattled. It had all been a lie. He'd been hidden, cursed, made to forget who and what he was. He'd hidden behind the hawthorn bush, told never to leave, to hide there... forever.

And he would have, until the day came when Dante's friend had taken Havok's eye. He'd left then, fled straight into Reina's waiting arms, into her twisted truths.

She laughed now. "He'll come for you, forgotten prince that you are. He'll burn this world and all of us in it. You are nothing against his might. Ice cannot withstand his scorching flame."

Gasping, Havok dropped onto a hand. Ice crawled over his fingers, holding him down. He plucked himself free, but ice crawled up his knees. He tore his legs free. Ice grabbed his boots, his tail, plucking and pulling, trapping him. It would devour him, the city, its people. He was the jailor, he was supposed to protect them, but this... It was unstoppable. Like the truth. And it was all his fault.

Reina's laugh sounded through the groan and crack of heaving glaciers. But when he looked for her, she'd gone, and he was alone, trapped as the ice closed in.

Dante... Had he escaped in time? Havok ripped his legs from the hungry ice, pulling himself free, but even as he tried to stagger toward the frozen doorway, sheets of ice barred his way. Why couldn't he control it? It was his, wasn't it? So why then was it trying to smother him and everything he knew?

He was broken.

Was that why he'd been sent away?

Nothing made any sense. The memories swirled inside his head, hissing where fire met ice. The mark. If he could retrieve his mark, hide behind its curse, all of this would stop. The ice would leave again.

"Havok." Dante's distorted figure loomed on the other side of a wall of ice. So close, but out of reach. "Can you break it?"

He punched the ice wall. Pieces of it shattered and splintered, but the wall held. Above, the ice had curved over him, sealing him inside a dome. There was no way out. The space around him grew smaller, shrinking, creaking, groaning.

"Your mark." In Dante's hand, the little mark gleamed its crimson fire. A gift and a curse from the Crimson Lord.

"Dante, listen." Havok pressed a hand to the ice and watched its crystal veins consume his claws and fingers, absorbing him into its frozen grasp. "I am not who you believe me to be."

"I know—It doesn't matter now." His voice wobbled, muffled behind the ice wall. "We need to get you out. How do we make it stop?"

Havok smiled. The ice warped Dante's face, smudging the details, but he knew he'd have that defiant expression, the one where he wasn't going to let anything stop him. Stupidly stubborn. "The story you told me when we were young, of the king who lost his marks? Your parents told it to you and you to me. You recall?" Havok's own voice echoed in the shrinking dome.

"What? Havok—the spire is crumbling, there's ice inside it. The ice... it's everywhere. It came out of the ground. You have to stop it."

"The ice is looking for me, Dante. It won't stop until I'm captured." It crawled up his arm now, wrapping around his shoulder. Panic almost pushed a cry from his throat, but he swallowed it back. "The story of the king's lost marks, the lost marks weren't stones, they were princes, and... it's too much to tell you now, but I was cursed, cast out, made to be forgotten. By my brother, the Crimson Lord. If I am to survive this, I fear only he can free me."

"Havok..." Desperation shook Dante's voice. He slammed the mark against the ice. "Just break the ice!"

"Go through the tunnel, find the Crimson Lord, find the truth."

Ice locked around Havok's legs, trapped his tail, climbed his hips. It chilled his veins, slowed his heart, squeezed his lungs. The next words would be his last. They had to mean something more, they were his last hope in a world that had forgotten him. All but Dante.

"Save me," Havok whispered and could only hope Dante had heard. Ice crawled into his mouth, down his throat, stole his voice, and froze the final beat of his heart.

CHAPTER 40

ante

THE COLD WAS SO intense it rattled his veins and burned his lungs. But he couldn't leave. "Havok?" Havok didn't reply.

He wasn't far, just beyond the vertical sheet of ice, his outline warped and cracked, motionless, as though he'd been trapped in glass. "H-Havok..."

The mark thrummed in Dante's hand. Useless.

Havok wasn't... dead. Not that. Havok survived everything. He was just... trapped, like Dante had been trapped. There would be a way out.

Dante plucked his tingling hand from the ice and wrapped his arms around himself. His teeth rattled. His breath misted. If he stayed much longer, the ice would claim him too. He stepped back. Ice crunched under his boots. The shattered remains of the house had been frozen in place, locked inside a single moment. There was no way to reach Havok. He had to leave. "I'll come back. I promise. I'll come back for you."

Stumbling outside, he slipped over layers of ice coating the street. "You know I always come back..."

Tiny icy dust motes floated in the silence. Ice had trapped people midrun, their expressions frozen in fear. Every house, every person, every stone, every lamp, even the grass and flowers—everything was sealed inside its own crystal prison. Everything except Dante.

He stumbled into a run. The farm. Ricard and Jean. They had to be there, they had to be safe. The ice receded the farther he ran from the city, but its cracking and hissing followed him along the old road. And when he reached the farm, a glance toward the emerald pond confirmed it too had frozen. Lenola's silence was complete.

"Jean?" He pushed inside the house to find a roaring fireplace and Ricard in the chair, his leg up, partway through being bandaged.

"Dante, you're all right!" He moved to stand but Dante waved him back down.

"No, stay there. Rest. You're safe, I think."

"The ice, is it still out there?"

He nodded. "Jean?"

"The kitchen."

Dante hurried through the house, grabbed an old saddle bag from the stairs, and after entering the kitchen, he shoved a stale loaf of bread, some dried fruit, and a canteen of water into it as Jean washed bloody bandages in the sink.

"Are you hurt?" he asked.

"Just a few scrapes. But Ricard's leg is badly bruised. He'll need to rest. What's happening out there?"

"It's gone." He kept his voice low to keep Ricard from hearing, and to keep his own panic from seeping through. "We need to pack essentials and leave."

Jean grabbed his arm. "What do you mean, *it's gone?*"

"The ice took everything."

"*Everything?*" She exhaled hard. "And Havok? Is he gone too?"

"It took him. The people, they're... they're all frozen. We need to leave before the same happens here." He pulled from her hold and continued adding items to the bag. He grabbed several knives; they'd be useful.

"By the powers," Jean muttered, slumping against the kitchen counter. "Are they all dead?"

"I don't know." There was a lot he didn't know. But he'd find out. "I don't think so. There's a tunnel. In the ravine to the east. We need to go there. Havok said... He said that's where the answers are." He'd said a lot more, but Dante needed more time to unravel it all. A brother, a king, a curse. He'd known Havok hadn't belonged, that he'd been different, that he'd been... special. He'd always known either in his heart or by some other means that he couldn't recall. Either way, to save Lenola, he had to save Havok.

"None of this makes any sense—"

"Of course it doesn't, it's Havok!" The damned *monster*! Why— Why had this happened, why was it left to Dante, and why did he even care? The people needed saving, but he was lying to himself if he believed that was the only reason he was chasing some distant Crimson Lord for answers. He braced against the counter and tried to gather his thoughts, keeping himself together, tried to push the sight of Havok frozen in ice from his mind.

"Ricard is hurt, there could be survivors—"

"There's nothing left to save back there." Calm. He had to stay calm. Breathe.

"There could be! Did you even look?"

"Jean, there isn't anyone there. It's all ice." His voice stuttered. "And the ice might come here. We have to go." He shoved the bag into her hand and found another. "Hurry. Take anything you think—"

"No, I can't." She dropped the bag, her face pale with fear. "Lenola is my home. It's all I know."

"It's gone!"

"No! I can't leave!"

He reeled. No, she was right. Ricard was wounded. A quick glance through the window revealed the ice had stopped its crawl from the city. Perhaps it was done, for now. Jean and Ricard would be safer inside the farmhouse. "Then I'll go. Keep the fires lit. You'll be all right. I'll go to the tunnel..." And onward, to Havok's land. To his *real* home. He'd said a home didn't exist, because he'd been made to forget his.

"What tunnel?"

"The story of a king and his lost marks. We read it, as boys..."

"A story? Dante, you're not making any sense." A tear escaped her eye. She swiped it away.

"Wait here..." Dante hurried up the old stairs and into his parents' bedroom. Not much remained from their time, but he'd kept a chest of old books and papers. He hauled it out from the old cupboard, opened it up, and rummaged through documents and moth-eaten books.

A small, roughly carved wooden butterfly tumbled from its hiding place.

Dante picked it up and brushed his thumb along one of

its wings. Havok had given him the carving when they'd first met, as a peace offering, or because he'd seen how Dante had stared at his collection of tiny carved animals. Dante had later learned that the butterfly, and the many wooden animal companions, had been Havok's only friends.

The sight of it now choked him. He'd failed Havok, like he'd failed his whole life.

Khandra flitted from whatever hiding place she'd found on his body and bobbed in the air, reaffirming what he already knew. He had to save Havok.

"Still with me, I see." That was good. Khandra was a tiny piece of Havok's magic, and if she was alive, then so was he.

He tucked the wooden butterfly into his coat pocket and dug around some more in the chest. There, the book lay on the bottom, dust-coated and forgotten, like the prince it told the tale of. Inside the front cover, Dante's mother had written his name, but in faded pencil, alongside his name, she'd written: *"The mark is a lie."*

He hadn't connected it before, he hadn't remembered, until now.

The rolled-up note in the well, the handwriting he'd found so familiar. It was his mother's. She'd known who Havok was, she'd been in that same well, a prisoner among monsters, and she'd died there, leaving her final words for Dante to find. She couldn't have known he'd be there, that he'd find it; perhaps fate had made it so.

His parents had known about the sacha boy who lived near the pond; they'd probably also known how Dante had visited him. But had they been Havok's guardians or his jailors?

Havok had been Dante's secret, and theirs.

Dante tucked the storybook inside his coat along with the wooden butterfly.

He needed to go through that tunnel, and he needed to find the Crimson Lord and the truth. *"Save me."* For Havok.

CHAPTER 41

eina

"You did well." The Crimson Lord's voice sounded like honey on darkness and never failed to pour a slow shiver down Reina's spine.

She kept her head bent and her wings spread, even as bruised and torn as they were. She hadn't survived Beric's revelation or Lenola's uprising unscathed, but each scar she cherished. Each was a badge she wore proudly, in service to her lord. She'd kept her lord's secret, captured and then watched over his kin, made it so Beric never knew who or what he was. Her lord would be grateful, he'd praise her. Reward her. And she ached for his giving touch, the touch of her creator, her maker.

"How much does he remember?" the Crimson Lord asked.

Beric had come undone before her eyes and the result had been spectacular. But it was clear, the lost prince's sudden revelations were more likely to drive him mad than pose a threat. "Perhaps everything, my lord, but the knowledge overcame him. He's weak. His mind buckled. He's no threat."

"Of course not," the lord snapped.

Was the Lenolian worth mentioning? Havok's obsession. *Dante*. If she didn't, and the fool later made trouble, she'd pay by the razor's edge of the Crimson Lord's whip. "There was a problem."

"Hm?"

She lifted her head to find the Crimson Lord closer. Sunlight poured through the balcony window, as though setting his wings ablaze. He wore a crown of flame and was draped in molten silks. If sacha had gods, then he was surely one of them. "A man. The lost prince's fascination. Some called him Fireheart. He had a bond with your brother."

The Crimson Lord sighed. His face remained hidden in the day's harsh glare. "A man?"

"I only thought to mention it—"

"Hush." The lord's touch warmed her face and lifted her from her knees, to her feet. His power weakened her, made her want to weep in his presence. His gifts had made her who she was. Her body had been a gift. The palace had been a gift. She owed him everything.

"My lord, I have his heart…" From inside the folds of her gown, she withdrew the leather pouch, and inside, the black heart thumped. "It was a gift to him, and now I give it to you. With this, you will find him."

His fiery eyes shone. He took the bag and raised it, tilting his head back, horns shining. "My darling Reina, you were made to serve. And now my brother remembers, you have served your purpose."

"My lord, I—"

When his blade tore through flesh, she didn't know it. When her body fell, her head severed, her spirit was already gone, torn from this earthly plain.

The Crimson Lord carried Reina's head to the balcony and cast his gaze upon his people below. They cheered and roared. He lifted the head, and rapturous howls piqued. He tossed it over the balcony into the fray, and the crowd swallowed what was left of his pet.

Beric had awoken.

Inevitable, really. He always had been a thorn of trouble.

A moth fluttered and danced from some unknown crevice, drawn to the Crimson Lord's light. He watched it a while, then extended his hand to allow the moth to land softly on his fingertip.

And as for the man... this *Fireheart*. The Crimson Lord spread his wings, dripping flame from each feather's edge—A pathetic man could not stand against a prince, a king, a god. A man was nothing more than a moth attempting to capture the moon.

The Crimson Lord clamped his fingers closed, crushing the moth inside. He smiled and sprinkled the dust into the wind. Beric had escaped his destiny before. His brother would not be so fortunate again.

Havok and Dante's epic tale continues in *Dante's Outcast, The Jailor #2*.

ALSO BY ARIANA NASH

Please sign up to Ariana's newsletter so you don't miss all the news and get a free ebook!

www.ariananashbooks.com

Want more amazing gay fantasy?

Award winning Ariana Nash has everything from a star-crossed elf assassin and dragon prince pairing, to the infamous and epic enemies-to-lovers story of Prince Vasili Caville and his reluctant soldier, Niko Yazdan. There are even demons in disguise as angels!

Search for:

Silk & Steel

Primal Sin

Prince's Assassin

Or dive into the stunning fae fantasy standalone:

The Final Masquerade

ABOUT THE AUTHOR

Born to wolves, Rainbow Award Winner Ariana Nash only ventures from the Cornish moors when the moon is fat and the night alive with myths and legends. She captures those myths in glass jars and returning home, weaves them into stories filled with forbidden desires, fantasy realms, and wicked delights.

Sign up to her newsletter and get a free ebook here:
www.ariananashbooks.com